JACK SHIAN AND THE DESTINY STONE

JACK SHIAN
AND THE
DESTINY STONE

Book 3 in
The Shian Quest Trilogy

ANDREW SYMON

BLACK & WHITE PUBLISHING

First published 2014
by Black & White Publishing Ltd
29 Ocean Drive, Edinburgh EH6 6JL

1 3 5 7 9 10 8 6 4 2   14 15 16 17

ISBN   978 1 84502 756 8

Back cover artwork and inside illustrations by Rossi Gifford.

A CIP catalogue record for this book is available
from the British Library.

ALBA | CHRUTHACHAIL

Typeset by RefineCatch Limited, Bungay, Suffolk
Printed and bound by Grafica Veneta S.p.A. Italy

To Maggie

And thanks to Ian Black for all his help over the years

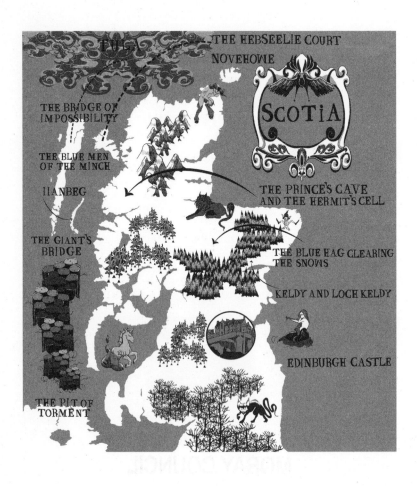

Contents

List of Characters from the Shian Quest Trilogy

Doonya	Jack's uncle
Doxer	An apprentice to Gilmore the tailor
Enda	A McCool
Endora	From Tula
Fenrig	Briannan's son
Festus	Freya and Purdy's father
Finbogie	A tutor
Finnegan	A McCool
Freya and Purdy	Jack's neighbours
Gilmore	The tailor; husband to Barassie
Gilravage and Stram	HebShian youths; friends of Ossian
Grandpa Sandy	A senior Congress member
Grey Wolf	A Shian 'from across the ocean'
Harald	The Norse leader 'from the fjords'
Hart and Dorcas	Jack's uncle and aunt in Keldy
He Who Waits	A Shian 'from across the ocean'
Hema	From Tula
Henri	Claville Shian leader
Iain Dubh	The HebShian leader
Ishona	Wife of Iain Dubh
Jack Shian	Our hero
John	A seer
Karl	A NorShian
Kedge	A Shian youth from near Edinburgh
Kelly	A McCool
Konan	A Brashat lieutenant
Luka	A seer (see *Jack Shian and the Mapa Mundi*)
Magnus	From Novehowe; leader of the NorShian

Malevola	An enchantress; from Tula
Malicia	From Tula
Marco	A seer (see *Jack Shian and the Mapa Mundi*)
Matthew	A seer (see *Jack Shian and the King's Chalice* and *Jack Shian and the Mapa Mundi*)
Mawkit	An inhabitant of the Shian square
Morrigan	Fenrig's sister; a Brashat
Murkle	Tutor of Shian tales
Oobit	A Cos-Howe lad
Ossian	Jack's cousin; son of Hart and Dorcas
Papa Legba	An enchanter
Petros, Rana and Lizzie	Jack's cousins
Phineas	Jack's father
Sanguina	From Tula
Saorbeg	A HebShian lieutenant
Stegos	A Kildashie
Tamlina	An enchantress
Telos	A McCool
The *cailleach*	An old healer
The Grey	An enchantress
The Twa Tams	HebShian youths

Shian (pronounced Shee-an [ʃiː + iən]):

n, the otherworld; creatures living in or coming from the otherworld. Also called daemons, fey, gentry, *daoine matha* [*good men*], portunes, etc. (C. 14; origins debated)

www.shianquest.com

The Shian Quest Trilogy is on Facebook!

Prologue

Jack flung the stone into the rock pool as hard as he could. The splash soaked his shirt, but he didn't care. This waiting around was so *boring*.

Midsummer – now *that* had been exciting. Hunting the swordfish of fortune; finding the *Mapa Mundi*; raising the giant's bridge; defeating Malevola and the Grey; rescuing his father.

My father . . .

But he's still so weak, thought Jack; *all these years I've longed to find him, and it was two months before he could even talk. I still hardly know him.*

But I've got Tamlina's ring.

Jack took the ring from his Sintura belt, and stared hard at the Triple-S spirals. What did they mean?

'Good things come in threes', Tamlina had said. *Well, there's three spirals. Is that really the Destiny Stone, the Chalice, and the* Mapa Mundi?

The sun glinted off the ring, and with a jolt Jack saw the spirals begin to turn. He felt a sudden whooshing sensation – like the low road, only faster. Instinctively he closed his eyes, but instead of the blur of shade and light of a low road journey, in his mind's eye Jack could see the street outside Cos-Howe in Edinburgh.

> *Two men, each tied to a chair, and facing each other. There's snow all around them, and a burning brazier next to one. The picture's blurred; I can't make out their faces . . . There's three tall men approaching . . . That's Boreus! And he's slapped one of the prisoners hard . . . Now he's holding the man's head so it faces sideways. Someone else is coming . . . he's put a sword in the fire. He's holding the hot blade up to the prisoner's eyes . . .*
>
> *Bleeurgh! That's gross!*

Jack opened his eyes, and took a deep breath. He felt sick.

That was disgusting!

Jack shook his head, trying to clear the image seared into his mind, but it was no use. Like a film loop in his head he kept seeing the sword slicing into eyes.

He puked.

1
Frustration

"What's the matter, Jack?" asked Rana.

Jack started, and wiped his mouth. Had she seen him puke? He wished his cousins wouldn't creep up on him like that. Glancing apprehensively at the ring, he noticed that one of the spiral arms had faded. He tried to concentrate.

"I thought I saw something. There was snow."

"Snow? What planet are you on? It's not even autumn yet."

"Shut up, Rana." Lizzie sounded concerned. "Jack doesn't look well."

"I'm all right. I was thinking about the Kildashie."

"That uncivilised bunch," snorted Lizzie. "It beats me how they can order the Thanatos around."

"It's the Tassitus charm," said Rana confidently. "If they can control sound, they can do what they want."

"And they're near the Stone too," added Jack. "That must make them stronger."

The Stone of Destiny. Jack hadn't seen it that many times, but he'd *known* it was giving power to the Shian square. Only now the Kildashie and Thanatos were there; and they were torturing people.

I'd better not say anything about this to Dad. He's still not strong enough to handle this – whatever this is.

"More Darrigs and dwarves have arrived," announced Rana. "There's some nearly every day now."

"This little one said he came from Lomond," said Lizzie. "It was freezing there."

"It's freezing wherever the Kildashie are," said Jack, thinking of the snow in his vision. "I wish we could do something to get them out. This island's getting crowded."

"You're just in a bad mood because you've had to start lessons again," mocked Rana. "Mum didn't waste any time getting you and Fenrig back to work when Gilmore arrived, did she?"

"It's not fair. Petros doesn't have any lessons. I've got to spend every morning stitching."

"At least that gets you away from his wife," pouted Rana. "Barassie's so *fussy*. All that stuff about what we can wear in the tents, what we can wear outside ..."

"And all her rules about behaviour," interrupted Lizzie. "They're a pain. She never stops criticising."

"Gilmore's all right, I suppose," said Jack. "Good luck to anyone who escapes from the Kildashie. I just wish we were planning how to stop them getting the Destiny Stone and the Chalice."

"At least we've got the Sphere, the *Mapa Mundi*," said Lizzie. "They can't make the magycks complete until all three are together."

Jack smiled at the thought. He'd been the one to defeat the Nucklat and retrieve the Sphere. To begin with, Marco and Luka had even said he should keep it. But it had been an open secret that he had it; and each day Jack feared someone coming to steal it. All these Shian arriving on the island: maybe there were spies among them? In the end, Jack had entrusted the Sphere to Marco, but so far he'd kept Tamlina's ring. Tucked away in his Sintura belt it was invisible; but people must know he had it . . . He'd got a strange buzz from it sometimes; but nothing like that vision –

. . . *That was an execution* . . .

"Anyway," continued Rana, "the Sphere showed us leaving here in the autumn."

"I've never said I wanted summer to finish before," said Jack. "But Marco's season-wheel is turning so slowly. I just wish we could get on with it."

In his heart Jack knew that the Sphere had shown an autumn departure; but each week brought more news of Kildashie atrocities. Surely it was time to fight back?

"Can you tell me where Sandy of the Stone is?" A tall stranger had approached without any of them noticing.

Jack hurriedly thrust Tamlina's ring back into his Sintura belt. Had the man seen it?

"He'll be up at the house. Past those trees." Jack pointed; the man nodded, and moved off.

"He's new, isn't he?" said Lizzie. "There's loads of people I don't recognise these days. D'you think we can trust them all?"

"You don't think he could be a Thanatos spy, do you?" asked Jack.

"I don't fancy meeting those Thanatos again," shuddered Lizzie. "You've never seen the unforgiven dead. Believe me, you don't want to."

"And there's Boaban Shee too," said Rana. "Mum told me they're like vampires. And there's Red Caps in the border lands. Most of the country's Unseelie now."

"It's hard to believe it's like winter almost everywhere," said Jack looking up at the clear sky. "It's nice here. Bit cooler, though."

Jack resolved to give Tamlina's ring to Marco for safekeeping – for now. Like the *Mapa Mundi*, it was too much responsibility. And that vision had been scary.

"I bet Cos-Howe's doing OK, though." Jack tried to sound hopeful. "Cosmo can hold out as long as he wants."

"If the Thanatos . . ." Rana was silenced by a shove from her sister.

"Let's get back to the house," said Lizzie. "It's getting chilly."

The youngsters wandered along to Marco and Luka's house, surrounded as it now was by tents.

"Good news, kids," called out Aunt Dorcas. "Marco and Luka are coming back tonight."

"You mean the low road's open again?" Jack's eyes lit up.

"No, it's still out of action. Anyway, they hardly ever use it. Enda's bringing them over from the mainland."

"They're calling more McCools over too," added Katie.

Aunt Katie's changed in some ways, thought Jack. *More McCools must mean they're planning something, and once upon a time that would've got her frightened. But with Uncle Doonya a prisoner, she's not scared now, she's . . . determined.*

"Does that mean we're leaving soon?"

"You'll have to see what Marco says, Jack dear. A grig told us they'll be here this evening."

Grigs are flying again, even outside the low road. That definitely means things are on the move.

However, Jack's new-found optimism was to be short-lived. When Marco and Luka arrived that evening, all they would say was that the time was not yet right for a counter-attack. It wouldn't be long –

(Where've I heard that before?)

– but things had to be in place, otherwise the whole mission might fail.

Despite yet another 'not yet', Jack was glad to see Marco and Luka again. Since midsummer they had hardly been on the island. And things on the mainland obviously hadn't improved. The Kildashie and the Thanatos had most Shian – few as they were – under the thumb. Stories of imprisonment, torture – even murder – were commonplace now. A few areas had managed to resist, but isolated and scattered, and with bitterly cold weather, this was not much use for a counter-attack.

Marco and Luka brought many tales of horror from the mainland. And while the Seelie Shian bore the brunt of the ferocity, the Unseelie made no bones about their hatred for the humans. Every opportunity to cause mishap or mayhem among them was grasped readily; stories of disasters on the roads, or in darkened streets at night, showed that the Unseelie had few qualms and even less remorse. Stabbings, crashes and vicious 'accidents' had doubled since the Kildashie had united the Unseelie.

As they sat outside to eat, Jack saw Marco and Enda talking

earnestly. Jack hadn't had a chance to speak with the McCool leader since he'd arrived back; but he was pleased that more McCools were on their way.

They'd be more than handy in a fight. We need them. And it looks like we're going to get the go-ahead tonight.

But if I'm honest, I still don't rate our chances – not if the Unseelie are as powerful as people say. Dad's loads better than when we rescued him, but he's still weak. Uncle Hart's not ready yet; Grandpa looks so old, though the Phosphan curse is out of his system at last. Finbogie will be useful, at any rate. Ossian too – if we can get him away from Morrigan.

"Friends," called Marco, standing up at the end of the meal. "You will know that more help is on its way from Ireland; and the growing numbers here on Ilanbeg represent an impressive force."

Jack screwed up his face. *Impressive force?* Most of the ones who'd got away were women and children. *We need to pull in extra help from somewhere.*

"We must stop the Kildashie and the Thanatos, before they get ideas about expanding further," stated Enda. "We have troubles enough in Ireland with our own Unseelie. If they combine with the Kildashie, then nowhere will be safe."

"The Seelie around the country will unite," continued Marco, "but only if they believe the Kildashie can be defeated. That is why some of you must undertake a quest, to recruit allies. When the right force is ready, then it will be time to strike back."

"Who are these allies?" demanded Telos the McCool. "Why haven't they made contact with us?"

"The Unseelie control most of the mainland," replied Luka sternly, "but not the islands. However, there are Unseelie spies everywhere. Some of you will journey north. Others will stay here and join in later. The low road will open when the time is right."

"In the meantime," continued Marco, "the young ones are to continue their studies. Weather permitting, some of you will leave in a month or so."

A whole month? Jack ground his teeth. *I thought we were going to get the green light now.*

2

Sheena of the Shadows

Gilmore had done his best to recreate a workshop, but it wasn't up to much – just a table and a bench; and yet he was somehow managing to add to his materials most days. Despite his gripes about lessons, now that Jack was finally learning about charmed cloths, he knew he was getting somewhere. Invisibility cloth might still be some way off, but shrinking and growing and healing cloths showed great potential.

Shame Freya's not here, mused Jack as he stitched a blood bandage. *I miss her.*

There had been no news of Freya, or her sister Purdy, since the forced evacuation of the Shian square in Edinburgh nearly four months earlier. Jack had heard that they'd got away; but whether this was true, or where they'd gone, was really anyone's guess.

Fenrig was first to finish that morning. Presenting his newly stitched cloak to Gilmore, he simply nodded, and left.

Jack tried to finish the stitching on his blood bandages. The edges were important – Gilmore had stressed that; otherwise the blood just gets out of the side. But that's just the cloth – even humans have them; I need to learn what makes them special, what makes them *Shian*.

Jack didn't notice his tutor watching him closely as he laboured over his task. When Jack had finished, Gilmore placed his hand upon the youngster's shoulder.

"Well done, Jack. The bandages will help to stem the flow of blood, but only if they're charmed properly. I think you're ready to move on now."

"Are we going to do the charms?" Jack's heart began to race.

"It's time. And we'll have to pick up speed if we're to have enough for our journey."

"Are . . . are you coming on the boat?"

"I do have some uses, you know. And there'll be plenty of need for charmed cloths where we're going. Not to mention good swordsmen. Speaking of which . . ."

Jack turned round to see his father standing in the tent entrance. He *was* looking stronger.

"Luka and Armina are good doctors," he said, reading Jack's mind. "It's been slow, but I can feel the strength returning. But don't let me stop you."

"I was just about to teach him the haemostat charm. Sit and watch if you like."

Despite the novelty of seeing his father watching, the morning passed quickly as Jack learned how to prepare the bandages for charming. The haemostat one was quite easy, but the Cu-shee ones were tricky. Jack had never come across this famed Black

Dog of the North. More werewolf than dog, if half the stories told about it were true.

"Gilmore's right about having to stock up well," noted Phineas, as Gilmore went to get his lunch. "There's some rough journeying ahead."

"Have you been where we're going?" asked Jack. "The McCools told me it's wild up on the north coast – but nice."

"Enda's a good man; but he's only travelled that route in the spring. Autumn winds and winter gales are very different."

"If it's that hard, why are we travelling that way?"

"Because that's the right time to get what we need."

"The *Mapa Mundi* showed us going north in autumn," said Jack. "What do we need to get?"

"Well, there's 'what'; and there's 'who'. We have several places to see before we get to the north islands. Our first stop will be to raise the Hebseelie, and we'll have to time that right. If we get them on board, we've a good chance with the Norseelie. But there's somewhere else we need to go in between."

There's tears in his eyes; but he doesn't look sad. Quite the opposite, in fact.

"D'you know a lot about the island Shian, then?"

"A little. But there's one island that's going to be a real problem. I believe something I went looking for a long time ago is there. That's when I ended up being suspended by the Grey. Me and Konan."

"Konan told us where Marco was. He said something else too, only Grandpa said it was just a story."

"The Stone key?"

Jack nodded.

"It's no story. In fact, it's why your mother and I quarrelled."

Jack took a deep breath.

"I know you want to ask about her. And it's right you should know."

"Grandpa told me she was . . . highly strung."

Phineas' laugh was hollow. "Well, that's one way of putting it."

He's still got tears; but his eyes aren't so happy now . . .

"Jack, I don't know how much you know about families. They're complicated; your mother certainly was."

"Was?"

"Is, for all we know. Life in Rangie just didn't suit her. She'd found someone else."

"Who?" Jack clenched his fists.

"A human. She was going to leave."

"Leave me too?" Jack's voice was no more than a whisper.

"I don't know. But she said she would leave me if I ever went to see Tamlina."

"You knew Tamlina?" gasped Jack.

"I'd heard of her; and I'd heard she had something that makes the Shian stronger. The Raglan stone was a chance I couldn't pass up."

Raglan stone . . . Jack's mind raced. Tamlina had said that when she'd come out of her trance, the first time he'd seen her.

"The Raglan stone helps Shian to get stronger . . . but how?"

"I couldn't tell you how it works. But it's powerful. I wanted to show Father – your grandpa – that I could do something worthwhile. When Sheena found out, she said she would go."

Sheena. Jack had almost never heard his mother called by her name. It had always been 'your mother'. It was strange to think that she even *had* a name. So many things about his family were . . . uncomfortable.

"What about my sister? Is she . . . you know?"

Phineas laughed, heartily this time.

"Yes, she's really your sister. But that's all I know. You've both grown up without your father; and I'm truly sorry. I can try to make some of that up to you. As for Cleo, well I suppose she's had her mother . . ." His voice trailed off.

Jack closed his eyes, hoping things would go away.

"Does Grandpa know all this?"

"About her human? No, I never told him."

"Grandpa and Uncle Doonya just told me that she couldn't cope after you'd gone. They looked everywhere, but couldn't find her."

"They wouldn't have thought to look in the human spaces. She didn't let that on to anyone. She was always very . . . secretive."

"'Sheena of the shadows'?"

"You heard that one, did you?" Another hollow laugh. "It's what some people in Rangie used to call her."

"So the Raglan stone would help you to become powerful?"

"Not me: I meant it for the Congress. I thought that would show your grandpa what I could do. But the Grey got to me before I could find Tamlina. And Tamlina didn't have it when you last saw her, did she? Grandpa used the Pulviscin charm to cremate her; but the Raglan wouldn't have burnt. I'm guessing Malevola took it."

"But Rana finished Malevola off on the giant's bridge at midsummer."

"She'll have taken it back to her own home – Tula. That's why we've got to go there and get it back."

"How hard's that if Malevola's dead?"

"She may be gone, but her cronies will be there. They're Boaban Shee, Jack. That's why we'll need the charmed bandages."

"Boaban Shee? They're like vampires, aren't they?"

"Sort of. They drain their victims' blood; but they don't bite them. They use their nails. That's why the haemostat bandages are vital. And the swords – they can't stand Shian steel."

"Gilmore talked about a swordsman, just before you came. Is that you?"

Phineas stood, and adopted an *en garde* stance, imaginary sword in his right hand. Then, swiftly advancing, he cut and slashed the air, vanquishing make-believe enemies.

Then he stopped, puffing. Sweat trickled down his brow.

"I'm not as strong as I thought I was."

He sat again.

Great, thought Jack. *We're about to take on vicious enemies, and he gets tired fighting the air.*

"Don't worry," said Phineas. "We've a few weeks before we leave. Plenty of time for me to get fit again. And it's the equinox tonight. That'll help."

"So where's Tula, then?"

"Difficult to say. It's off the north coast, but it's almost impossible to find. It's always covered in cloud, or fog. Some even say it moves around. But that's where Malevola came from; and that's where she'll have hidden the Raglan stone, I'm sure of it."

"Because it would make her powerful?"

"Some say it's like the Destiny Stone in Edinburgh. It's got a real power."

"Shouldn't we be concentrating on getting the Kildashie out of Edinburgh, then?"

"The Destiny Stone's protected, Jack; the Kildashie may never work out how to get it. But if the Boaban Shee are using the Raglan stone, that's bad."

"If they keep it on their island, what's the harm?"

"Sooner or later the Kildashie will get it. Remember they seem to be controlling the Thanatos: they can be very persuasive."

Jack thought back to Tamlina's ring, and the execution scene it had shown. He shuddered.

"Come on," said Phineas, standing up again. "We'll get some lunch. Then you've got lessons with Finbogie this afternoon, haven't you? He's going to show you lot something special today."

3

Autumn Equinox

Finbogie's lesson *had* been good, even if it hadn't been a one-to-one. Learning how to use a sword, now that had been cool. Rana and Lizzie showed some promise too, and Fenrig. Finbogie had stressed that this was just basics, but even in a few hours, Jack felt he had mastered them. He'd stayed practising for ages with Finbogie after the other apprentices had given up, and now resolved to show his father what he could do. After all, he was a swordsman too.

Jack strode from the field where they'd had their lessons, and made for the house, swishing the blade Finbogie had given him. He noted the activity outside the house as tables and chairs were set out, and garlands strung over branches, but as Jack stepped through the doorway his shouted 'Hello' got no response, and his enthusiasm faded. The island was so busy these days that it was unusual for the house to be empty.

Probably getting ready for tonight's party . . .

Temporarily at a loss, Jack wandered along, examining the book shelves. So many books; how did they find time to read them all? He noted the wall-mounted season-wheel, which showed that they were indeed turning towards autumn. There was something reassuring about the wheel; it didn't lie. His eye was caught by an old leather-bound tome. Picking it idly off the shelf, Jack sat down and flicked through.

This new section's got a picture of an eagle. 'In the beginning . . .' But it's near the end, thought Jack. *And it's long. It would take years to read this one.*

He flicked further back. The people's names were strange. Jack flicked on, trying to find something he recognised. *Ah! Something about a riddle, that should be good.*

"Out of the eater came something to eat . . ." Jack read aloud.

"It's good to see you reading that."

Jack dropped the book as he jumped up and turned to face Marco.

"I . . . I was looking for my father."

"It's all right." Marco stooped down and picked up the old leather tome. "I don't mind you reading. But take care of the books, please."

Jack blushed, and avoided Marco's gaze.

"Your father's down at Trog's Bay with Murkle. They're practising their duelling. You can wait for him here. He shouldn't be long."

Jack sat down, and accepted the book from Marco.

"I think you'll find you were . . . there," said Marco, opening the book at the page Jack had been reading.

Jack was relieved when Marco left, and he resumed his reading. *Strange riddle . . . ah. There's the answer. Huh?* Jack read back a bit, to find the start of the story. *A lion? Coincidence that, seeing as Marco's a . . .*

"*En garde!*"

Jack turned to see his father in the doorway, brandishing his rapier. He looked suddenly . . . *alive*. Proudly, Jack got up, and held his own sword ready, facing his father.

There was a blur, three sharp metallic twangs, and Jack felt his sword fly out of his hand.

"I couldn't resist that," laughed Phineas.

"You don't look so tired now."

"I can feel the equinox coming; it's healing me. I'm glad to see Finbogie has started you on some useful stuff."

"He's already taught me loads of useful stuff," pouted Jack. "But the swords are cool. He said we would need them against the Boabans."

"That's only half of it," replied his father. "You need to be able to use the sword, but to banish them you have to . . ."

"Cut off their feet, and use some kind of hex. Finbogie told us."

"Did he teach you the hex?"

Jack shook his head.

"Well, I'll teach you that soon. Maybe when we're travelling. It'll take some time to get there. We'll need to teach you the hexes for Cu-shee as well."

"The Black Dog of the North? Gilmore showed me the bandage hex."

"That's for the wounds they cause; you need to know how to fight them too. They don't like Shian steel either. We'll cover that when we're sailing."

"Are you coming on the boat with us?"

"I'm sure I'll be strong enough in a month's time."

Jack thought back to how tired his father had become just fighting the air. A gruelling sea journey, with vicious enemies along the way, seemed a tall order. Still, he seemed to believe he would get better.

Supper was eaten as the falling sun neared the horizon. The whole Shian congregation were present, now about 100 in all. By the gloaming hour, the revellers sat replete, wistfully watching the darkening sky.

"Friends," called Marco, "you are all most welcome to this equinox feast. I know that some of you felt we did not celebrate midsummer properly. I hope tonight has gone some way to making up for that."

A whoop of delight from Rana.

"I am also aware that many of you are keen to reclaim your homes from the Kildashie and their allies. I would ask Kedge to bring us news of the situation."

Jack blinked hard. In all the excitement of the party he hadn't even seen Kedge . . . but there was no sign of Ploutter. He hadn't seen either of them since their jaunt in the High Street more than a year earlier.

"I am Kedge, from Rangie, near Edinburgh." Kedge's voice was faint. "The Kildashie have the city in terror. No Shian is safe; and the areas outside the city are nearly as bad. It's been freezing since the Kildashie took over."

His clothes tattered, and his right arm hanging limp by his side, he cut a pathetic figure.

"Tell them what happened." Luka spoke gently.

"They caught me trying to get into Cos-Howe with my brother. Sometimes they use Thanatos to give out punishments.

They tied me to a chair; then they took Ploutter . . ." He paused a moment and took a deep breath. "They sat him in front of me, and put his eyes out. Then they took a sledgehammer . . ." He sobbed, his shoulders heaving.

"Urrgh!" Lizzie covered her face at this picture of torture.

Jack felt his scalp go cold. He'd seen this . . . or some of it: when he'd looked at Tamlina's ring. He tried to swallow, but his mouth was dry.

"I never liked Ploutter," whispered Rana, putting her arm around her sister's shoulder. "But no one deserves that."

"What the Thanatos did to Ploutter has been done to many others. They *are* a vicious enemy, fearing only the death that awaits them in Sheol." said Marco.

"Murkle told us about Sheol once," said Jack. "It's Shian hell. And if you're nearly dead when you're sent there, you'll die, soul and all."

"The Kildashie," continued Marco evenly, "seem to have turned the seasons back."

"Then how'd we get them out?" shouted Ossian.

"Only with the right force, and at the right time." Marco spoke evenly. "You will need many more to have any chance of regaining your homes."

"But they have the Tassitus charm," yelled a voice.

"Perhaps," replied Marco evenly. "They *are* strong, have no doubt of that. And especially in the bitter cold, for that is their element."

"More friends are coming from Ireland," announced Enda. "In the next few weeks they will teach you about life on a boat. Some of us will sail to the north islands."

"Seven boats will go north," stated Marco. "Their fate will

determine when others can go to the mainland. As you all know, certain feast days are more auspicious."

"Who's going by boat?" demanded Ossian. "And what kind of tasks will they have?"

"Those who are being considered will know soon enough, for they will have to undergo training. But your knowledge of some of the island Shian will be valuable."

Jack wondered about getting up and repeating what his father had said about Tula island; but a stern look and a slow shake of the head from his father changed his mind.

What's he got to hide? thought Jack. *We're all in this together, aren't we?* He resolved not to mention his vision of Ploutter's death – for now.

"Your first stop will be Nebula," stated Luka. "There you must consult the Hebseelie Court, for with their help you will find other allies."

"Where's Nebula?" hissed Petros. "Sounds bloody uncivilised to me."

Jack shrugged his shoulders. He didn't care where it was; just so long as they got going; but he could sense Petros' reluctance.

"Those who sail north will begin training tomorrow," stated Marco. "Your enemy is formidable; but know too that you have right on your side."

"The next few weeks will be tough," added Enda sternly. "Only those who prove themselves, and those with a special role to play, may come."

I'm not missing out on that, thought Jack.

"And now," proclaimed Luka, "I see that the merging of day and night is almost upon us. Would Phineas please come forward?"

Jack frowned as his father got up.

What's this about?

Phineas seemed to know what was required, for he stepped smartly forward, and knelt before Luka. Armina rose too, and stood behind the kneeling figure.

"You all know how Phineas was kept by the Grey for ten years," announced Luka. "When Jack rescued him, he was at the point of death. But Jack's determination, and his love, won through."

He placed his hands on Phineas' head, at which Armina did the same. There was an expectant hush; people stood up to see what was happening.

For a moment there was a silence; then a soft shimmering sound, like faraway thunder.

Jack looked on with fascination. *What's going on?* He glanced over at Marco, who was looking straight back at him. Marco smiled.

And then Phineas stood up; shook himself, and stepping forward reached under his chair for his sword. Grasping it firmly, he swirled it around his head with a flourish, before looking over to Jack. His eyes were beaming.

Jack started forward, hesitantly at first. He reached his father, glancing nervously around at the expectant crowd.

Phineas stuck the sword into the soft ground, knelt down and looked Jack straight in the eyes. Jack saw for the first time that his father had the same piercing right blue eye as him.

"I'm back."

4

Sabotage

Each day now was a punishing routine of physical exercises, boat drills, and cleaning. Enda and Marco had been clear at the equinox feast: they were up against vicious enemies, and the boat journey north was not for the faint-hearted. *But why do boats have to be kept so clean?*

Still, Jack knew he couldn't complain. The mainland was not an option yet; and there was no sign of the low road opening up. So, boats it was. Heading north, and just as autumn turns towards winter. Exactly what the Shian people *don't* do. Or at least, the Seelie people.

Space on the boats was limited, and there was competition for places. Jack knew all the Shian who'd come from Edinburgh; but people had escaped from all over. Jack had an uneasy feeling as they trained each day: could everyone be trusted?

Jack enjoyed the sword practice; but the physical training

was exhausting. Almost all the others were bigger than him, and Jack secretly worried that he wouldn't be judged strong enough.

Ossian relished the training, and took great delight in showing off his considerable sailing skills to Morrigan, who, for her part, seemed besotted. Fenrig made no attempt to conceal his disdain, and spent most days sulkily going through his tasks.

"I like this," shouted Rana across to Lizzie as the two of them sat on the quayside and sewed patches onto torn sails. She glanced surreptitiously over at Dermot to make sure he had heard. There was no way *she* was getting left behind when the boats left.

"D'you think they'll let us?" whispered Lizzie, as her sister came over.

"They'd better." Rana huddled down with Lizzie under a sail as a squall blew up. "After all the work we've done on the boats. Besides, they'll need someone to help around."

"I'm not so sure. And Mum's never going to agree."

"We'll just have to show them we've got the skills they need," huffed Rana. "It's up to Mum to stop us if she can."

"It's going to be cold." Lizzie shivered in anticipation. "Winter on an open boat'll be freezing."

"Gilmore's making us special warm clothes; I heard him telling Barassie. And we're not going to spend the whole time on the boats. Enda said the islands are safe: we'll be able to sleep ashore most nights."

"Hope so." Lizzie was clearly less thrilled than her sister at the prospect of the journey north.

The rain eased off, and she threw the sail aside.

"Have you heard?" asked Jack as he came and sat with them.

"Arvin and Daid have arrived. They were using a human car on the mainland."

"Where were they hiding?" asked Lizzie. "Are they all right?"

"They hid out with some human musicians Daid knows near Lomond. Even the humans have noticed something's up. Daid showed me one of their newspapers – 'Climate chaos' it said."

"It'd be nice to have Arvin on the boat," mused Rana. "I mean, he'd be able to play music to us while we were sailing."

"You still planning on coming, then?" Jack tried to sound nonchalant.

"Why? You heard who's going?"

"No, but there's going to be seven boats; so that means about sixty. And Enda said you had to prove yourself if you wanted on."

"Well, we're being useful, aren't we? There's more to life on a boat than hauling ropes and sails. Who's going to cook, for instance?"

As long as it's not your mum, thought Jack.

"Come on you lot; break time's over."

A new arrival slapped Jack playfully on the shoulder as he passed. Jack eyed him suspiciously. He *said* he'd come from near Eildon, but he'd arrived alone, and nobody really seemed to know who he was.

But then that goes for lots of people here.

As the day of departure drew near, autumn gripped the island. Glorious golds and browns transformed the landscape, but they came at a price. Bitter winds blew in from the Atlantic, and squally showers became longer and more frequent. Despite this, there was a growing sense of excitement. Who would be chosen to go?

"I'll be all right," announced Ossian carelessly as the apprentices gathered in the field for supper on the eve of departure. "I know some people on these islands."

"Can't you say you have to take us?" asked Jack, without any real conviction.

"It's no' up to me. You heard Enda: everyone who goes has to have a reason."

"I suppose Morrigan's got a reason, then?"

Rana's question was both a challenge and a rebuke, but Ossian refused to rise to the bait.

"She's handy enough around a boat. And you never know: we might end up needin' some Brashat when it comes to takin' on the Kildashie."

Aye, right, thought Jack.

"Can I have your attention, please!"

Marco's voice was loud and authoritative, and the Shian crowd fell silent.

"Tomorrow, some of you will leave on your quest. You know by now that Luka and I only rarely interfere directly in Shian affairs. We have tried to guide you, and prepare you. But the task is yours to accomplish."

"We thank you for your guidance, and your hospitality," replied Enda.

"The McCools' sailing expertise will prove invaluable in the weeks ahead." Luka stood now and faced the assembled throng. "There are seven boats; two will be exclusively for their own use, and they will crew the others; that leaves twenty-four places."

"We have watched all of you in the last few weeks, and know what we need," announced Dermot. "But first, you must understand our quest. We seek the help of the Hebseelie Court.

They have no cause with the Kildashie, but neither do they like to leave their islands."

"You may know of the Hebseelie's reputation," said Enda. "We ourselves met some of them earlier this year. To persuade them to join us will not be easy; but we have no option. The Unseelie threat grows by the day, as Sandy of the Stone will confirm."

Jack had seen little of his grandfather in the preceding weeks. And when he *had* seen him, Grandpa Sandy had been busy, discussing matters with Marco, Luka and Enda; or helping Armina with her preparations – for there was no doubt that *she* would be one of the travellers.

"The Hebseelie Court holds the key," stated Grandpa. His voice was strong, and there was no sign now of the debilitating Phosphan curse that had so weakened him. "Although Seelie, they are mistrustful of people from the mainland. To persuade them to join us, we need to retrieve a treasure lost by them many years ago: a flag, held by the humans. Some of you may have learnt this story from Murkle."

Nope, thought Jack. *One of many things I can't remember from Murkle's lessons.*

"To get the flag, we will need the help of the giant Caskill; and to get his help, we must find a charmstone. That is our first task."

"You *will* need the island Shian," agreed Marco. "But not only from the west. You must also recruit the Norseelie: united, you will be a powerful force."

"A few islanders and us against the Kildashie and all their allies?" cried a voice from the crowd. "And in the winter? We've no chance."

"Winter may seem to be the Kildashie's ally," explained Marco, "which is why the Kildashie will never expect an attack then. And while they have formidable allies, you have great strength here too. Jack, please come forward."

Jack hadn't expected this, and he blushed as Rana shoved him to make him stand up.

"Most of you know how Jack came to be here," proclaimed Marco. "Wisely, he entrusted this to me." Marco now reached into a sack and withdrew the *Mapa Mundi*.

There was a general buzz among the crowd, as the more recent arrivals whispered amòngst themselves and strained to see the treasure. Jack walked slowly towards Marco, feeling the eyes of all there upon him. He glanced nervously up at his grandfather, then across at his father. His father smiled.

"The Sphere: the *Mapa Mundi*, that shows its holder their true path," announced Marco. "It has already shown Jack the route to the north islands. Jack is clearly meant to go; and his father and grandfather too. You have seven boats, as you know. The McCool leader of each of these will now name his crew."

As Marco tied the flag around Jack's neck, Enda faced the crowd, and announced in a clear voice, "Jack, his cousin Petros, and their grandfather; Armina, Gilmore and Barassie; and Fenrig."

Barassie and Fenrig?! Jack felt his stomach turn, but his disgust was overtaken immediately by a loud explosion from the harbour. The sheet of flame that shot into the night sky drew gasps of astonishment . . .

The boats!

5

Stowaways

After the explosion came the confusion, as almost the entire crowd rushed to the harbour. Though it was too dark to assess the full damage, accusations, claims and counterclaims were hurled, resurrecting old resentments. The night passed with mutterings and talk of conspiracies.

By morning, few had managed to get much sleep; but at least the situation was clearer. Only one boat had been destroyed, more a result of luck than intention. The charges that had been placed along the quayside had failed to ignite after the first explosion.

"Amateurs!" spluttered Finbogie as he surveyed the scene in the early dawn light. "Whoever it was, I hope it wasn't someone I taught."

"It is clear that someone does not wish this venture to succeed," said Grandpa as he walked back up to the house with the youngsters. "But we cannot let that delay us. We only have three days in which to reach Nebula. We must catch the morning tide."

Rana and Lizzie hung back. Jack had been puzzled the previous evening by their quiet acceptance of the news that they had not been selected to travel. After a perfunctory 'It's not fair!' (... *almost their theme tune*, Jack had thought ...) they had retreated to their tent and had not been seen again before breakfast.

Jack wound the Sintura belt around his waist, and checked its contents: jomo bag – *good, I've got three dirts in there now* – the lucis powder and Tamlina's ring. Then he strapped Trog's steel knife to his calf, stuffed his few belongings into a satchel, and went to the house to say goodbye to Marco and Luka. He found them waiting by the door.

"The news that someone here does not wish your quest to succeed will not have reassured you, Jack. But wear the *Mapa Mundi* as you did when you first got it. And use Tamlina's ring to tie it," said Marco.

Jack did as he was bid, and was astonished to see the flag around his neck vanish as he pushed the ring up towards his neck. He couldn't even feel it.

"Don't forget it's there. There'll be times when you'll need it."

"Go well, Jack," said Luka kindly. "And know that you serve a just cause. Keep that always in your heart. Our brother will help to guide you."

Jack looked in puzzlement at the two of them. "You mean Matthew's coming?"

"No, not Matthew," smiled Marco. "Remember I told you there were four of us? Our brother John will be watching you, from a distance."

"Is he . . . a shape . . ."

Luka smiled. "I think you'll recognise him when the time is right."

Fiddling rather awkwardly with the flag around his neck, Jack shook hands with the two old men, and turned away.

I've got to say goodbye to Trog's Bay, he thought. *I owe him that.* Jack fingered the steel knife that Trog had bequeathed to him as he made his way for the last time down to the shoreline.

By the time Jack reached the quayside an hour later there was a palpable sense of excitement. The damaged boat lay, partly submerged, but the other six were crowded with people and belongings. Being Shian size, they looked tiny: Jack had grown so used to being human height on the island. His heart began to beat faster.

"Come on! We need to catch this tide!" Grandpa's exhortations were strident.

Phineas came up and embraced Jack.

"We're on our way. I'll be on Dermot's boat, but we'll see each other whenever we put into shore. They've sorted out the places for the eight whose boat was sunk. It'll mean we're all a bit more crowded, but we can't help that now. Oh, and ask Enda to teach you the Cu-shee hexes."

Jack saw Ossian and Morrigan step onto Telos' boat, shrinking down to Shian size as they did so. With relief he saw that Murkle was with them. *At least we won't be getting his lessons on board.*

"Where's Barassie?" Gilmore sounded desperate. "She should be here!"

His concern was matched by Aunt Katie, who asked anxiously

of Jack, "Have you seen the girls? They disappeared after breakfast. I hope they're all right."

"They'll be fine, Auntie. You know what they're like; they'll have wandered off to a beach somewhere."

Petros was sitting in the prow of the boat, looking pensive. *He doesn't really want to be here,* thought Jack. *But he must've been chosen for a reason.*

"Have you seen my wife?" Gilmore accosted Fenrig as the young Brashat climbed into the boat.

Fenrig sullenly shook his head, and threw his satchel down.

There'll be a reason for choosing Fenrig too. Someone must know something I don't.

Grandpa and Armina climbed – none too sprightly – onto the boat, resuming their Shian size. Armina's large bag clunked loudly.

"Come on; the tide's turning," Enda snapped, as he stowed Fenrig's satchel carefully away. "Who're we waiting on?"

"Barassie. I haven't seen her for an hour." Gilmore's voice was frantic.

"Well, she's five minutes to get on board; then we're leaving."

Enda's tone did nothing to ease the tailor's anxiety. Jack decided to go and sit with Petros.

"Exciting, eh? It's nice being real size again."

Petros grunted.

"You want to help get the Kildashie out, don't you?"

Petros sniffed, and looked away, out to the open sea.

Sensing that he would get no more out of his cousin just now, Jack set to watching the other boats. Telos had already manoeuvred his boat out, and was starting to hoist his foresail with Ossian's help. Arvin had a squeeze box out, and was playing a human hornpipe while Daid clapped along. Murkle's grimace indicated his distaste for such un-Shian arrangements.

Dermot's boat was next out, followed by the others. Jack waved as he saw his father hauling on a rope to release the foresail.

Enda strode up to Gilmore.

"We can't wait any longer; the tide's running fast. And there's no time now to replace her. I'll take over the cooking."

Gilmore's pained expression showed his feelings, but he nodded.

With large paddles, Enda and Grandpa steered the boat away from the quayside. The tide was running freely now, and with just the foresail released the boat moved swiftly out of the harbour and into the open sea.

"Shall we bring the mainsail down?" shouted Jack as they encountered deeper waters.

"Aye, we're ready for that. Like I showed you."

Jack and Fenrig, well trained now, released the locks that held the mainsail ropes. As the great white sail billowed out, there were two thuds on the deck, and two squeals of pain.

Armina, instantly alert, held her sceptre out. "*Ostentus!*"

The girls, still in a heap on the deck, materialised.

"What in the name of Tua are you two doing here?" Grandpa's outraged yell was echoed by mocking squawks from two seagulls.

Rana and Lizzie sat up, their green bonnets now scalded red by Armina's hex.

"We've come to help," said Rana defiantly.

"Turn around," Grandpa shouted across to Enda. "We'll have to take them back."

"We can't. The tide's running too strongly. There's no time if we're to make Nebula in three days."

With an exasperated roar, Grandpa Sandy upbraided the two girls. Lizzie's eyes filled with tears, and she looked down at her feet; but Rana's face showed no sign of regret. There was a twinkle in her eye, and she glanced slyly across at Jack and smiled.

"What have you two done with my wife?" demanded Gilmore.

"She's back at the house," answered Rana calmly. "She'll wake up soon."

"What do you mean?" roared the tailor.

"It's not a bad hex. We used one of Armina's potions."

"You did what?" squeaked Armina, reaching for her bag and examining the contents. "And what else have you stolen?"

"Listen," commanded Enda. "This is not the start we'd planned. But we have to get along. So that's the last of the shouting. We'll find plenty to keep these two occupied."

Jack moved up to the back of the boat, where Petros had remained a silent spectator to these events.

"What're they like?" smiled Jack as Petros turned to look at the receding island. "Your mum's going to go spare. Oh well, say goodbye to Ilanbeg."

Petros said nothing, but wiped his mouth slowly.

He's not looking that well, thought Jack.

"Aren't you going to say goodbye to the island?"

"Goodbye breakfast." With that, Petros leant over the side and heaved.

Petros was not the only crew member to get seasick. As the boats passed each other tales were swapped, and it became evident that the sea's swell had identified those who lacked 'sea legs'.

Fenrig's initial delight at Petros' misfortune didn't last long, and before they made landfall that night at Soabost, he too had succumbed. Kelly, relocated from the boat that had sunk, tried to console him.

"Don't feel so bad. Plenty of sailors get seasick."

"Leave me alone."

"Ah, don't take it like that. We've days on this boat together. It's autumn, see; we can't go nearly as fast as we can in the summer."

Fenrig scowled and turned away.

"The best thing you can do is concentrate on something else. Like that selkie, for example."

Fenrig squealed in alarm as a face appeared beside the boat. The selkie began swimming alongside the boat, almost touching it.

"She's sheltering," stated Kelly. Looking around, he fixed his gaze on a boat some distance away. "Human fishermen," he went on. "They shoot seals. Looks like they've mistaken the selkie for one."

"I've never seen a selkie." Jack made his way to the side of the boat, and looked down at the graceful creature. He noticed a dark mark on the creature's back. "I think she's hurt."

Kelly peered down. "She's been shot all right. We can't do much while we're sailing. But she's safe now, as long as she stays with us. We'll check her over when we reach land."

"I know about selkies," announced Fenrig to Jack's astonishment. "They're cool; they steal the humans' fish."

When they made landfall, Kelly and Fenrig stayed behind in the boat as the others went ashore. The selkie, bleating harshly, remained close by in the bay.

Suppertime was a chance for those on the other boats to get

the full story of Rana and Lizzie's escapade. The inevitable rows from some of the adults were balanced by respectful (but silent) praise from most of the youngsters. And with the winds set as they were, the only chance of getting word down the coast to Ilanbeg had been to send a seagull.

After supper, Ossian stepped onto a fallen tree trunk and shouted for order. Grandpa Sandy stood beside him.

"We've one good day's sailin' behind us; and two more to Nebula. Tomorrow we make landfall at Canna; and the next day by Talisker. There we've to get Caskill's charmstone. We've a selkie for company; she's been shot, but only in the shoulder. Kelly and Fenrig have seen to her wound. We'll see if she wants to come further with us."

Jack looked across at his grandfather; then over at his father. Why weren't they explaining all this?

"We all have different reasons for being here," added Grandpa. "Ossian's friendship with some Nebula people will help us. So, to your tents, and rest well. Tomorrow night we'll reorder the crews for Thursday's sail."

"What's so special about Thursday?" grumbled Petros as he and Jack bedded down for the night.

"So that we know who's doing what when we get to Nebula. Anyway, it's not Thursday that's special; it's Friday."

"Friday?"

"That's Hallows' Eve."

Petros started guiltily. He was a quarter human, after all: had living at human height for so long really made him forget?

6
Fishermen's Blues

The sail up to Canna the next day was uneventful, except for the puzzling appearance on the boat of a shy young woman. She sat huddled in the prow, pale-faced, watching the other boats carefully. Kelly stopped any of the youngsters from approaching her, explaining that she had to rest.

The seagulls that periodically followed the boats, hoping for scraps, looked huge to the Shian, but were no trouble as long as no food was visible. But if the seagulls were not threatening, the sight of an eagle soaring overhead was the cause of animated discussion.

"They take lambs," announced Petros. "They could easily take one of us. Or one of you," he said pointedly to his sisters. "You're the smallest."

Lizzie cowered as he said this, but Rana was made of sterner stuff.

"It's a sign of good luck. Marco told me about an eagle once

– he even showed me a picture in one of his books. They're special."

That's right, thought Jack. *In Marco's book.*

The day passed slowly. After Enda had taught Jack and Fenrig the Cu-shee hexes, they had an unofficial competition to see who could react fastest to Enda's orders. Each considered himself the winner, but their keenness provided great entertainment for the others.

Except Petros. If Fenrig had got used to being on board, *he* hadn't, and he spent another miserable day gazing at the heaving waters – and heaving back. If nothing else, it gave everyone something to talk about.

Rana and Lizzie, kept busy initially with as much swabbing, scrubbing and cleaning as Grandpa could think of, had weathered that particular storm, and spent the afternoon sitting in the small rowing boat that was pulled along in the boat's wake, trailing a hopeful fishing line.

But two days' good sailing was as long as their luck was to last, and Thursday morning saw leaden skies and a fierce north-westerly wind that prevented them putting to sea. Ossian had selected Jack to come on his boat, swapping with Finbogie, and the two of them sat by the boats and looked morosely at the churning sea.

Jack, finding himself seated next to Gilmore, couldn't think of a way to open the conversation. What do you say to a tutor whose wife has been abducted by your cousins? Gilmore saved his blushes.

"Jack, I'll be going on one of the other boats. You'd better take this for your new guest." He slipped some cloth into Jack's palm.

Jack's puzzled expression told its own story.

"It's a special haemostat bandage: it works against bullet wounds. The one we used yesterday will need replaced sometime."

"But I'm not going on Enda's boat," said Jack. "Ossian wants me to go with him to Talisker."

"I'll give the bandage to Fenrig, then. It could be useful having a selkie around. They know the waters here better than any of us."

However, when Ossian and Enda decided at noon that they had little option but to take to the boats and head north, the selkie woman was nowhere to be seen.

"She'll have gone back to her people," said Enda to Rana and Lizzie, who were looking anxiously for the selkie. "Her wound was a lot better after we used Gilmore's bandage. Come on, we need to get going."

What had been planned as a reasonably gentle few hours' sail to Nebula became a fraught marathon endeavour against surging swell and bitterly cold rain. Never had Jack thought that the sight of a rocky outcrop would be so cheering, but when Ossian ordered him ready to take the mainsail down, Jack knew they were safe. As they sailed up the coast Ossian kept a keen eye on the shore. Finally, he let out a whoop of joy as he saw a flare from a secluded bay. Turning the boat into shore, he guided the craft gently in.

Jack turned round and was surprised to see the other boats continue up the coast, their mainsails still up.

"Where are they going? I thought we were going to get Caskill."

"We'll meet them up at Ardmore. That's where the flag is. But we need to get the charmstone first. This is Talisker."

As the boat drifted in, Jack saw two figures huddled on the shore. The wind had died down, but it was still cold.

"We thought ye werenae comin'," grumbled one of the shore figures as Ossian steered the boat in.

"The wind was up. Have we still time?"

"Oh aye. They'll be there until it gets dark. An hour, anyway."

"Jack, you come wi' me. The others'll meet us at the head of the loch later."

"Can't I come?" wailed Morrigan.

Jack had hardly noticed her throughout the day. She had spent the time hunched down as far out of the wind as she could get.

"I want to show Jack this. You'll be fine wi' the others. See you in an hour or so."

Ossian, Jack and Telos clambered into the tiny rowing boat, and made the short distance to shore. As they made the shoreline, Ossian and Jack jumped out, leaving Telos to return to the main boat.

"Jack, meet Gilravage and Stram."

Jack waved as the two locals shouldered their knapsacks.

"Why d'you not want Morrigan to come?" Jack knew that she and Ossian had been well nigh inseparable since midsummer.

"She's gettin' on my nerves. Never leaves me alone."

"Ye an' yer girls." Gilravage punched Ossian matily on the shoulder as they set off up a woodland track.

"Where are we going?" asked Jack. He was cold and tired, and wanted a hot meal more than anything.

"To get the charmstone," answered Gilravage. "It's no' far. Least, the man that's got it isnae."

"How did you know we needed it?"

"We've been weeks arrangin' this, Jack," said Ossian. "D'you think we were just trainin' all that time? I've been up here a couple o' times sortin' this out."

"So who's got the charmstone?"

"A human," growled Stram. "He's an eejit. He's no idea what he's got."

"Ossian," whispered Jack as Gilravage and Stram strode ahead. "They are Seelie, aren't they? I mean, this whole thing is about being Seelie."

"Doesn't mean you can't get the humans that deserve it. This guy's a real prize – you'll see. And anyway, we're stuffed if we don't get this charmstone."

With that, Ossian jogged to catch up with his friends, leaving Jack to bring up the rear.

They had walked for twenty minutes when they came to another shoreline.

"It's a loch," explained Stram. "This guy fishes on the other shore."

The four clambered into a small boat, and Gilravage and Stram expertly rowed them across the misty loch. In a few minutes they were within thirty yards of the far side, and in the fading light Jack could make out half a dozen people sitting on the shoreline with fishing rods.

"They're all humans, yeah?"

"Just watch," said Ossian, "you'll like this."

Jack strained to see what was happening, but for several minutes there was nothing more exciting than one of the men getting up and having a stretch. As he turned to sit down again he held his hands about two feet apart, gesturing to one of his friends. Loud braying laughter echoed over the water.

"Boastin' again," muttered Gilravage.

"You call this entertainment?" Jack rubbed his icy hands together. "Even Murkle's lessons are more exciting. And I'm starving."

"Just listen," said Stram. "He'll start any minute."

Sure enough, a loud imperious voice carried over the water to the small boat.

"My great grandfather bought the estate back in the '30s. We come up once a year for the fishing."

Jack looked more closely. The man was clearly holding court.

"He thinks he's the laird," whispered Ossian. "The best dressed bad fisherman in the country – and his cronies are no better. He just brings them here to impress them. They can afford anythin' they want, but they know the value of nothin'."

"The old house had lain empty for ages. Great grandpapa had to gut the place, basically. But he planted some apple trees – that's when he came across this."

The 'laird' showed his friends a quartz amulet which he wore around his neck.

"He found it in a chest buried in the garden. Sort of shaped like a pot, or something. No idea what the symbols are – look like ancient runes to me. Some local chappie says they're crescent moons . . ."

Jack's ears pricked up. *Crescent moons?*

". . . anyway, hundreds of years old. But I've always believed it brought me luck when fishing. Never fail to catch a whopper. Hwuh, hwuh."

He sat down again, pleased with his little joke, and picked up his rod. The amulet sat on his ample chest, glinting in the fading light. Lazily, he took a long swig from his hip flask, then passed it along the line to a chorus of 'Thank you, sirs'. His face radiated contentment.

The 'laird' had been sitting there for only a minute or two when suddenly he leapt up as his line went taut. He let the line play out for a while, then, as it slackened, started to reel it in. Jack watched as the other fishers gathered around to offer advice and encouragement.

A thought occurred to Jack.

"Can they see us?"

"'Course not," replied Ossian. "The boat's charmed, it's invisible. Those Dameves are in for a shock."

Jack watched as the fisherman slowly reeled his catch in, the splashes getting larger as the fish neared the shore.

"What's he caught?"

"More than he bargained for," said Ossian, as the fish was reeled in.

One of the other fishermen let down a net, and scooped up the catch. The 'laird' lifted the furiously wriggling fish – at least two feet long – out of the net, and held it aloft. Its wriggles slackened off, and the group passed around congratulations and estimates of weight. As the 'laird' reached into the fish's mouth to release the hook, the fish began to grow.

Within seconds it had doubled in size, and the laird struggled to keep a grip. The fish lifted its head, gave an almighty shake and dislodged the hook in its mouth; then, it made to bite the laird, who dropped it and fell over. The others had all stepped back in amazement as the fish, landing on the ground, exploded into several smaller fish. These now began to squirm and flip down the bank to the water's edge. Reaching this within seconds, they slid quietly into the dark water.

There was a moment of absolute silence: the fishermen stood transfixed by what they had seen; the 'laird', still on the ground, stared, open-mouthed at the now still water. Without warning the fish – restored to its swollen size – poked its head out of the water, and uttered a deep roar that echoed across the loch. Then, sliding down into the water again, it swam away. The 'laird' looked as if he was about to die.

Ossian laughed wildly, rocking the boat from side to side.

"That'll teach 'em to brag about the one that got away," he said, wiping tears from his eyes. "They're boastful, that lot, always goin' on about how they nearly broke the record. Serves 'em right."

"Time to get the charmstone," said Stram matter-of-factly, and he and Gilravage rowed to within a few feet of the shore. Jumping out of the boat, Gilravage made his way determinedly towards the stunned fishermen.

If the exploding fish had been cause of enough surprise and shock, the sight of a two-foot man emerging from the loch put paid to all notions of a peaceful night's sleep to come.

"He's stayed Shian size," hissed Jack. Having been so used to growing to human size when in the human parts of Edinburgh – and on Ilanbeg – Jack had almost forgotten how much smaller Shian were than humans.

Gilravage strode boldly up to the 'laird', and bent down. With a flick, he produced a small knife, and swiftly cut the chain holding the amulet. Then, grabbing the laird's hip flask, he made an exaggerated swigging motion with his right hand, before heading back for the water and – to the watching humans – disappearing.

As Gilravage clambered back into the boat, Ossian and Stram took the oars. All four were laughing uproariously.

"Can't they hear us?" asked Jack through tears of laughter.

"Aye, but they still can't see us," replied Stram happily. "What're they goin' to say? A big fish exploded into lots of wee fish, and yelled at 'em? Then a wee man appeared and stole his lordship's charm? That's one story they won't tell; nobody'll believe 'em."

"That's Phase One complete, Jack. Glad you came? Now we can go and find Caskill."

7

Waking Caskill

As Ossian and Stram rowed along the loch, Gilravage turned the amulet over in his hands, delighted with his prize. Still being Shian size, the amulet more than filled his hand.

"How'd you know his lordship had the charmstone?" asked Jack.

"Your tutor's been comin' along this last while," replied Gilravage. "You'll see him soon."

My tutor? Jack's mind whirled. *It must be Murkle. That's it! He told us about the crescent moons.*

"It does look like a pot," said Jack.

"It's a cauldron, not a pot," replied Gilravage. "And those aren't runes. But it *is* Norse, I know that much."

"The Norsemen came all the way down this coast, hey? I mean, Dunvik's not far from here, is it?"

"They left behind all sorts. This should be worth a bit."

A jetty at the mouth of the loch appeared out of the mist, and the boat nudged into it. They all clambered ashore.

"They'll be waiting for us. Come on." Stram took the lead, striding quickly through the dusk.

The mist had settled, taking visibility down to a few yards, and Jack could barely see Ossian ahead of him as they made their way through dense undergrowth. Jogging to keep up, he gradually became aware of the sound of cascading water.

"What's that?"

"It's whit keeps most folk out o' the cave o' the wells," replied Gilravage.

Jack's mind was working overtime. *The cave of the wells.* It was another name he knew from Murkle's dreary lessons. Murkle was definitely nearby.

Sure enough, as they reached a gnarled oak tree, Jack saw several of the Shian square residents huddled over a fire. There was Grandpa, and Murkle and Daid, Gilmore and Finbogie; and about a dozen McCools. The smell of roasting meat assailed Jack's nostrils, and his stomach rumbled.

"Sit down, sit down." Gilmore fussed around as the new arrivals gathered round the fire. "We'll get you some food. Did you get the charmstone?"

Gilravage produced the amulet, but hesitated for a moment.

"Do you not trust us?" Grandpa Sandy appeared out of the mist. "I take it Ossian has explained the necessity of this action. Believe me, if there was another way we would not be here."

"How much is it worth?" asked Gilravage.

He had no time to respond. There was a swish, and two seconds later he lay on the ground, with Finbogie standing over him, sceptre pointed at his throat.

"More than your life is worth, fisherman. Hand it over."

Gilravage proffered the amulet, and got to his knees.

"I was only jokin'."

"This is not the time for jokes," spat Murkle. "Who knows what waking this giant may do? But we have no choice. We must get the flag."

"I think we could all do with some food." Grandpa Sandy spoke evenly. "And I urge you all to save your energies for tomorrow. There is a bothy nearby where we can sleep."

"Grandpa, where are the others? Dad, and Petros and the rest of them?"

"They have gone ahead to prepare for tomorrow. The Hebseelie will convene at Balbegan. That's not far from Ardmore castle, where the flag is kept."

"But shouldn't we stick together?"

"We have to be cautious; they're mostly Seelie here, but they're different. Each boat crew will seek their own shelter. Phineas is scouting ahead; he'll make sure we're all in the right place for tomorrow."

"So who's going to wake this giant up?"

"Oh, that's easy. It's you and Murkle."

Jack did not sleep well that night. For one thing it was cold, and even in a bothy crammed with people, there was precious little warmth. But what really kept him awake was the thought of going into a cave with his least favourite tutor to wake up a giant. How was that for a Hallows' Eve surprise?

Breakfast was eaten in near silence, everyone preferring the company of their own thoughts to the conversation of others.

"Grandpa, we've got the amulet to wake Caskill. What am I supposed to do?"

Grandpa Sandy looked hard at Jack.

"Jack, waking this giant will not be that simple. The legend says that we must charge his heart – that's what the amulet is for."

Jack's astonished expression told its own story.

"The amulet has the power to awaken Caskill, but only with the right charm; and you must find him first."

"But he's in the cave; you've already said."

"Jack, that cave stretches far into the mountain; and it's dark. There are tunnels and wells in there; it's dangerous."

"Then why don't we all go in and look for him?"

"We need to win him over. Giants aren't used to crowds. If we all go in, he'll think he's being attacked, especially if he sees fire torches. That's the surest way to turn him angry."

"Can't I have a sceptre if it's dark in there?"

"You're not allowed one; you know that."

"So what do I do in there?"

"Marco and Luka have great faith in your ability to see the right way. You must use the Sphere. There's no harm in you knowing now, but while Marco was keeping it safe, several of the Congress tried to use it; and we couldn't."

"You mean I'm the only one who can make it work?"

"Jack, our powers are not as strong here. Maybe we're too far away from the Stone in Edinburgh – the Kildashie have the benefit of that now; but you have the benefit of the Sphere."

"Young man," said Murkle quietly, "your role in that cave is to keep me on the right path. This is not something I ever expected to be asking of an apprentice; but your grandfather is correct: the powers we would normally use do not work well here."

"We can take you as far as the great cataract; we will wait for you there." Grandpa smiled at Jack.

"And Caskill will get us the flag from Balbegan, which means we can summon the Hebseelie Court?"

"Yes," said Murkle, becoming excited. "My first trip here. I'll be the first one to waken Caskill in 100 years . . . Caskill – the only one who can get the flag because of . . ."

Grandpa Sandy's hand extended out and gripped Murkle's arm. The tutor stopped abruptly, then swallowed hard.

"Because of what?" Jack fought down a rising sense of panic. "What's stopping anyone else from getting the flag?"

"One task at a time, Jack. Just be true to what you know is right." Grandpa looked Jack directly in the eyes, and smiled. "We're relying on you."

Jack thought that Murkle was looking sheepish. Had he something to hide? And what did he mean – this was his first time here? Hadn't Gilravage said his tutor had visited Nebula already?

It was with a heavy heart that Jack made his way with the others to the foot of the great cataract. Thousands of gallons of water gushed between the two rock faces, falling 100 feet before crashing into the waters of Loch Lin. A fine spray met them as they got close.

"Murkle will summon us if we are needed. You go and show him the way."

Jack looked at the waterfall. There seemed to be no point at which you could walk under it – it fell straight into the loch, with a noise that drowned out all conversation, and a force that ruled out any notion of swimming under it.

"Come along, come along," mouthed Murkle. "Let's be getting in there."

He walked to the side of the great cataract, where a barely discernible path disappeared under the torrent of water. Unable to hear him, but taking his cue, Jack followed. Holding his sceptre forward, Murkle shouted,

"*Obturamentum!*"

It came out as a high-pitched shriek, and an inverted V-shape formed in the curtain of water, just three feet high. Murkle grabbed Jack's arm and dragged him through. The moment they were on the other side, the V-shape disappeared.

The cave was curiously quiet after the deafening noise on the outside; and almost pitch dark. Murkle struck his sceptre on the ground, and held it aloft. The crystal glowed brightly, throwing a dim circle of light around them. The circle didn't extend very far, however, and Jack wished he'd been allowed to have his own sceptre.

I don't know why they're so strict. I'll be fourteen in a few months.

He had no time to muse on these things, as Murkle was evidently keen to proceed.

"Come along, young man. We need to find this giant."

Murkle started off on a narrow track. Even at Shian height, there was little room to either side.

"Let me get the Sphere, and I'll see what it shows," cried Jack plaintively as his tutor disappeared into the gloom.

It made little difference. As Jack unwound the *Mapa Mundi* from his neck, he only knew where Murkle was because of the tiny bobbing light from the tutor's sceptre. Jack felt the flag turn into the Sphere, but it was too dark to make anything out.

"Murkle! Wait for me!"

He headed for the sceptre glow ahead, but the glow kept moving. Murkle hadn't even stopped.

Muttering under his breath, Jack edged forward as quickly as he dared. He hadn't gone more than a few paces when his right leg plunged knee-deep into a freezing pool. Clutching the Sphere frantically, he clambered back onto the narrow path.

A shout of pain from ahead suggested that Murkle had also come off the path. Jack made his way towards the glow of his tutor's sceptre, and found Murkle sitting down, clutching his left ankle and cursing softly. Jack fought back a giggle.

"I'll use the Sphere."

He held the Sphere forward, and in the sceptre's light saw the map's two large circles.

They helped us get across the giant's bridge at midsummer. What are they showing now?

For a while, nothing was visible. Then a slumbering figure appeared, with a glowing path leading up to him. Jack looked at the picture. *A glowing path?* The sceptre was no good; and they weren't allowed to use fire because it would frighten Caskill.

Murkle's cursing had lessened, and Jack looked curiously at his tutor. Despite his obvious pain, he looked . . . well, excited.

"My first giant," said Murkle happily, in between gasps of pain.

"Murkle, have you never seen a giant before?"

"I've read more about giants than you'll ever know, young man. I was researching giant lore before you were even born."

"But you've never actually met one?"

"I've got the amulet; it will waken his heart again. I know what to do. Now, can't you make that thing show us where he is?"

Jack thought. A glowing path . . . Then his mind cleared. Of course! Finbogie had given him the lucis powder. Quickly, Jack reached inside his Sintura belt and took a pinch of the powder. What was it Finbogie had said? 'Only a pinch; make it last'.

Jack looked at the Sphere again. It showed the cave's multiple paths, and great pools in between them all. Which path was the right one? As Jack turned to face different directions, one of the paths on the map glowed.

That must be it. I'll have to use the Sphere to keep me on track.

Edging cautiously forward, Jack threw the lucis powder onto the path in front of him. As he did so, the path glowed for about a dozen yards ahead.

"Keep the sceptre's light on the path too," he instructed his tutor.

Murkle's mutter of contempt was unmistakeable, but he did as the young apprentice said. As Jack reached the limit of the glowing path he checked the Sphere again.

The path veers off to the left here. Oh well. As long as the lucis powder keeps working, and Murkle holds the sceptre low to the ground.

Jack threw some more of the powder in front of him.

"This way!" he shouted triumphantly.

Every twenty steps or so Jack had to throw another pinch of the powder down, but the path was light enough now for them to see their way, even without the sceptre.

But I've got to make this powder last . . .

They moved forward more quickly, Murkle limping behind Jack, but still brimming over with enthusiasm.

"I've got the amulet, and I'll place it in his chest and wake him. Oh! It will be a sight to see!"

He's never done anything like this before, thought Jack. *All he's ever done is read stories.*

Although the cave ceiling was high, the path led them under rock overhangs, and Jack found himself brushing cobwebs away.

Ugh! I hate spiders! I wish Murkle was going first.

Murkle too seemed to want to take the lead, for he suddenly pushed past Jack.

"He's near! I can hear him!"

Indeed, an echoing sound of snoring drifted from nearby. And clambering over a rock, in the glow from the sceptre, they saw him. The cave ceiling rose sharply again, creating a cavernous chamber. And there, in the middle, flat on his back, bare-chested, mouth slightly open, a slumbering giant.

"How big is he?" whispered Jack.

There was no reply. With a cry of elation, Murkle hobbled forward, and clambered onto the chest of the sleeping figure. Reaching down into the pouch on his belt, he grabbed the amulet, and thrust it into the tiny depression over his heart.

"No!"

Jack's warning came too late. The giant remained snoring on his back, but his right hand reached up and grabbed Murkle tightly. The tutor's body just filled the great creature's fist, but looked like it wouldn't be a body much longer. Murkle's eyes were nearly popping out of his head, and even in the dim light, Jack could see his face turning puce.

Jack reached into his Sintura belt again, grabbed the Aximon figure and shouted,

"Salvus! Salvus! Salvus!"

There was a moment of stillness, then Caskill's grip lessened. Murkle's body slumped, his head striking the ground with a dull thud. His sceptre rolled to the side, and he lay, motionless.

Great. Now I've stunned the giant; and Murkle's probably dead.

Murkle, however, was not dead. A deep agonising intake of breath was followed by a prolonged hacking cough; then he sat up, rubbing the side of his head. He looked accusingly at Jack.

"Did you do that?" His voice was croaky.

Jack felt the blood run to his face.

"He was going to kill you! And you were supposed to wake him gently. Don't you remember what you teach us?"

Momentarily rebuked by Jack's harsh tone, Murkle muttered, "Whippersnapper," but said no more.

"So what d'we do now? How long's the Salvus charm work?" Jack thought back to the only other time he'd had to use it, when Konan had been fused into the oak at Dunvik. Uncle Doonya hadn't allowed the charm to wear off.

"I've never seen it used before," muttered Murkle.

"Well, I'll try the amulet again," said Jack firmly. "Properly."

He climbed up onto the giant's slumbering body and levered the amulet out of the depression in which it nestled. Then, muttering a "Please make this work; we need this", he placed it back gently in the hollow on the giant's chest, then jumped back down onto the ground.

Nothing happened.

What's missing? thought Jack. He looked at the Sphere again. The picture of a flower appeared; a purple flower with a drooping head. *Oh, yeah! Armina was telling us about this.*

Jack picked up Murkle's sceptre, and tapped the giant's body with it.

"*Digitalis!*"

There was another moment of stillness.

Then the amulet began to pulsate, and a glow appeared around the giant's body, illuminating the cave in a restful light. The giant blinked; then sat slowly up. Rubbing his eyes, he yawned expansively, and smacked his lips together. Then, peering at Jack and Murkle, he blinked. A menacing growl began at the back of his throat, and his eyes narrowed.

Murkle reached and grabbed the sceptre from Jack's hand.

8

The Road to Ardmore

The giant rose slowly to his feet, staring all the while at Murkle. At least twelve feet tall, his head reached the rock ceiling, and he dwarfed the two Shian creatures. Jack saw Murkle's fingers twitch as he grasped the sceptre and looked up.

"We need him on our side," hissed Jack.

Murkle didn't seem to hear. Overawed by Caskill's enormous size, he trembled slightly. When he started, shakily, to raise the sceptre, Jack moved forward.

"Thank you Caskill," he shouted. "We promise to leave you the heart stone and the charm it needs if you get us the Shian flag from Ardmore castle."

There was a pause, while the echoes rang around the cave. Then Caskill looked down at his chest and saw the amulet pulsating. His great hand passed over it, touching it lightly. He stared at Jack, then knelt down and patted him on the head. Jack felt as if the cave ceiling had fallen on him; his head pounded, and his ears thrummed. Then, turning to Murkle, Caskill snatched the sceptre from the old tutor's hand, peered at it briefly, then snapped it as if it were a twig.

Murkle let out a gasp of surprise, but seemed unable to move.

He's never dealt with anything like this before, thought Jack, his head pounding less now. *All those stories, but it's like he's never been out of his house.*

"Ar'mor'." It was more a grunt than a word.

Caskill picked Jack up gently, cradling him in the crook of his right arm, snorted, and set off for the waterfall, his great strides echoing around the cave and making short work of the distance. Startled out of his reverie, Murkle began to run after them, shouting,

"Hey! Wait up!"

Caskill paused briefly, and glanced over his shoulder. As Murkle approached, the giant stretched his foot out and nudged the tutor into a rock pool. With an undignified yell, Murkle fell in, splashing water everywhere. Jack sniggered. This wasn't such a bad Hallows' Eve after all.

The rock pools were little more than puddles to Caskill, but now he began to wade into deeper water. Jack saw the waterfall curtain ahead, and looked around to make sure Murkle was there. His tutor was jogging painfully, trying to keep up, making the best of the path's glowing residue of lucis powder.

As Caskill approached the waterfall, he placed his left hand over Jack's head, sheltering him from the torrent of water, and they passed through. Emerging into the morning light, the great giant lifted his left hand to shield his eyes.

Jack's first sight was of Finbogie, Gilmore and the McCools crouched down, military-style, their sceptres at the ready. Grandpa stood behind them.

"It's all right!" shouted Jack. "He'll help us!"

A cheer rose from the ranks.

"But where is Murkle?" demanded Grandpa.

The bedraggled figure of the old tutor now emerged from the edge of the waterfall. Soaking wet, and limping heavily, he cut a sorry figure, and it took him some time to hobble over to where the others were gathered.

Caskill deposited Jack beside the others, and patted him on the head once more. It was kindly meant, but just as clumsily done. Jack felt as if a ton weight had fallen on him again.

"Caskill, I am Sandy of the Stone, from Edinburgh. You must retrieve for us the Shian flag in Ardmore castle."

"Ar'mor'," came the grunt again. "U'isk."

"We know of your battles with the Urisk. We promise to give you the charm that will keep your heart working if you get the flag for us."

The giant passed his huge hand over his heart once more, and appeared to consider this.

"Uh!" he grunted, before nodding, and settling himself down on the riverbank, and bathing his face.

"Well done, Jack lad!" said Grandpa, turning to Jack, his eyes beaming. "I knew we could count on you."

"What's all that about a Urisk?"

"It protects Ardmore castle. It's a creature we just can't fight, Jack: not without the power of the Stone. No amount of hexing can defeat it. And the castle has iron everywhere. Only a giant is strong enough to get in."

"That giant," spat Murkle with disgust, "is a menace. He tried to kill me."

If he'd tried to kill you, thought Jack, *you wouldn't be here.*

Grandpa placed his hand reassuringly on Murkle's shoulder.

"But he's with us; that's what counts. Now, let us get to Balbegan. We'll need to meet up with the others."

The group started to make their way up the glen towards Balbegan. Murkle, still limping, hobbled at the back, keeping a wary eye on Caskill, who seemed content to amble along at the slow Shian pace. Jack fell into step with his grandfather.

"Grandpa, has Murkle been here before? Gilravage said my tutor had been here making arrangements; but he was useless in that cave."

Grandpa Sandy stopped and looked hard at Jack. He began to walk again.

"Murkle knows a great deal," he said evasively. "That's why he's a tutor to you apprentices. But it's Daid who's been coming here."

Daid? Jack had barely been aware of Daid on Ilanbeg. If he'd been away a lot, that would explain things.

"Daid knew the story about the charmstone being found by humans. That charmstone has become a local legend."

"Gilravage said the charmstone's Norse."

"That's quite possible. As you know, the Norsemen were here long ago. And the Kildashie fear them coming back, too. You did well to get it."

"What do the crescent moons mean?"

"You'd need to ask Murkle. Whatever, this charmstone's the difference between life and eternal sleep for Caskill. And we really do need him to get this flag."

"How did Caskill lose his heart?"

"That wasn't his heart, just the charmstone that stops him sleeping forever. No one knows how it happened – it was long ago. But once we found out from Daid about that human wearing it when he went fishing, we had to arrange to get it from him."

"That was funny," said Jack happily. "You should've heard this guy."

"Oh, I have – twice. I'm sure he deserved everything he got."

"So has Murkle really never done anything like this before?"

Grandpa Sandy was silent for a moment. "He's more of a theory tutor, I suppose," he said eventually.

Jack didn't reply. The road along the glen was rocky, and he had to pick his way carefully to avoid twisting his ankle.

"Ah! There's your father," said Grandpa, breaking the silence.

"Come on. Ardmore's a good few hours away," said Phineas as they approached.

"Can't we use horses, then? Or a low road?" asked Jack plaintively. After the excitement of the cave a long walk was a big anticlimax. And on Hallows' Eve, too.

"The low roads here aren't working," replied his father. "Not even today. And we must move carefully: the local Shian are mostly Seelie, but they're protective of their world here. Groups on horseback would be seen as hostile."

"Fenrig says the Shian here are more like Brashat than like us."

"Well, the island Shian don't have much to do with the humans any more, it's true. But not out of animosity. At least, not for a long while."

"So what's the story with the flag, then?"

"It's Shian, only they lost it hundreds of years ago; it's been kept in Ardmore castle since. We're banking on it persuading the local Shian of our good intentions."

"And it's surrounded by iron?"

"That's right. The locals would have loved to get it back, but the human family who keep it are canny enough to know how to stop that happening. Also, they have a friendly Urisk."

"Murkle talked about a Urisk once. They're pretty fierce, yeah?"

"Most certainly. For some strange reason, some attach themselves to human families. In this case that means the castle has an added defence for the flag."

"But Caskill can beat him, can't he? I mean, that's the whole point."

Phineas considered his reply. "He's our best bet."

Jack's heart sank. Wasn't this supposed to be a formality? What if Caskill failed?

The long walk continued after a break for lunch, and by the time the afternoon sun started to dip, Jack was really tired.

"Is it much further? My feet are blistering."

If Jack was looking for sympathy, he was looking in the wrong place. With a great shout, Caskill began to move swiftly. For hours he had dawdled along, seemingly content to gaze at the autumnal countryside. But now his lumbering pace quickened to a loping run, and he uttered a series of yells.

"He's caught the Urisk's scent," said Phineas. "It must be out of doors."

The earth shook as the giant's heavy footsteps thudded into the ground.

"Our presence here is not going to be a secret for much longer," observed Telos wryly. "How far's Ardmore?"

"A quarter of a mile. Ten minutes to walk it."

"We've better get a move on, then."

The company broke into a run. Rounding a bend, Jack saw his father and the others who had sailed up from Ilanbeg. Silhouetted behind them, in the grey evening light, was the castle, atop a cliff that fell sheer to the beach. And on the foreshore were Caskill and the Urisk, locked in battle.

9

The Urisk

Half human, half goat, standing eight feet tall, the Urisk's long hair swept from side to side as it dodged the branch which Caskill swung around his head. The giant's swipes were fast and powerful, but lacked precision, and the Urisk hopped and skipped nimbly out of the way each time.

"Caskill's bound to get him," said Petros with satisfaction.

"I'm not so sure," replied Rana. "He's clumsy – look."

Caskill raised the branch above his head, and brought it down with a crashing blow, but once again the Urisk avoided this, hopping into the shallow water. Then, seeing Caskill overstretched, it leapt forward, snarling ferociously. Its jaws locked onto Caskill's neck, and the giant dropped the branch. Caskill pulled at the beast's body, trying desperately to tear it away, but it was obvious he was unable to breathe. Finally, with a thundering swipe and thump, he succeeded in dislodging the Urisk, which fell to the side, yelping and whimpering.

The two creatures circled each other now, each looking for an opening. Blood spurted from Caskill's neck into the oncoming waves, and also trickled from his chest and sides, where the Urisk's hooves and claws had slashed him. The Urisk dragged one leg as it circled cautiously.

"Won't the humans hear them?"

"They can't see the beach from the castle," replied Phineas. "They'll put any strange noises down to the wind."

"Can't we help?" Jack tugged his father's sleeve.

"Against that thing? We've no chance. Look at the size of him."

"Won't your sceptre work?"

"Not here. The islands just don't work for us."

Jack looked with dismay at the two battling figures. Although taller, Caskill was slow and lumbering; and he looked exhausted already. But if he didn't get past the Urisk, he'd no chance of getting into the castle.

Please. It's what must *happen!*

Jack felt powerless. And when the Urisk leapt again, his heart sank.

The Urisk knocked Caskill to the ground, and began to tear noisily at his throat. Caskill flailed at the beast's body, landing punch after punch. The Urisk, though savagely wounded by these blows, still clung on. Caskill's swipes became weaker . . .

No!

Jack closed his eyes and concentrated hard.

Marco taught me to think positively. To get the Kildashie out, we need the Hebseelies' help; and we can't get to them without the flag. So we must *get that flag. Which means Caskill must win this fight . . . He will win it! I know he will!*

A screech from the air distracted Jack, and he looked up. An eagle!

The great bird swooped down and fastened its claws on the Urisk's face. The Urisk, startled by this sudden change of tactics, yelped in pain and released its grip on Caskill's throat. Thrashing with its claws, it succeeded in freeing its face from this unwanted attention. But one eye had gone; and the eagle's retreat was just momentary. In a flash it had jumped forward, locking its claws into the Urisk's remaining eye.

With a great roar the beast fell back, swiping manically at the bird; but the damage was done. Blinded now, and exhausted by the multiple body blows, he tried to crawl away.

Caskill, seeing his adversary weakened like this, found new strength, and stood up. Picking up the Urisk, he flung it hard against a rock. The beast had no time to recover, for Caskill was on it again, grasping and hurling it down again. The Urisk made a final attempt to defend itself, snapping its jaws ferociously. But Caskill was out of range; and, retrieving the branch he had used earlier, he swept it up into the air before bringing it crashing down onto the Urisk's skull. Blood, bone and brains flew up.

The crowd watching stood up, expectantly. The Urisk lay, lifeless; Caskill, leaning on the branch, gasped in pain and exhaustion. Then he let out a roar that echoed around the bay.

Armina was first to move. She bounded down towards the shore, quickly followed by Phineas and Jack.

"You did it!" yelled Jack as they drew close.

Caskill, still gasping for breath, did not seem to hear. Jack saw with alarm that the charmstone in his chest was hanging loose.

"Will he be all right?" he asked anxiously.

Tutting, Armina drew a jar of paste from her sack, and started to smear this on the wounds on Caskill's leg.

"I can't reach his chest or neck; and he's losing blood! Can't you get him to lie down?"

Jack stood in front of Caskill and waved to him. A pause. Then Caskill appeared to recognise the tiny figure before him, and he grimaced.

"Lie down!" shouted Jack. "We need to fix your cuts!"

Whether he intended to or not, Caskill now toppled backwards onto the ground. Gilmore ran up, unwinding strips of cloth from his knapsack.

"Let me through!" he demanded. "I've got the haemostat bandages!"

He swiftly compressed the worst bleeding points, and tied swathes of bandage around these. The blood, which had flowed freely, now ceased. Armina, making swift work of spreading jyoti paste onto the less severe wounds, muttered under her breath, "If only my sceptre worked properly; then I'd have this fixed in no time!"

The crowd grew around the giant's recumbent body. He seemed to be sleeping.

"What a fight!" gasped Petros. "Did you see the brains go flying? Wicked!"

"It was the eagle that really helped," said Jack. "Where'd it go?"

In all the exhilaration of the end of the fight he hadn't noticed the bird fly off. Now he saw it, perched on a rock not far away. Jack waved at it.

I don't know why I did that. It's not like it understands.

The eagle inclined its head, hopped off the rock, and took a few steps towards Jack, its dark brown plumage looking ominous in the fading light. Jack's mouth went dry. From a distance he hadn't appreciated how huge this bird was.

I'm no bigger than a lamb to this thing. And it eats them for breakfast.

The bird, however, stopped; then spread its wings out . . .

Loki's tricks! They're enormous!

. . . and gave a shrill cry, before turning and taking off. Within seconds it was lost to sight.

"It sounded like it was talking to you," said Rana.

Jack didn't move. Was that the same eagle which had followed the boats? And what was that tied to its leg?

A rumbling sound from behind him made Jack turn round. Caskill was trying to sit up; the effort was making him splutter and cough. The giant sat for a moment, and stretched his neck. Then, turning, he spat. Copious amounts of phlegm and blood sprayed onto the ground.

"Urrgh!" squealed Lizzie. "That's gross!"

However, Caskill seemed to feel the better for it. He wiped his mouth with the back of his hand, and smiled.

"U'isk." The grunt had a definite note of satisfaction.

"Caskill, we need you to get the flag now. We must get into the Hebseelie Court by midnight. Can you get to the castle?" Grandpa's voice was tense, urgent.

Caskill looked up at the castle on the promontory above the shore.

"Ar'mor'."

"Yes, Ardmore. You must retrieve the Shian flag for us. If you do that, we will give you the charm that makes your stone work."

Caskill looked down at the charmstone in his chest. The fight had dislodged it, and it hung loose. He looked around anxiously. Then, seeing Jack, he pointed at him.

"Uh!"

Me?

"Come on Jack. He wants you to tell him." Grandpa reached out and took Jack's arm, pulling him forward.

"Me tell him?"

"Come on! There's no time to lose! We must get to the Hebseelie Court!"

Jack stood before the seated Caskill, and spoke in as clear a voice as he could.

"Caskill, I vow that we will give you the charm you need. But please, fetch us the flag. Then you will be free to go."

Caskill reached forward, and made to pat Jack again. Remembering the last two crashes on his head, Jack's first instinct was to duck; but he saw that the gesture was kindly meant, and he gritted his teeth.

Thump!

Oww! Jack screamed inwardly, but determined not to show this. Caskill, satisfied with the arrangement, levered himself into a standing position, and looked up towards the castle. He paused and looked thoughtful (or as thoughtful as a giant can). Then, apparently deciding on his course of action, he set off along the shoreline to where a rough track led up to the castle walls.

"Come along! We'll wait for him by the bourtree. And the tide's coming in; we need to get off the beach."

Grandpa led the crowd past the track Caskill had taken. At the end of the bay, another path led up to a small enclosure, in the centre of which stood a gnarled bourtree.

Fifty Shian was a big crowd to gather around the one tree, but the spot was sheltered, and gave a good view of the castle.

"How does he get in?" asked Jack of his father.

"I'm guessing he's been in before. He's certainly the only one here who can brave the iron. None of us would get very far in there."

"So why'd the humans have the flag?"

"Lost in the mists of time, I'm afraid. They've had it centuries, mind. And they've even used it in their own battles. It's their talisman."

"So why's it so important to the local Shian?"

"It was theirs to begin with. Or so legend has it. At any rate, it's the best way we have of gaining an audience with the Hebseelie Court. But I hope Caskill's not long in there. We'll need to get to Balbegan by midnight; otherwise the game's lost."

It's not a game, thought Jack. *I've seen the Kildashie. And what the Thanatos are doing is no joke either. We need this.*

Twilight faded to night, and a fine drizzle settled on the waiting crowd. Jack shivered.

Some Hallows' Eve.

Then he remembered that he'd spent most of the last Hallows' Eve in a tree trunk at Dunvik.

This isn't so bad, I guess. At least there's a little moonlight.

But it was a long time before there was any sign of activity. A church bell rang the hours with increasing frequency. Eight o'clock came and went; and nine; and ten.

Jack looked over to where his father and grandfather were conversing with the McCools. *Are they planning an attack?*

Eleven o'clock.

If we don't get it soon, we might just as well admit defeat.

Quarter past.

Out of the gloom came a loud belch, and a growling laugh. Then, lumbering towards them came the figure of Caskill. He swayed gently as he approached, and belched again. In his left hand he proudly carried what looked on him like a small pennant . . .

The Shian flag! A cheer went up from the crowd.

. . . while in his right hand he clutched loaves of bread, two hams, and several bottles of wine.

Caskill flung down his booty, and hiccupped happily.

"He's drunk!" shouted Armina. "Do you mean he's been in there having a party while we've been out here waiting for him?!"

Grandpa Sandy bent down and scooped up the Shian flag.

"We must get to Balbegan. There's no time to lose!"

Turning to Jack, Phineas said, "Perhaps you'd give him the charm, Jack? I think he'd like that."

Caskill had sat down, and was trying to persuade those looking on to share his food. Jack strode up. Despite the gnawing hunger in his stomach, he spoke resolutely.

"Caskill, we thank you for the flag. We must leave and go to Balbegan now. You may go where you wish. The charm you need is 'Digitalis'. Do you understand?"

" 'Talis." Caskill nodded, and belched again.

"'Digitalis', Caskill."

"We haven't time for this," said Grandpa, tugging Jack's sleeve. "We must get to the Hebseelie Court, or all is lost."

10
The Hebseelie Court

In the gloom of the night, the fifty Shian made their way north over the short distance towards Balbegan. Grandpa Sandy proudly held the Shian flag aloft as he urged them on, but tiredness was taking its toll. Lizzie was almost walking in her sleep, and was only kept upright by Rana's determined grip on her arm.

"The Hebseelie Court meets under the silver bough," said Grandpa encouragingly, and striding forward. "They'll be there for Hallows' Eve."

"Couldn't we grow to human size?" asked Petros, struggling to keep up. "We'd get there quicker."

"For centuries the Hebseelie Court has had little to do with humans," replied his grandfather. "If we were to try that, they would conclude it was human trickery."

"But we have the Shian flag," pointed out Petros. "They're bound to let us in."

"If they see humans with their flag, that won't look like an act of friendship," stated Phineas coldly. "We must be careful."

"There it is!" cried Ossian triumphantly. Having run ahead, he was now pointing to a striking silver tree that glistened in the pale moonlight. "Let's get inside!"

"Wait," urged Grandpa Sandy. "They're bound to know we're coming. We need to approach deiseil."

"Deiseil?" asked Jack, turning to his father. The bough was not twenty yards ahead of them.

"Sunwise – it shows we come in peace. Grandpa's right: they're bound to have had people watching us. Caskill's battle will have woken every Shian for miles around. Our presence here is no secret."

"But we don't have time for niceties," snapped Murkle. "And in any case there's no sun: it's nearly midnight."

"If we go in without doing this, we'll throw everything away," stated Phineas firmly. "I'll lead."

He started forward, and the whole crowd fell into line behind him.

"What's deiseil?" Lizzie yawned expansively as she accompanied her sister.

"We have to go clockwise around the tree, three times: west, then north, then east, and south. That way they'll know we're not attacking." Jack proudly showed off something he'd remembered from a Murkle lesson.

But that doesn't explain why he doesn't remember it himself, he thought. *Honestly.*

Murkle's enthusiasm was indeed once again running ahead of his book learning. The expert on Shian tales fidgeted, keen to get inside the tree; but progress was not smooth. By the time the crowd had all gone round the tree, the head of the queue had met the tail, and there was some confusion over who had gone round how many times.

"This is ridiculous!" shouted Murkle as people at the back collided with those ahead of them. "We must get inside!"

Having finally satisfied himself that everyone had indeed completed the three circuits, Grandpa Sandy halted and held the flag up.

"This had better work," muttered Jack.

Grandpa held the flag out towards the silver bough and shouted, "*Effatha!*"

"Will the charm work here?" whispered Rana to Petros.

She needn't have worried. The tree glowed, and a door in its side opened, revealing a staircase leading down.

"Inside! Quick!"

Jack was in just behind his grandfather as he stepped into the tree. The spiral staircase was steep, and he nearly lost his footing as they clattered down the stairs.

"What time is it?" asked Murkle anxiously as the last one reached the foot of the stairs.

They were in a long chamber, lit only by a single burning torch.

"A few minutes before midnight," replied Phineas testily. "Let's get in."

Jack was dimly aware of music, but he couldn't locate its source.

"What is this place?" asked Rana.

"It's like the chamber outside the hall at Cos-Howe," said Ossian. "Look, there's the door."

Jack had been unable to see the dim outline of a large wooden door in the gloom, but now his grandfather strode up and struck the door with his sceptre. The sound echoed around the antechamber.

The door opened with a *whoosh!,* spilling music and light. Framed in the doorway was a tall red-haired man, who briefly contemplated the crowd before him. Then he saw the flag.

"You . . . have the flag? On Hallows' Eve?"

Quickly, he indicated for the crowd to enter.

If the antechamber had been like the one at Cos-Howe, there the resemblance ended. This was the biggest hall Jack had ever seen − or imagined. Burning torches lined the sides, throwing out heat and light. The celebrations were in full swing. Jack was overwhelmed by the number of people, the music, the laughter − but mostly by the smell and sight of the food. His stomach rumbled, and he moved involuntarily towards a table with food scattered over its surface.

His father's arm restrained him.

"Later. We have business to conduct first."

Grandpa Sandy stood at the front of the newcomers, and held the flag aloft.

"I am Sandy of the Stone, from the castle in Edinburgh. We crave an audience with the Hebseelie Court." He waved the flag.

The music died instantly, and all eyes turned on the new arrivals.

"And where is Atholmor?"

A fair-haired woman had come forward, and she stood now before Sandy.

"He was taken by the Kildashie; maybe killed. We crave the Hebseelie Court's help in regaining our castle, and the Destiny

Stone within it. The Kildashie will not stop if they get the Stone."

The woman turned, fixing her gaze on a distant figure. Then she turned back, and nodded at Sandy.

"You may come to plead your cause with the praesidium. Bring your son, and his son. Coll here will see to the rest of your group."

Jack saw the red-haired man beckon the others to some nearby tables. Grandpa Sandy nodded at Enda, who had moved forward.

"We have no option. Do as Coll says; and see the others are fed."

Enda stared for a moment, but then turned on his heel, and indicated for the others to follow Coll.

"I am Ishona. Come."

The fair-haired woman led Jack, his father and grandfather along the length of the hall. The music restarted, but without its previous fervour. Jack could feel eyes following them as they proceeded with the flag.

I'd feel happier if we'd all stayed together.

It seemed like ages before they reached the end of the hall, and Jack had lost count of the number of tables they had passed. His hunger hadn't lessened, though.

At a raised table sat three well-dressed men. They were middle-aged; older than all the people they had passed on their walk up the hall; but, like the other revellers, they looked healthy and well fed. Each faced an array of discarded plates and goblets. Silently, Ishona joined them.

"Hallows' Eve is nearly spent." One of them rose and spoke evenly. He had an untidy mane of jet-black hair. "What wish you of our Hebseelie Court?"

"The Kildashie have taken Edinburgh ..." began Grandpa Sandy, but he was silenced by a raised hand.

"Not you; the youth. By what name are you known?"

"Jack. Sir." Jack gulped.

"Well, Jack sir; pray tell me why you interrupt our Hallows' Eve feast."

Jack looked nervously at his father, then his grandfather. Phineas smiled encouragingly.

"We are the Watchers of the Stone. Last Hallows' Eve we defeated the Brashat, and got the King's Chalice. But the Kildashie have taken the Shian square, and they have turned summer back to winter. If they get the Stone and the Chalice from the humans' castle, they will be unstoppable."

"You are Jack Shian who retrieved the Chalice, then," said the man with a smile. "Your fame precedes you, young man. I am Iain Dubh – Black John. Welcome to our feast. Would you eat?"

Jack wanted to shout "Yes!" as loud as he could, but with difficulty he just nodded, and the three of them were invited to join the top table.

"You will indulge me, Sandy of the Stone," said Iain Dubh with a glint in his eye; "but we have heard of your grandson's exploits last Hallows' Eve. I had to hear from him myself. And you have brought back our flag."

"We bring this as a sign of our good intentions. We know that this flag was precious to your Court."

"The flag gains you entry here," said Iain Dubh firmly. "But how did you get past the Urisk?"

"We engaged Caskill the giant. He is free now."

"You have freed the giant?!" One of the others shouted, spraying wine over the table.

"We pledged him his freedom if he would help us. Our task is urgent; we had no option."

"Then tell me why you need our help so," said Iain Dubh. "The giant we will deal with later. Speak freely: Saorbeg and Clavers here are my right-hand men; and Ishona shares all our discussions."

As they were brought fresh food and drink, Grandpa Sandy explained the history of the Kildashie takeover, and the urgency of evicting them before they harnessed the Stone's power.

Iain Dubh sat thoughtfully for a few moments, then leant over to speak to his colleagues. When he faced Jack and his family again he was stern-faced.

"The Kildashie are Unseelie, and no friends of ours. But they have abandoned their island home now; whatever they are doing to the weather affects only the mainland. What is that to us?"

"They will not be content with that," urged Phineas. "They lead an alliance of the worst Unseelie. You must have heard what is happening."

"With our flag again, we can defend our islands against anyone," sneered Saorbeg. "Even with the Stone, the Kildashie cannot touch us. For that they will need the third treasure; or maybe you city Shian have forgotten our history."

Jack was about to speak when he intercepted an urgent stare from his father: *No!*

Jack had become so used to the flag being around his neck that he was only rarely aware of it now. But he fingered his neck nervously. The flag was invisible, but Tamlina's ring seemed so obvious: surely they were bound to see it?

However, Iain Dubh and his colleagues seemed oblivious of the presence of the third Shian treasure.

"You have our Shian flag," said Clavers slowly. "And you have walked into our Court unarmed."

Jack felt his stomach fall several feet. Beside him, his father gripped the handle of the sword he had secreted within his cloak.

Iain Dubh stood up again, and faced Jack.

"Have no fear, young man: Clavers is jesting. Under our laws of hospitality, you shall not be harmed. And if you have retrieved our flag, stolen by the humans so long ago, then clearly you are meant for great things."

"But will you join us against the Kildashie?"

Iain Dubh paused, and looked at Saorbeg and Clavers.

"We must discuss that. But even with our help, I fear you cannot hope to defeat the Kildashie."

No hope? We came all the way here to be told there's no hope?

"But," continued Iain Dubh, "if you could recruit our Norseelie cousins, that might suffice. The island Shian united will be formidable."

"*All* the island Shian?" demanded Phineas, standing up now. "Are you aware that the Tula Shian may have the Raglan stone?"

"I know of no Raglan stone." Iain Dubh's eyes narrowed. "But what know you of the Tula?"

"They live off the north coast, but they are not Norseelie; and I have heard they hold a charmed stone."

"The Tula Shian are content to stay on their miserable bog-island." shouted Saorbeg, rising to his feet. "Going there can only make us more enemies. It's madness!"

Iain Dubh raised his arm, and Saorbeg sat down again, scowling.

"If what you say is true, then your task is harder still. We cannot allow a powerful enemy to be at our rear."

"The Tula Shian have . . ." began Clavers, but he was silenced by a thump on the table by Iain Dubh.

"The Raglan must be retrieved from Tula," said Phineas firmly. "I have heard that there is a secret route there – a bridge."

Iain Dubh eyed Phineas suspiciously.

"That bridge is dark magycks; and I have no idea how you would even know of such a thing. In any case, your task is to persuade Magnus of Novehowe to join you," added Iain Dubh. "If he agrees, we will join too."

Jack was baffled. How many 'ifs' and 'buts' were there?

"We know well what the Kildashie and their allies have been doing," continued Iain Dubh. "To defeat them will require Shian from all the islands; and help from elsewhere too, if we can secure it. We must discuss this ourselves, so we will let you rejoin your group. Hallows' Day is here."

Jack saw his grandfather lean over and whisper in Phineas' ear. When Grandpa Sandy sat up again, Jack saw that he was furious.

Phineas looked slyly across at Jack, and winked.

11
Island Time

As Jack walked between his father and grandfather back down the hall, he was acutely aware that they were not even looking at each other. *What had all that been about?*

"Come on, Jack. The food's great." Rana shoved Lizzie up to make room for Jack on the bench.

Jack threw his cloak onto a pile of other cloaks.

"What happened up there?" asked Ossian. "Why'd Grandpa leave the flag with them?"

"The flag got us in here," explained Jack, crumbs spilling from his mouth. "But it's theirs, so they're keeping it." He gulped down some elderberry juice.

"Are they going to help us?" queried Petros. "I mean, that was the whole point."

"It's complicated," replied Jack between gulps. "They might, if we get the Norseelie to join in; but Dad says we've got to go to Tula as well."

"Tula?" shouted Ossian. Then, lowering his voice, he went on, "I've been all over the country, but that's one place I never want to go."

"What's wrong with it?" asked Lizzie.

"The Boaban Shee are there; and the worst kind of witches. We'd be lucky to get out alive."

"It's something about the Raglan stone," went on Jack. "My dad said the Tula Shian have it. Grandpa was furious."

"Tamlina had the Raglan stone, didn't she?" said Rana thoughtfully. "When we first saw her she talked about it – when she came out of her trance."

"I think my dad was trying to get it when he was captured by the Grey," added Jack. "But I don't think he ever told Grandpa, because he didn't seem to know about that."

"I've heard o' the Raglan stone. It's special," said Ossian wistfully.

"Well, that's more than the Congress then," said Jack. "Grandpa doesn't even believe it exists; and Iain Dubh didn't know about it either."

"If the Raglan was Tamlina's, Malevola must have taken it when she killed her," said Lizzie. "Only Malevola can't have had it when Jack killed her . . ."

"When *I* killed her, you mean," said Rana indignantly.

"You just finished her off," interjected Jack. "Anyway, if Malevola'd had it on the giant's bridge we'd never have defeated her. She must've left it on Tula. And now we've got to get it back."

"Where *is* Tula?" asked Lizzie, straining to keep the exhaustion out of her voice.

"Way off the Cape Wrath coast," said Ossian. "But it's impossible to find; it's always covered in cloud. No two maps agree where it is."

"Dad said something about a bridge."

"The Bridge o' Impossibilities?" said Ossian scornfully. "If there's anythin' less safe than sailin' to Tula, it's usin' that bridge to get there. It's no' for the likes o' us. You'd need special powers to make that work."

Morrigan stroked Ossian's arm tenderly, and he turned and gave her a kiss.

Rana nudged Lizzie, and mimed 'I'm-going-to-be-sick-I've-got-a-finger-down-my-throat'.

"Iain Dubh said something about dark magycks," said Jack, smiling at Rana's mime. "But that's for Unseelie. We couldn't use that; we'd be dismissed by the Congress."

Doubts gnawed away at Jack. If his father and grandfather were arguing, what chance had they of keeping everything together? He looked around, but couldn't see either of them. The rest of the Ilanbeg crew seemed to be enjoying the festivities. Some had mixed with the HebShian, and were sharing stories and songs. Ishona approached with a jug.

"Hallows' Day special," she announced, pouring a little into the goblet in front of each person. "We'll have a toast."

Jack noticed that the jug didn't seem to get any emptier, despite Ishona pouring out liberal quantities. When everyone at the tables had a goblet-full, Iain Dubh strode up.

"A special toast for Hallows' Day: Toussin gloria!" He raised and drained his goblet.

Encouraged, Jack swigged his goblet back. As the bitter taste hit the back of his throat, he spluttered. The room began to swim, and his vision blurred.

A roaring sound, like the loudest traffic noise Jack had ever heard.

Jack saw a blurred Rana and Lizzie fall off the bench.
Then . . . *birdsong*?! Then . . . silence; and darkness.

When Jack came to, he was lying on a low bed in a darkened room, covered by a thin blanket. A small candle beside his bed threw a dim glow, and he could just make out another bed a few feet away. Petros lay, snoring gently. With a sudden sense of panic, Jack's hand went up to his neck. *Phew!* Tamlina's ring was still there, holding the *Mapa Mundi*. *They didn't find it. That's something.*

Jack tried to sit up, but immediately regretted it. His head thumped.

What's going on? Where are we?

As if in answer, he heard Rana's urgent whisper.

"Jack! Can you hear me?"

"Rana? Where are you?"

"It's like a prison cell. There's two beds, and a door."

"Is Lizzie there?"

"She's asleep. They must've drugged us."

Jack peered through the gloom. He could just make out the shape of a door ahead of him, and he tried to sit up again. The clanging in his head made him lie down instantly.

"I can't get up. Every time I try my head feels like it'll burst."

"I'm scared. I thought they were on our side."

"So did I. It'll be all right. Once Dad and Grandpa sort it out. We'll be fine; you'll see."

But as Jack lay there in the gloom, he felt anything but reassured. What had they got themselves into? He felt his eyelids closing . . .

★ ★ ★

When he awoke again, the room was unchanged. The candle sputtered gently.

There must be a breeze. It's certainly cold enough.

Jack shivered, and pulled the threadbare blanket around him. *If only I had one of Gilmore's warm cloaks . . .*

Jack looked around.

What is this place?

"Petros! Are you awake?"

"He's asleep."

Jack started, and looked up. In the gloom he could just make out a figure standing over him. It sounded like . . .

"I am Ishona. Have you slept well?"

Slept well?! You drugged me, and my head's pounding.

"You've been asleep for a while. I hope our Hallows' Day toast hasn't left you too thirsty?"

Jack licked his lips. His mouth was parched.

"Why'd you drug us?" His throat felt like sandpaper.

"You weren't drugged. You just had some island potion. You're obviously not used to it."

"How long . . . ?"

"Have you been asleep? A few days. It's for the best. Now, have some water, and I'll see you again soon."

She bent down, placed a small jug and two goblets on the bedside table, and started to leave.

"Where are the others?" Jack's voice was little more than a croak.

"They're safe. You'll understand when you're all awake. Now, get some rest."

Jack drank a little water, but found he still couldn't sit up. He yawned. *Maybe just a bit more sleep.* The room began to swim. His eyelids felt heavy . . .

"Jack!" Petros shoved his cousin as he lay curled up on the low bed.

Jack stirred, and slowly opened his eyes.

"Whassup? What . . . ?"

"We're prisoners. And I'm starving. Even Ilanbeg was better than this place; at least we could move around."

Jack blinked. The room was still dark; the candle sputtered softly on the bedside table.

"Ishona came in a while ago, but I couldn't even sit up. How long've we been here?"

"Dunno. But I don't want to stay any longer. Let's see if we can get out."

To his surprise, Jack found that he could sit up without his head bursting; but when he tried to stand his legs wobbled and he stumbled, knocking the candle over.

"Oh, that's brilliant!" shouted Petros. "Weren't things bad enough that you had to take away the one thing here that might help us?!"

"It wasn't my fault; my legs just collapsed." Jack hauled himself back onto the bed.

A tapping sound came from the wall beside him.

"Jack! You awake?"

"Rana? Is Lizzie OK?"

"We're all right. What happened in there?"

"Jack knocked the candle over," shouted Petros.

"Shhh! We don't know who might be listening." Jack tried to

quieten Petros, but the sound of footsteps outside the room made him catch his breath.

"If anyone comes in, we'll rush them," whispered Petros.

Keys jangled; and the door creaked open, showering light into the tiny room. Unaccustomed, Jack and Petros shielded their eyes. Peering cautiously, they could make out a figure silhouetted in the doorway.

"Come on; you lads must be hungry. I'll take you to the others."

"Clavers?"

"Aye, that's me. They're ready for you upstairs now. Come on; get your shoes on."

Jack tied his laces and got uncertainly to his feet. His legs felt weak, but he steadied himself against the bed, and edged over to the door.

Clavers clapped an arm over Jack's shoulder.

"Ishona tells me you've been asleep for days. Not used to island potion, eh?"

"Why'd you give us it? What happened to your laws of hospitality?"

"We shared our meat and drink with you; and you've been safe. Come on, I'll take you up to Iain Dubh."

Jack stepped out into the corridor, and saw that the bright light in fact came from just one burning torch opposite each doorway. Petros followed him uncertainly, his eyes slowly adjusting to the light. Clavers opened the door to Rana and Lizzie's room next door, and they peered out nervously from the doorway. But something bothered Jack: Clavers looked somehow . . . older.

"It's OK." Jack tried to cover his sense of foreboding by sounding cheerful to Rana and Lizzie. "We're going to see the others."

The four youngsters followed Clavers warily as he made his way to stairs at the corridor's end. Climbing up, they were ushered into a long room.

"Is this the great hall?" asked Rana, peering in the gloom. "It's totally different."

You're not kidding, thought Jack. *It's freezing.*

"You saw it at Hallows' Eve," replied Clavers. "That's a special night for the HebShian, when the Hebseelie Court meets. Most of the time we're not so well . . . catered for."

The room was an almost total contrast. Gone were the lights, the tables, the food and drink, the sense of joyous celebration. Several HebShian milled around in the gloom, but none acknowledged the youngsters.

"There's Grandpa!" shouted Lizzie.

In the dim light, Jack could make out his grandfather and father ahead of them.

"Dad!"

Phineas turned as he heard Jack's shout, and smiled.

"Did you sleep well?

"We were poisoned; or drugged. We've been asleep for days."

"It seems strange to us; but they'll have their reasons."

Jack squinted up at his father. *What did he know?*

"This is a different place, Jack. They have their own way of doing things here. Iain Dubh will be along shortly; he'll explain."

A door to the side of the hall opened, and Jack saw Iain Dubh and Ishona stride in, accompanied by four men carrying burning torches.

"I trust you are all rested?" asked Iain Dubh warmly.

Rested? Jack felt the hackles on his neck rising. This was getting beyond a joke. Then he saw that Iain Dubh's hair was flecked with grey.

"You call poisoning us restful?" shouted Petros.

If Iain Dubh's glance at the youngster was puzzled, Phineas' glare was pure daggers.

"You may not appreciate our situation," went on Iain Dubh evenly, his voice huskier than Jack remembered it. "The Hebseelie Court has now agreed to join you, providing you enlist the Norseelie; but not everyone here agreed. You may notice that Saorbeg is not with us."

Jack could see that Clavers and Ishona were beside Iain Dubh, but he hadn't realised the significance of Saorbeg's absence.

"So you drugged us while you had your arguments?" he spat.

"Jack, hold your tongue!" retorted Phineas sharply.

"You are under a misapprehension," said Iain Dubh calmly. "Nobody has been drugged. You were clearly unused to our island brew."

"Not used to it?" Jack's temper refused to subside, despite his father's injunction. "We've been asleep for a week. What's that if it's not poisoning?"

"You are a stranger here, young Jack." Ishona spoke up now. "You clearly have never experienced island time before. You were not drugged; only asleep. And it was for the best. We had to discuss matters further here; I'm afraid with our meagre resources we would not have been very good hosts to you."

"Look around you, Jack," said Phineas. "Hallows' Eve brought this place alive; but it's only like that for a few days in the winter. The rest of the time it's like this."

Jack looked around the room. Despite the glowing torches he could see that the room was pretty bare. A small group of local Shian had brought some food, placing it on a table. But far from being the young and happy well-fed people he had seen when they arrived, Jack saw now that they were thin creatures, whose pinched faces showed their age and their hardship. They looked like they needed the food more than he did.

"Food is scarce here during the winter months. We spend much of our time resting; it conserves our energy for when we need it. And if we are to attack the Kildashie before the spring, then we must conserve it well." Clavers spoke slowly, emphasising his points.

"Sorry," mumbled Jack.

"That's all right. Most of your colleagues are still asleep. But there's things we need to discuss with you now. Like why we need to get to Tula."

We?

12

The Gusog Feather

Iain Dubh smiled as he saw Jack blink in surprise.

"That's right; we're coming with you."

"Tula's more complicated than we thought Jack," said his father softly. "But the Hebseelie will help us. Come on; let's eat."

Iain Dubh then waved his sceptre in an arc above his head, and the HebShian that had been milling around in the dimness now appeared bearing more trays of food. Jack's stomach rumbled at the prospect, but when he saw the meagre fare on offer his hunger almost left him. It was scraps – scraps that looked like they were leftovers from Hallows' Eve.

"Not very sumptuous, I'm afraid," admitted Iain Dubh. "But you've seen the best we can offer; we won't see the likes again until the winter solstice."

"By which time we need to be at Novehowe," added Grandpa Sandy firmly.

"But first we have to get to Tula," added Clavers, at which Grandpa Sandy snorted.

Jack looked at his grandfather. *He seems . . . distant; as if he doesn't matter. But he's a senior Congress member; he* must *be important.*

"You are not the only ones to seek treasure in Tula," said Iain Dubh. "After we lost our flag, much of our strength went too. Soon after, our one remaining treasure was stolen. A golden feather, one that belonged to our ancestor Gusog."

"Murkle will have told you all this, won't he, Jack?"

Jack turned to his father and shook his head.

"No. He never talked about that."

"A pity," noted Clavers. "One of the great Shian tales. With his wings Gusog could control the passage of time; even the one feather that remained to us allowed us to speed our way through the harshness of winter until the return of spring. But it was taken, many years ago; which is why you see us like this." He indicated the gloom of the hall.

Jack looked around the hall. It was the gloomiest place he had ever seen. Then his eye caught something on the far wall.

"Is that a season-wheel?" he asked. The symbols at the base of the wheel looked familiar.

"It is. And you'll see that it shows a long winter for us; and winter is death for many. The return of the Gusog feather would be as important for us as you getting the Stone back." Iain Dubh spoke wistfully.

"You see, Jack," said Phineas, "we both have a reason to go to Tula."

Did Grandpa just snort again?

"But we need your help, Jack. You've got something that will help us."

Jack's heart raced for a moment, and he looked across at his father, and without thinking he put his hand up to Tamlina's ring on his neck.

"They know about the *Mapa Mundi*, Jack."

"Of course we knew you had it. Did you think we wouldn't hear about something as important as that? People have been going up and down the coast since midsummer talking about it. And it will certainly help us – if it shows us our true path."

"Why didn't you take it when I was asleep?"

"Our laws of hospitality would not allow that, even if we'd wanted to. We'd rather ask you to join us."

"They haven't woken the others, Jack; Murkle, and Finbogie and the rest. The Hebseelie need to know what you'll do with the *Mapa*."

Jack looked around as one of the attendants coughed. He looked ill, even malnourished.

"And getting Gusog's feather back will help you to endure the winter?"

"It's no ordinary feather, lad. It's the last of his wings; the last remnant there is of our ancestor."

"The gold feather's charmed, Jack. It allowed Gusog to control time. Just that one feather meant we could survive the winter without starving: we could speed our passage through time. Without it – well, you can see what we've become."

Jack had to admit that the Hebseelie, after the Hallows' Eve party, were a sorry sight. He grasped Tamlina's ring and tugged it down, allowing the *Mapa Mundi* to fall about his neck. He pulled the flag until it was free, and offered it to Iain Dubh.

"Marco told me it shows true believers their path."

"We know. And for us, that must be the path to the Gusog feather."

As Iain Dubh took the flag gently, it formed into a sphere, showing the two great map circles . . . but they were blank.

"What does the map show?" Phineas leant forward to get a better look.

"Nothing," said Iain Dubh, handing the sphere back to Jack.

Jack stared hard at the circles. Slowly, a dark castle formed in one of the *Mapa Mundi* circles; but not a regular picture: it seemed to be made up of tiny fragments.

"It's Fractals' Seer," said Clavers softly. "Malevola's castle."

There was a thump as Grandpa's head met the table, and he rolled to the floor. Jack jumped in surprise; but he was even more astonished by the next sensation.

Phosphan?!

Rana's gasp confirmed to Jack that he was not mistaken.

Ishona moved quickly to check Grandpa Sandy's breathing. Kneeling down in the dim light, she listened intently; then sat up and smiled.

"It's all right. I think he's just fainted. Probably hungry."

But Jack wasn't so sure. There had been something unusual about his grandfather. Normally, he would take charge of things. Here he'd been . . . sidelined. And he'd definitely not been keen on going to Tula.

Phineas bent down to scoop up his father's body.

"Just let me get him back to his room. I'll see he's all right."

"I think we'd better get Armina, Dad," said Jack. "I can smell Phosphan. It's like his wound's opened up again."

Phineas grunted.

What's up with him? thought Jack.

Armina, Finbogie and Murkle were quickly summoned, and while Armina and Phineas attended to Grandpa Sandy, Finbogie drew Jack aside.

"They certainly have an unusual way of treating guests here. I'm sorry that I didn't foresee the dangers of the island potion. But I wasn't expecting trouble from the HebShian. They *are* Seelie, after all."

"Dad says they're all right; they've just got their own way of doing things. But if we're going to Tula, we'll need to be well prepared, won't we?"

"Going to Tula is not possible, given our timescale," butted in Murkle. "We must be at Novehowe before the solstice. Winter's closing in; there's no time for detours."

"But can't we slow time down, like we did at midsummer last year?"

"You should have noticed by now that our charms barely work here," snapped Murkle.

"Murkle's right," interrupted Grandpa Sandy. His voice was weak, like when Malevola's hex had opened his wounds again on the giant's bridge. "We have no time for diversions; and especially not to somewhere like Tula."

"But don't you see, father?" said Phineas, trying to keep the heat out of his voice. "Tula is the key. If we can get the Raglan . . ."

"The Raglan is nothing," shouted Grandpa, sitting up despite the pain. "One of Tamlina's charmstones, no more. If it meant anything, the Congress would have known of it. Am I not right, Murkle?"

Murkle pondered for a moment.

"You are. In all my experience of Shian tales, I have never come across this stone."

"But the HebShian know about the Raglan," warned Jack. "And they said we shouldn't leave enemies like the Tula behind us."

"The island Shian will squabble and fight, like they've always done," said Murkle coldly. "The Tula Shian have no reason to leave for the mainland."

"Nobody predicted the Kildashie coming," urged Jack. "And if they ask the Tula Shian to join them, well . . . We should destroy them now."

"Destroy the Tula?" scoffed Murkle. "Have you any idea what you're saying? You wouldn't know where to start."

And I suppose you knew exactly how to deal with Caskill. You were hopeless in that cave.

"But I can help there," pointed out Finbogie. "Phineas and I have worked on the swords. They're ready; we can at least take the Tula Shian on."

"Regardless of that, there is not time," stated Grandpa firmly. He rose unsteadily to his feet now. "It could take weeks to sail to Novehowe at this time of year. Tula is a distraction; and a dangerous one at that."

"But father, Iain Dubh was right: the Tula Shian are a dangerous enemy to leave at our rear. And if we get the Raglan stone, that will multiply our chances."

"Enough! I will not hear of it. We sail for Novehowe. Our task is to persuade Magnus to join us. That's the key to getting our homes back – and the Stone, and the Chalice. All else is just distraction."

Grandpa Sandy sat down, quickly weakened by the effort.

He's wrong, fumed Jack; *and we've* got *to get the Tula Shian out of the way. Tamlina knew the Raglan was important . . .*

"Come on, Jack." Phineas tugged Jack's sleeve, and the two of them left the room.

"Why's Grandpa so against us going to Tula, Dad?"

"Time is tight. If we're to make Novehowe by the solstice, we'll have to leave soon. But there's other problems too."

"I don't understand."

"Families, Jack. If anyone ever said they were straightforward, they were lying. One of the reasons your grandfather doesn't like the idea is because it came from me."

"Why's that a problem?"

"It goes back a long way, Jack. You know your Uncle Doonya was chosen as the Stone Watcher over me? I didn't like that – so I decided to show them."

"When you went off to find Tamlina and the Grey suspended you?"

"That's right. I found out that Tamlina had discovered a fragment of the Destiny Stone. I thought if I got that, it would impress your grandpa."

"Part of the Destiny Stone!? You mean the corner that's missing?"

"That's right. It's only a small piece; but imagine the power that would give you."

"But if Grandpa had known the Raglan was part of the Destiny Stone, he would've told the Congress."

"Hardly anyone except me and Konan knew about it. He'd found out from Malevola. He wanted to impress Briannan; and I guess I wanted to impress the Congress. We both thought we could get it from Tamlina, and take it home to show it off."

Jack thought about this for a moment.

"You mean we could actually get part of the Destiny Stone? Why don't the Tula Shian use it for themselves?"

"They'll know it's important, because it was Tamlina's. But away from the sandstone near Edinburgh it won't work so well. Just like when it was in London. I'm guessing they haven't worked out it's part of the Stone."

"Well, let's tell Grandpa. If he knows what the Raglan is, he's bound to want to go there."

"There's something else. Didn't you hear it in his voice?"

Jack thought back to the way his grandfather had sounded just now, then to the giant's bridge at midsummer. *I'll never forget that smell of Phosphan.* His grandfather had been scared then; terrified, even. Terrified of Malevola and her demons.

"Malevola came from Tula, right?"

Phineas nodded.

"And Ossian said the Boaban Shee are there, and really bad witches. Grandpa's scared, isn't he? I always thought he was so . . . strong."

"What Malevola did to him is unimaginable, Jack. We shouldn't think harshly of him for that. Deep down he connects Tula with what Malevola did to him. Whether he knows it or not, that's why he's determined to avoid going there. Maybe it's for the best."

"But that'll mean splitting up. Shouldn't we stay together?"

"Not if we're arguing all the way. Sometimes a smaller force can achieve more."

"Can't we at least tell him why we're going to Tula?"

"He won't believe that – he's terrified of Tula. But he might accept that the HebShian have to go there. The Gusog feather is part of their history."

"But it only took us three days to sail here from Ilanbeg. Even allowing for bad weather, we could get to Novehowe in a week or so."

"The sail from Ilanbeg was a breeze, Jack. From here on it's really tough."

Jack thought about Petros being seasick. *It wasn't a breeze for him.*

Seeing Jack's look of disbelief, Phineas continued, "It's going to be much harder, and not just because of the weather. Whether we head for Novehowe or Tula, we need to leave before too long. Before the Blue Men of the Minch wake up, anyway."

13

The Cailleach

As Phineas went to find Iain Dubh and Ishona, Jack wandered back into the room where his grandfather lay.

When Grandpa Sandy saw Jack, he reached out for his hand.

"You are the only one who can make the *Mapa Mundi* work," he gasped. "What does it show you?"

"Iain Dubh's got the *Mapa*, Grandpa. He was looking at it when . . . when you fainted."

"Then maybe he can see it too. Our powers do not work well here. That is why we must enlist the Norseelie to help us retake Edinburgh. Now, let us rejoin our hosts."

Sandy sat up painfully, steadied himself, then stood up. Armina *tsk*ed as he wobbled slightly, and moved forward to provide support. With Murkle on the other side, the group made their way back to the great hall.

At least the smell of Phosphan has gone.

"And how is our honoured guest?"

"I apologise; a recent illness lingers within me. But we must discuss our plan."

"We have gathered your other companions," said Iain Dubh, indicating Enda, Telos and the others, seated at nearby tables.

Jack, his father and grandfather sat themselves at Iain Dubh's table as Telos stood up, and announced, "Your island brew was a little strong for most of us. Let us repay your compliment with some traditional Irish poteen."

He produced a flagon and proceeded to pour its contents into the goblets on the top table. As he poured into Jack's, he paused and stumbled forward, grasping the goblet in his right hand.

"Clumsy!" he said cheerfully, as he righted the goblet. "Don't want you getting drunk. Go easy on that."

"I propose that we divide into two groups," said Phineas, rising, and holding his goblet aloft. "My father will take one group straight to Novehowe; the other will come with me and the Hebseelie to Tula first, then Novehowe. From there we can make our way to Edinburgh."

"Phineas is right!" announced Iain Dubh, also rising. "The Tula Shian must be dealt with; only then can you take on the Kildashie."

Grandpa Sandy sat silently, staring ahead of him.

"Sandy!" hissed Armina from the next table. "Speak for the Congress!"

Grandpa Sandy got unsteadily to his feet, clutching his goblet weakly.

"I . . . I know that some here feel the need to go to Tula. Very well; but I cannot sanction this detour for my grandson. Phineas may travel with you; I will take the rest to Novehowe."

Jack saw his father's eyes narrow, and his mouth set.

"Let us consult the *Mapa Mundi*. If there is a true path, that will show it," said Iain Dubh.

"But it only shows itself to Jack!" screeched Murkle.

"And to the Hebseelie," added Phineas. "Is that not right, Iain?"

"Only when Jack is present. It would not work for us, while you were down below. But we have seen Fractals' Seer on it. The HebShian will go to Tula with Phineas."

"Then what of Jack?" shouted Murkle again.

In response, Iain Dubh produced the *Mapa Mundi*, and handed it to Jack. It lay limply in his hands for a moment, before curling up into a sphere. But for a while, there was nothing to see in the two circles.

"This accursed place!" bellowed Murkle. "The magycks do not work here!"

"Wait!" Gilmore silenced Murkle with a glare. "See! The pictures form!"

Sure enough, into the circles came the image of Fractals' Seer, and a feather. A gold-tipped feather.

"Then it is settled!" announced Iain Dubh triumphantly. "We take Jack and the *Mapa Mundi* to Tula! Your health, young Jack!" He raised his goblet, and drank deeply.

Jack avoided looking at his grandfather as he sipped from his goblet.

That's not bad!

Then he clutched his head, as a roar assaulted his ears. Like the loudest traffic noise he had ever heard . . .

Oh no! Déjà vu.

In slow motion, Jack imagined Rana and Lizzie falling off their seats.

I know what's coming next . . .
Yes: birdsong. Then . . . darkness.
My head hurts already.

Jack was dimly aware of voices; and of being carried. Over the next while – minutes? hours? days? – he was aware of arguments above him. Snatches permeated his consciousness . . .

". . . *poisoned him!*" "*Traitor!*" "*This is a plot!*" "*Unseelie spy!*"

. . . but mostly the sounds wafted over him, like the angry buzzing of wasps. He felt sick, and stomach cramps gripped him.

When he could finally open his eyes, he felt roasting hot; and yet cold, at the same time. Armina's blurred face hovered over him, and he could hear Ishona intoning a song, or a prayer, or something, beside him. He'd never felt so ill in his life. Opening his eyes made him want to be sick; but closing them made his head swim. In his head he begged for recovery.

". . . quite clearly poisoned . . ." Armina's firm voice again. "Like before."

"We have never poisoned him. Someone must have slipped something into his goblet . . ."

Jack's mind wandered off again. His forehead felt like you could fry eggs on it.

When he awoke, it was to the uncomfortable jolting sensation of being carried up steps.

"Where . . ." but he got no further.

"Don't speak; save your energy."

Evidently his father was carrying him.

Then a blast of icy air as they emerged into the open. Jack felt himself bundled onto a cart, which pulled away. Ishona knelt beside him and mopped his brow.

"We're going to see someone," she said calmly. "The *cailleach* will know what to do."

Cailleach? Jack had only heard that name at the start of spring, when Grandpa Sandy had taken him and Lizzie to see the Blue Hag clear the snows.

They trundled for what seemed like hours, finally stopping beside an old stone house. There were two tiny windows, and a low door which seemed overgrown by the thatched roof. Jack heard someone knock; then Iain Dubh's voice murmuring. Shortly after, Jack was lifted from the cart and carried inside.

The house was dark, and reeked of peat smoke; but at least it was warm. Iain Dubh remained by the doorway.

"Put him doon."

"*Cailleach*," began Ishona as she set Jack down on a low bed, "this boy was poisoned. He has the key to the safety of our people. He recovered the *Mapa Mundi*, and it will only work when he is there. We need his help to retrieve our Gusog feather."

The *cailleach* muttered inaudibly, but came into Jack's vision. *Was it her?*

"Mmmph." The old woman peered at Jack, examined his eyes and tongue, then lifted his shirt and palpated his belly. Jack squirmed as his tender abdomen was prodded and poked, but he determined not to cry out.

"Aye, it's me," she said, reading his mind. Then, turning to Ishona, she barked, "And why is this mainland boy here? He should be in his city home."

"He fled the Kildashie. And he seeks to return home, and send them away."

"Kildashie – Raca!" The old woman turned and spat.

"They have stopped the seasons turning, *cailleach*. Their work is *infama*."

Jack watched the *cailleach* get up and go over to the dresser. When she returned, she held a small wooden wheel, which she held above his head.

"Do you know this, boy?" she demanded.

Jack nodded. "It's a season-wheel. Marco's got one; and Iain Dubh." A spasm of pain racked him, and he retched, a painful dry heave.

"And what happens if the wheel stops turning?"

Jack shook his head.

"You have a special ring there, boy," barked the *cailleach*. "Show me your use of it."

Gasping for breath, Jack tugged Tamlina's ring off his finger. He gulped hard. *The last time I did this I saw Ploutter being tortured . . .*

"Show me!" The order brooked no denial.

Fighting back the sickness, Jack grasped the ring and stared hard at the Triple-S pattern. One faded spiral arm, two bold ones. Slowly, the shape began to spin, and Jack closed his eyes. Between spasms of nausea, Jack could make out . . .

Edinburgh's High Street. There's torrential rain: rain so hard it bounces off the ground. Gutters overflowing. A newspaper shop; the sodden headline on the A-board says 'Capital chaos – monsoon's fifth day.' There's something bloated in the gutter – a child's body!

Jack opened his eyes, and vomited.

"Well?" snapped the old woman, when Ishona had wiped his mouth.

"Floods. Edinburgh's under water. And a child drowned."

The *cailleach* sat and thought for a moment. Then she leant forward, and whispered to Ishona, "He has the sight; he is the one. But the remedy he needs will not be ready for three weeks; when the mistletoe blooms."

Three weeks?!

"I can keep him comfortable until then. Send for his family."

"His family are keen to leave now, to get to Novehowe," said Ishona. "But his father will stay."

"Three weeks is too long," protested Iain Dubh. "The weather's closing in. We need to get to Tula, then Novehowe by the solstice."

"He cannot leave until he is cured. If he is necessary to your journey, then you must postpone your departure!"

"Very well," said Iain Dubh slowly. "But Phineas will be needed to help us plan. Perhaps one of his cousins can come."

As Iain Dubh left, Ishona offered to stoke up the fire.

"The peats are in the corner," grunted the old woman. "But they must last me the winter."

Once the fire was blazing, Jack dozed off. When he awoke, the *cailleach* offered him some broth.

"It'll help," she said gruffly.

Jack sipped the piping-hot liquid, and was surprised that he did feel a little better. *What did the cailleach mean – the peats must last her the winter?* He raised his head and looked at the old woman.

"You send the snows away in spring. Can't you control the weather?"

"I am the sign of the seasons, boy. I do not control them. To interfere with time and the seasons is against nature – *infama*."

Jack thought for a moment. "But the Hebseelie want the Gusog feather so they can speed up the winter."

"It does not speed up time; merely their perception of it."

"Like when we slowed down time at the midsummer festival? And we speeded it up at Oestre. I even used the fugitemp charm against the Grey."

"Old witch! I hope you banished her!"

Jack pondered this. Had he banished the Grey? The McCools hadn't believed she was gone for good.

"Are the Kildashie controlling the weather, then?" Jack lay down again. His brow was burning.

"I thought maybe they had – for a while. But I do not believe so now. They think that winning Shian treasures will give them power – and so it will. But there's something they'll never understand, the fools."

Jack sat up eagerly.

"They don't realise that the creator force binds everything together. Their treasures will give them nothing unless they are in harmony with that. And ye know about that, eh? Your ring tells me you do."

Tamlina's ring? Jack had no time to follow this thought, as another wave of nausea broke over him.

"But the rascals are dangerous," continued the *cailleach*, oblivious to Jack's torment. "And they have allies, too. One of your group is a traitor. You were poisoned."

"Poisoned?" Jack gasped as the nausea returned once more. "Why?"

"Somebody wishes to halt your quest."

"What did they use?" asked Ishona. Jack had not seen her in the gloom.

"Something crude. The mistletoe will purge his body; but the berries are not ready yet."

On cue, Jack turned on his side and retched. His guts ached; and his head felt like it would burst.

I wish I was off this island. I've been ill most of the time here.

"You need to rest," said the *cailleach*. "But it will be a long three weeks. You'd better sleep. Drink this."

Jack's throat was parched, and without thinking he sipped the proffered goblet.

The room swam . . . birdsong . . .

Oh no . . . Déjà vu all over again.

14
Recovery

Jack woke to the sound of his cousins fighting.

"Can . . . I have some water?"

Rana released her sister's head, and came over to Jack's bed.

"How're you feeling?"

"Water."

Rana splashed some water into a goblet, and held it to Jack's lips.

"What day is it?"

"Thursday. You've been sleeping."

"You wake up, and just go back to sleep," added Lizzie. "We've been here for ages."

Jack turned on his side. "How long?"

"Nearly three weeks. It's freezing here. That fire doesn't give off much."

"Where are we?"

"The *cailleach*'s house. Ishona brought you here; don't you remember?"

Jack's thoughts gradually settled. The cart journey, the fever, being sick. Then there were strange dreams – or were they dreams? Voices, people talking above him. '*The Creator Force*,' one of them had said, over and over. He felt so weak.

"Where's the old woman?"

"She went off to collect something; she was quite excited."

"It's the mistletoe, silly," butted in Rana. "She had this special golden knife."

The wind whistled as the front door opened, bringing in an icy gust.

"Brrr!" Lizzie shivered, and looked round.

"I've got the berries. Let me paste them."

The old woman went over to the stove, and clattered among the pots for a moment.

"Is that what Jack needs?" asked Rana.

The *cailleach* grunted, and continued to work away.

"Where's Dad?" croaked Jack.

"They're down at the Hebseelie place. They've been arguing since you left. Grandpa wants to leave, but Iain Dubh says we've all to leave together, and we can't do that until you're better."

"Out of the way, girl." The *cailleach* shoved Rana aside as she knelt down by Jack's bed. "Take this." She proffered a goblet to Jack.

It was the bitterest thing Jack had ever tasted, and he screwed up his face.

"All of it. Otherwise the poison can't leave you."

Jack grimaced, and took another sip, but this wasn't fast enough for the *cailleach*. She grasped the back of his head, and, lifting it up, forced the rest of the contents down Jack's throat. He gasped as the foul brew found every taste bud. Coughing and spluttering, Jack sat up. The liquid seemed to be in his stomach for no more than a few seconds before it was clear that it was coming up again.

Frantically, Jack reached for the bowl beside the bed, and was extravagantly sick.

"There. It's working." There was a tone of satisfaction in the old woman's voice which was completely at odds with how Jack was feeling.

He retched and spewed again, then lay back, gasping.

"Will that clear all the poison from him?" asked Lizzie timidly.

"It's the only way. I've kept him from getting worse these past weeks, but this is the only way to get the poison out."

Jack closed his eyes, and prayed for respite. *Please please please make this go away.*

He shivered, and fell into a fitful sleep.

When Jack awoke, he felt ravenous. Sitting up, he realised how weak he was, and he lay down again.

There was a clatter of pans from through the house, and he could smell cooking. His stomach rumbled. There was no sight of Rana or Lizzie, though, and with some trepidation he called out, "Hello? Anyone there?"

The *cailleach* emerged from the gloom, carrying a bowl. Steam rose gently.

"Sit up. I've made some broth."

Jack pushed himself up into a sitting position again, and gratefully accepted the bowl. When he had finished it, he was surprised at how much better he felt.

"Take a look at yourself," said the old woman. She indicated a half-length mirror by the wall.

Jack stood up slowly, and edged over towards it. His face was hollow, and his shirt hung from him.

"Some of that's from the poison," said the old woman, matter-of-factly. "But mostly it's because you've eaten little for a long time. Does it remind you of anyone?"

It didn't take long for the image of the emaciated creatures at the Hebseelie Court to flit into Jack's mind.

"You almost look like a local," said the old woman. There was no satisfaction in her voice; it was just a statement of fact.

"And my family?" asked Jack. "Have they been eating since . . . since I came here?"

"Every other day. It is the way of things here in winter – excepting special days. Now you will see why they wish to retrieve the Gusog feather. It will allow them to endure the winter. Ishona will be here soon; she'll take you back."

"You mean . . . I can go now?" Jack was surprised at how well he felt.

"It's special broth; you'll be fine to leave the island in a day or two."

"Thanks for . . . you know."

"It was my duty. Yours is to defeat the wastrels who desire a perpetual winter."

Jack thought for a moment.

"Those floods I saw, when I looked at Tamlina's ring. Are they what's happening now?"

"They are. The climate is disturbed; such things are rare; or should be. But the rhythm is changed. Was that the second time you used the ring?"

Jack nodded.

"The first time will have showed you something that had already happened; am I right?"

Jack gulped. "It was ... an execution. I didn't understand it; later, I found out it had happened."

"It's a triple spiral: two arms have faded. You have one vision left. The next time you use the ring it will show you something that is yet to happen. Use that wisely."

Jack fingered Tamlina's ring. *When's the right time to do that?*

"And don't forget your knife."

The *cailleach* handed him Trog's knife. He fingered it carefully, thinking back to the ancient Norseman on Ilanbeg. Then he strapped it to his right calf.

When Ishona came, Jack said his goodbyes, and climbed onto the cart. He hadn't been outside the gloomy cottage for three weeks, and the brightness of the day made him wince. The air was still, quiet; and bitterly cold. His breath formed clouds in front of him, and his nose dripped slowly. The desolate frosty countryside made him long for warmer days. He shivered and pulled his coat around him.

At least when I had the fever I was warm.

"They're desperate to get going," said Ishona. "Your grandfather fears you will never reach Novehowe in time."

"But the sail here from Ilanbeg only took three days," pointed out Jack. "It can't take more than a week from here?"

"The weather's turning; and the seas are rough. You will only manage short sails. You'll have your work cut out to make Novehowe in three weeks; but there was no choice."

"Who's got the *Mapa Mundi*?"

"Iain Dubh has it, but it shows nothing."

It began to snow; softly at first, then with more force. Jack shivered.

Seelie don't go out in weather like this.

Ishona looked at him. "It's the same for us," she said. "We should all be indoors now; but the winter is long and hard here. If we can get the Gusog feather, that will make it bearable once more."

"We've to stop the Kildashie as well," stated Jack. "The old woman was telling me: if they win, it'll be like this all the time."

He looked up at the snow-laden sky, then across at the white landscape. It was beautiful ... but such beauty is appreciated more when you're not perishing cold. Jack tried to pull his coat tighter around him, but it made little difference.

"How far's Balbegan?"

"Far enough. The *cailleach* doesn't like to be too close."

It was a good two hours before they reached sight of habitation, by which time Jack was almost frozen. He tried to move, but found that his feet would not cooperate. Ishona had to turn his body round so that he could dismount. On firm ground, he stamped his feet to try and get the circulation going. Ishona tutted, and led him to a small doorway.

"Come on. It's warmer down below."

They descended a wooden staircase which creaked horribly. Then along a low dark corridor, and finally into the great chamber.

It seemed to Jack that the chamber was smaller than before; two burning staves on the wall gave off a smoky light. People milled around aimlessly, gaunt creatures whose pinched faces betrayed their chronic hunger. Everything was so ... grey.

"Jack!" Rana bounded up and gave him a hug. "You were so sick yesterday; it was gross."

Jack's frozen nerves were starting to thaw out. His fingers and toes began to ache as the sensation returned. *It was almost better being cold!*

"Jack, my boy." Phineas strode up, and hugged Jack. "It's been a long time. But you're better now?"

Phineas led Jack over to the far side of the chamber, where several people sat at tables. Jack saw his grandfather in deep conversation with Finbogie and Murkle. Seeing Jack approach, Sandy stood up.

"Welcome back! It's good to see you."

There was real warmth in Grandpa Sandy's eyes, but Jack couldn't help thinking that his grandfather looked somehow smaller; less imposing.

"Jack!" Iain Dubh's voice called out firmly. "Sit down, lad, and we'll tell you our plans."

Jack did as he was bid, noting that the people were subdued. It was hard to make out how many were there, or who they all were, but in the gloom he saw Enda, and Dermot, and Ossian, with Morrigan and Fenrig. Petros came and sat by Jack.

"Your safe return gives us all great joy," announced Iain Dubh. "The unfortunate manner of your illness presented us with something of a challenge; but now I believe we can leave."

Enda stood up now.

"Jack, I can't tell you how sorry I am about what happened. It shamed all the McCools. But it's made us all the more determined to succeed."

Jack's body had warmed up sufficiently now for him to feel alive.

❀ 117 ❀

"Who poisoned me? I've a right to know."

"We have found and punished the guilty person," said Iain Dubh emphatically. "And let that be a warning to all who would try to thwart us, for this is a matter of life and death to us." He indicated the far end of the chamber, where Jack could just make out a figure, suspended from the ceiling.

"Is that . . . ?"

"It's Telos," whispered Petros. "He put something in your goblet. Iain Dubh took care of him."

"You mean . . ."

"Not even a Shian death; they're showing their contempt for him, leaving him strung up like a human criminal. And it's a warning to others."

Jack turned back to face Iain Dubh, who had silently observed Jack's reaction.

"Like I said; it's a matter of life and death. And while we'd not normally leave our shelter in the winter months, the return of our flag is an omen. The *Mapa Mundi* will show us how we can recover our ancestor's talisman. And now we must set sail, before the weather closes in. Your grandfather will take four boats directly to Novehowe. The other two Ilanbeg boats will take a select band to Tula. But we must all beware: it is now December, the Blue Men of the Minch will be there."

15

The Blue Men of the Minch

December already. Jack knew that he had been delirious or drugged for ages, and hadn't really been aware of time. But a whole month? Suddenly getting to Novehowe by the winter solstice looked a lot harder; and even more so with the planned detour to Tula.

Grandpa Sandy approached him.

"Jack, it's no secret that I do not approve of your going to Tula; but I have been overruled. I am asking Armina, as a personal favour to me, to accompany you."

"It's where the *Mapa Mundi* says we have to go. And if we get the Gusog feather and the Raglan, then we'll be better off."

"The Raglan ... I do not believe that is worth such a dangerous mission. But I must bow to our hosts here. Promise me you will avoid danger wherever possible. I will sail with your cousins for Novehowe. Weather permitting, we shall engage Magnus at the solstice there."

"Ready, Jack?" Enda's cheery voice boomed out. "We sailed the Minch earlier in the year. Some bad currents, but nothing we can't handle. Kelly will take the lead boat."

One of the McCools stepped forward, and shook Jack by the hand.

"I like a challenge. And I've sailed these straits before."

"Why aren't the Hebseelie taking the lead? They should know the seas here better than anyone."

"Ah, who knows? One of their boats will go off to Lyosach anyway, to recruit there."

"Who are the Blue Men?"

Kelly looked sideways at Enda, then back at Jack.

"Between you and me, I think this superstitious lot here have imagined them. I've sailed here many times without a problem."

"So who'm I going with?"

"Ye'll come with me, Jack, along with your dad and Armina," said Enda. "Dermot will take Ossian and the two Brashats. Are ye ready?"

"How long will it take to get to Cape Wrath?"

"A week at least. We can't hug the mainland coast: the Kildashie's spies might see us. We'll go north to Port Ness, then cross the Minch."

"But that's the most exposed part," said Jack.

"Like I said, the mainland coast's not an option. We'll have to take a chance with Cape Wrath."

"Where are the boats?"

"We've not been sitting idle while ye were away. The boats are all ready, below in the harbour. They're kitted out, and ready for sailing. Oh, by the way; Iain Dubh said you'd better have this."

He held out the *Mapa Mundi*, draped flag-like over his arm. Jack took it, wrapped it around his neck, and fastened it with Tamlina's ring. It felt chilly, and he wished he could get properly warm. Tentatively, he approached Gilmore.

"Umm, Gilmore. Do you have those warm clothes?"

Gilmore looked at him distractedly for a moment. "Of course, of course," he muttered. "The others packed them for when they're at sea. That's when it'll be coldest. Are you wanting to wear yours now?"

"Yes please. The ride back from the cottage was freezing."

"We're all ready now for the Minch; and Tula. Lots of haemostat bandages. And Finbogie has the swords all prepared."

Gilmore handed Jack a nondescript-looking jacket. Dull brown, and thin-looking, it didn't look like it would keep out anything much; but when Jack put it on he felt the benefit immediately.

"That's brilliant! I wish I'd had that earlier!"

Phineas came up.

"All ready? This is it, Jack. Time for a real adventure. I'm sorry Grandpa doesn't approve of you coming; but we'll show him, eh?"

"Got your sea legs?" Dermot's cheery shout echoed across the chamber.

And Trog's knife stuck to one of them, thought Jack happily.

He followed his father up the wooden staircase to the barn. Gilmore's jacket was certainly an improvement, but what it didn't cover still felt bitterly cold. The snow had stopped, and the wind had fallen. As the boat crews set off down to the harbour, Jack marvelled at the beauty of the scene.

Nine boats lay waiting in the harbour.

"Excited, Jack?" Lizzie gave him a hug. "Grandpa's going to take charge of our boats. We'll see who gets to Novehowe first, yeah?"

"We've a few days before we split," said Jack. "At least a week, Enda said."

"It's not fair that you're getting Arvin on your boat the whole time," pouted Rana. "I want to be able to hear his music too."

"He's not on my boat; he's on Ossian's. But anyway, we've got to learn to sail the boat as a team: Grandpa said. That means keeping the same crew, and not swapping around."

The flotilla was soon afloat, despite a swelling sea. Even in the comparative shelter of the harbour, Jack could tell that it was not going to be easy. He looked across at Petros on his grandfather's boat.

He doesn't look well – already.

The McCools' seamanship was put to the test straight away. Even with the tide running in their favour, the boats were only able to make slow progress north. Kelly bravely took the lead, and showed his mettle, finding the best path in the squally conditions. The small Shian craft bobbed up and down in the swell; at times the waves seemed like they would engulf the tiny boats, but experience – and perhaps luck – told. And all the while a lone eagle soared above them, seemingly keeping watch. Jack wondered if this was the same eagle that had attacked the Urisk.

It was big up close on the beach; I'm glad it's keeping its distance.

By the second night they had reached Antob, and the next night saw them beach safely on Scalpay. Here the third HebShian boat would leave them, setting a course for Lyosach, where they would attempt to recruit the outer isle Shian.

As the eight crews prepared to set out on the fourth morning, Iain Dubh gave a warning.

"The Blue Men are awake. Be on your guard. And remember, they are capricious. Have your answers ready."

"What's caprish . . . ?" asked Lizzie.

"It means they like to have fun," said Phineas. "But their version of fun is to drag boats down to the bottom."

"Kelly doesn't even believe in them," pointed out Jack. "He says he's been here loads of times and never seen them."

"He's never been here in December," noted Phineas. "You just be on your guard."

"How do they attack?"

"They ask riddles."

Jack laughed out loud. "That's silly! You mean they're jokers?"

"These are no jokers," admonished his father. "This day will be the toughest yet. Keep a careful watch."

Jack wasn't sure how much to believe his father's warning. How bad could creatures be if they asked riddles?

Lunch was a bouncy affair, which saw Petros forego his food. The youngster gazed glumly at the foam-flecked sea. Jack had just finished eating when he saw the eagle, flying to the east, and calling raucously.

He's never made that sound before; and he's always been directly above us.

Kelly had steered the lead boat into the Shiant Sound, where the water was briefly calm, but with a covering blanket of mist. Looking around, he called over with satisfaction to Enda in the second boat, "Told you I'd find a smooth path!"

The eagle called again, a harsh urgent cry.

At first Jack thought it was a selkie, and his heartbeat quickened. Then he realised that the creature whose head he could see was far from beguiling. Rising out of the water, its long grey beard partly covered a dark blue body. Splashing down again, it was joined by a second. Jack strained to see ... Then a face appeared out of the water, and called across to the lead boat. Kelly seemed dumbstruck.

His silence was fatal. The sea around the lead boat began to froth, and five of the creatures now rose simultaneously out of the water on the port side. They landed on the boat's edge, tipping it over. The McCool crew had no time to leap for safety, and were lost within seconds as the sea around them churned violently.

Jack looked around to see how Iain Dubh would respond, and was disconcerted to see the Hebseelie leader frantically trying to tack.

That's no good! We've no chance of turning round in time!

A blue face appeared out of the water again, close to Enda's boat.

"'Out of the eater came something to eat; and out of the strong came something sweet.' Answer me now, or drown like the first."

Enda looked helplessly around him. The sea began to churn again.

Jack heard the eagle calling again.

Got it!

Jack jumped forward to the prow of the boat and shouted down, "It's a honeycomb! The bees made a hive in a dead lion!"

The churning waters now settled, and the top half of one of the blue figures reappeared. It stared hard at Jack for a moment, then uttered a roar, before turning and splashing down dramatically and swimming away. The waters settled, and the mist started to clear.

Phineas looked at Jack with amazement.

"How in Tua's name did you know that?"

Jack had stunned himself.

"I ... I read it somewhere. It must've been one of Marco's books."

"Well, it's saved our bacon, that's for sure."

"What about Kelly?" Jack looked sadly over the side of the boat.

"They're gone," replied Enda. "They wouldn't last long; not the way those waters were churning around."

"Can't we at least look for the bodies?"

"No point. The Blue Men will have taken them to the bottom. We'll have a wake for them tonight."

Jack looked over at the now calm sea. *Kelly gone?* He hadn't even believed in the Blue Men. Jack was grateful for a smooth sail up the island coast; but what a price to pay. They hadn't even got to Tula, and they'd already lost a boat.

"Who are they?" he asked of Iain Dubh when they docked in a small bay for the night. "Those Blue Men."

"Some say they're fallen angels. They only emerge in the winter months. You could sail for years and never meet them."

"But you warned us against them. You must've known they were around."

"I did warn you all. But Kelly never believed me. You can't prepare yourself for an enemy you don't believe in."

"Couldn't you have told him what to say?"

"You never know what riddle they'll come up with. So well

done for knowing the answer to that one. Now, get some food, and rest well. We've another few days to reach Cape Wrath. I'll keep Enda and the others company."

As Jack nestled down that night, he was grateful for the insulated tent Gilmore had made. It was almost like being inside with a roaring fireplace. But the keening sound of the McCools as they mourned their dead comrades made him think back to funerals at Rangie. First Telos; now Kelly and his whole crew. Death was following them: how many would make it to Novehowe?

16
Kelly's Wake

Jack woke to the sound of a furious argument.

"To lose a boat and its crew is bad enough . . ." (Jack recognised his grandfather's voice) ". . . but to sacrifice another precious day is madness!"

" 'Twouldn't be right to go; not for a day or two. We must mourn them, and pray for their rest." Enda spoke equally firmly, and Jack heard his grandfather's exasperated gasp.

The scene around the bay was not quite one of chaos, but it was easy to see that the camp was divided. The McCools were refusing to leave until they had paid sufficient respect to Kelly and his crew; Grandpa Sandy was getting increasingly agitated about the delay; and the Hebseelie were divided. The different crews had lined up behind their respective leaders.

"Who knows what the weather will do in the days to come? We must make progress while the weather is fair." Sandy's voice urged action, but it was easy to see that this was having no effect on the McCools.

Fair weather? Jack looked up at the sky, and shivered. True, it was clear, but the cold wind was a forceful reminder that winter had now set in.

"Jack!" called Iain Dubh. "You must settle this. Your grandfather is all for leaving now. What does the *Mapa Mundi* show?"

Keen to keep the group together, Jack looked uncertainly at his grandfather, then at Enda. Nervously, he tugged Tamlina's ring from around his neck, and put it on his finger. The flag formed slowly into a sphere once more.

The two circles formed, but both remained blank. Murkle strode forward, demanding to see.

"Ach, these islands!" he spat, seeing the blank sphere. "Nothing works here."

The *Mapa* did indeed seem to be lost for pictures. Jack concentrated hard.

The Mapa *shows our true path. What do we really* need*? We have to raise the Novehowe Shian; but Dad says we have to get to Tula as well, to find the Raglan stone – and the Gusog feather.*

He stared at the sphere. Still nothing.

"Jack; use the ring." Ishona spoke softly. "The *cailleach* told me you have it, and that it can show the future."

Jack took Tamlina's ring from his finger, and stared at it. Two spiral arms had faded: the first had shown him Ploutter's execution, but that had already happened; the second was floods in Edinburgh, and the *cailleach* had said they were happening now. The third vision was to show him the future. The spirals began to blur, and he closed his eyes.

It's me! In a big hall . . . there's a huge fireplace; and snow on the window panes . . . I'm being forced to my knees . . . Boreus is standing in front of me . . . he's smiling . . . he's got a broadsword in his hand . . . He's raised it above his head . . . he's about to strike . . .

The tableau in Jack's mind froze; he remained, kneeling, waiting for the sword to fall . . . But then a soft voice called in his head: "And the father shall die for the son . . . the father shall die for the son . . ."

The tableau started to life once more, and Jack saw his father move forward purposefully, and stand immediately in front of Boreus . . . Boreus smiled evilly and began to bring the sword down . . .

Jack opened his eyes, gasping for breath.

No! Anything but that!

"The images are showing!" called Murkle with glee.

Sure enough, the circles in the *Mapa Mundi* were now revealing shapes. Boats . . . in both of them. Then the circles faded, one to reveal Fractals' Seer once more, the other to show Novehowe.

Jack was confused. The crews weren't supposed to separate until they got to Cape Wrath.

"It means we part company here; until we meet again at Novehowe." Enda spoke emphatically. "Sandy will take his boat and two others for Novehowe today. The other four boats will follow on later; but for Tula."

Jack nodded – he could put no other interpretation on the images. But what had his vision meant? He looked at Tamlina's ring: all three spiral arms were faint.

Phineas came up and put his arm around Jack's shoulder.

"Well? Are you going to tell me what you saw?"

Jack found it hard to look straight at his father.

"The image was fuzzy ... I couldn't make out much. Just a big hall, with a fireplace. There was snow outside."

Phineas looked hard at his son, then grasped him violently to his chest.

"I would do anything to protect you."

Jack felt tears welling up inside, and he pulled away.

"Is Grandpa going now?" he sniffed.

"Aye. The southerly wind will carry the boats far."

"But it's freezing."

"Believe me, freezing is when it blows from the north. We'll stay here for a day or so and mourn with the McCools. Then we'll head for Tula."

"Why's Fenrig coming to Tula? And Morrigan?"

"Jack, everyone was chosen for this quest for a reason; except Rana and Lizzie, obviously. Fenrig has qualities that you may not appreciate: he was good with the selkie, and he's been helping Gilmore with the warm clothes."

Jack thought with distaste of his fellow tailoring apprentice. *Is he really a better tailor than me?*

"What about Morrigan?"

"Maybe she'll be able to help us against the Boaban Shee," said Phineas evasively. "She's a nasty bit of work. And we may need that if we're going to fight really evil creatures."

"Fighting fire with fire?"

"I just sense that she can think like them. That may give us an edge."

"Well, what about Petros, then? He's been as sick as a dog most of the time."

"I wouldn't tell him this; but he's what they call a lightning rod. Him being so seasick makes everyone else feel better about feeling just a bit sick. It's an old sailors' trick; a bit mean, but it works."

Jack could see his cousins getting ready to leave. While Lizzie was hugging Ossian, Rana was noisily checking that they had enough food for the journey. Despite repeated assurances from her grandfather and Dara, she was insisting on checking the provisions.

Jack watched the three small boats leave the bay. As Phineas had predicted, they quickly caught the southerly breeze, and were soon lost to sight as they headed north.

"We'll maybe catch them up," said Phineas, joining him. "I know Grandpa's keen to get to Novehowe; but the McCools are excellent sailors. They'll get us there."

"Is the mourning like when someone dies at Rangie?"

"A bit. They'll tell stories of Kelly and his crewmen, then sing. And they'll probably have a drink or two to note the passing."

Jack could see the McCools building a cairn on the beach, beside which they stacked driftwood. Iain Dubh and the two Hebseelie crews watched, occasionally helping to drag a branch over. Armina was engaged in conversation with Finbogie and Gilmore, while Murkle sat at a distance and observed the Irish activity.

Building up his store of Shian tales . . .

As Phineas had indicated, they sat around the fire, and told stories. With each tale, a bottle was passed around the company, and the laughter got louder.

"I thought they were mourning Kelly," said Jack to his father. "It sounds more like a party."

"It's their way. Come on, let's practise our swordplay. We'll see if we can find Ossian and Fenrig."

However, Ossian was observed walking along the beach with Morrigan, and Fenrig was nowhere to be seen. Jack and his father moved to a sheltered spot above the bay and rehearsed their sword routines. After an hour, Jack was feeling hot and sweaty, and he sat down to rest.

"Phew! That's hard going!"

"You'll need to keep going a lot longer than that on Tula; I'm certain of that." Phineas sat down beside him and stroked his chin thoughtfully. "The Boaban Shee I think we can handle; but the witches – nobody really knows what they're like."

"Will they all be in Fractals' Seer?"

"Anyone's guess. But first we have to get to Tula, and that's not going to be easy. Come on, let's see how the wake's going."

When they got back to the bay, Arvin was playing on his squeeze box, and the McCools were singing along. Several empty bottles were strewn around.

"Come in!" said Enda cheerily. "Ah, it's a grand wake. Kelly would've loved it." He waved his arm extravagantly, indicating several sleeping figures around the fire.

"Are you going to be able to sail tomorrow?" Jack's tone was reproachful.

"Ah, we've only just started. But we'll be fine by the morning; I promise."

Enda turned out to be quite correct in his assertion: the McCools *had* only just started their celebrations. They seemed to take it in turns to sleep on the beach, while others sang, or told long, rambling stories. But, amazingly, all the McCools were awake at first light, and ready to leave.

"Well, Jack," said Enda as Jack emerged shivering from his tent, "'Twouldn't be true to say we're all bright-eyed this morning. But we'd be ready to leave, if only . . ."

"What?"

"Well, look at the sea."

Jack peered out to sea where the light danced off the water. It was another bright day, but still freezing cold. Jack pulled his charmed jacket closer around him. *There's white horses on the waves, but it doesn't seem so rough. Am I missing something?*

"The wind's from the north. We might get across the Minch, but then we'd have to hug the mainland coast north, and there's too much danger in that. We'll have to sit it out until the wind changes."

When this news became known, there was consternation.

"But we delayed leaving yesterday for your wake!" shouted Armina above the sound of the rising wind. "If we lose more time we may never reach Novehowe by the solstice."

"We've no option," said Enda emphatically. "We can't get north in this wind."

"These setbacks will ruin everything!" Murkle joined in now. "Sandy may even have crossed the Minch already and be making his way along the north coast; and we're stuck here!"

"Sure, we can't control the weather," butted in Finnegan. "We're not Kildashie."

"No one knows if they're controlling the weather," put in Arvin. "They just like the winter."

"And if we don't get back to Edinburgh and clear them out, then we could be stuck with winter the year round," roared Armina. "Who wants the Kildashie to be in control?"

"I don't." Morrigan spoke calmly.

Jack had not even seen her join the growing argument; but she stood, relaxed, her eyes glinting in the wintry December light. Ossian and Fenrig were beside her.

"And so what do you propose to do about it?" sneered Murkle.

"I'll take you to Tula. I know how to open the Bridge of Impossibilities."

17

Papa Legba

The Bridge of Impossibilities?!

"This is insanity," screeched Armina. "Only dark magycks can open that bridge; and who knows how much time would be lost in that vortex?"

"Do you want to go or not?"

Iain Dubh held up his hand.

"Look at the sky," he commanded. "The north wind may blow for six or seven days. We might not sail now for a week."

"A week!" spat Murkle. "Then we've no chance of making Novehowe if we delay for a week. I said that wake was a mistake."

"It delayed us a day. And the north wind will be delaying Sandy and his crews, wherever they are," stated Finnegan emphatically.

"Not if they got across the Minch yesterday," admitted Enda. "The coastline will shelter them – as long as they can keep out of sight of the Kildashie spies."

Ossian was looking strangely at Morrigan. "Do you really know how to open the bridge?" he said, a mixture of awe and fear in his voice.

She looked back at him calmly, but said nothing.

Phineas now walked up to her, and looked hard at her. There was a brief flicker of a smile, then he turned away. As he saw Jack looking on in astonishment, he winked quickly.

What's going on? Dad can't be doing deals with an Unseelie like Morrigan!

"I demand to know how this . . . this girl can work such dark magycks!" spluttered Armina. "It is far beyond her age!"

Without speaking, Morrigan took out a small crystal sphere from her pocket. She passed her other hand over it, and revealed a distorted image in the globe.

"It's Fractals' Seer!" exclaimed Gilmore.

Wordlessly, Morrigan threw the globe high into the air and clapped her hands. Instantly changing into a hoodie crow, she flew up, and caught the globe in her claws, before descending and hovering in front of Fenrig. With a squawk, she dropped the globe into her brother's waiting hands. Settling onto the ground, she changed back into her usual figure.

Jack was impressed. It was the first time he'd seen Morrigan shapeshift since Dunvik, more than a year before.

Fenrig smiled, and embraced his sister.

"Parlour tricks!" sneered Murkle dismissively.

In a flash, Morrigan had grabbed the globe back, and cast it at the Shian tales tutor. It hit him in the forehead, and exploded with a shower of sparks. When the sparks cleared, Murkle had vanished.

"Does anyone else doubt me?"

Morrigan's voice had deepened to a growl; fierce, powerful . . . and exciting. Jack felt the hairs on the back of his neck bristle.

"Where . . . where have you sent him?" asked Daid nervously.

"To the end of the bridge; if you wish to see him again, you'd better come to Tula."

"Enough!" Iain Dubh spoke firmly. "You have the gift; from where, I do not wish to know. So tell us: where is the start of this bridge?"

Morrigan eyed him playfully for a moment, enjoying her moment of triumph.

"It's nearby; it's always nearby, if you know where to look."

Jack thought he heard Armina mutter "Dark magycks!" under her breath.

"What about the boats?"

Morrigan now eyed Enda carefully. "Leave one man on each boat," she said simply. "The rest will come with us." There was no mistaking the authority of her voice.

Jack turned to his father. "What's so dangerous about the bridge, that Armina doesn't want to use it?"

"It plays tricks. For one thing, you lose all sense of time on it. Armina was right: we could be stuck on it for weeks. But we've no choice now: we can't sail, and we can't fly. So, the bridge it is."

"Why's it called the Bridge of Impossibilities?"

"Because it does things it shouldn't. I'm only going on what I've been told; and that was many years ago. The one thing you can count on is that it won't be like any other bridge you've been on. And there's no time to lose; our hand is forced. Do you agree, Enda?"

The Irishman looked back at Phineas.

"I hate to leave the boats; they're our home. But you're right. Let's get ready."

"We may be on the bridge for a while," barked Morrigan. "Take only fresh water and fey biscuits; anything else is too much to carry."

The crews had soon taken what they needed from the boats. While Gilmore distributed the food and haemostat bandages, Finbogie ensured that everyone had a sword.

"Remember the hexes," he warned. "And aim for their ankles."

"We'll sail for Novehowe when we can," promised Dermot, as the group set off.

When she reached the cliff face, Morrigan began to move along it, adjacent to the sea line. The pebbly beach scrunched as the crews followed her. Every few paces she would pause, and tap the rock face.

"Is she looking for a way in?" asked Jack.

"I don't know how the bridge is opened," admitted Phineas. "We were never taught dark magycks like this."

Murkle never taught us anything useful, thought Jack. Then he reflected that one or two lessons had managed to seep into his memory – such as waking the giant's bridge. *Columns awake!* he mused. *I wonder if this bridge is like that one?*

Morrigan had stopped and paused a number of times. The incoming tide was close to the rock face here; the water soaked their ankles.

I don't like Trog's knife getting wet, thought Jack, aware of the blade strapped to his right leg. *It'll rust.*

"Are you sure you know where it is?" asked Ossian, his teeth chattering.

Morrigan spun round and flashed a look of contempt that had Ossian turning scarlet. Mumbling, he looked down at his feet.

The sea was up to their shins now.

"It's freezing!" said Jack, as the feeling in his toes died away.

"Cold feet will be the least of your worries soon," cautioned Daid, as he moved up beside Jack. "This trip will beat even your flight to Dunvik last year. I hope you've been practising your swordplay."

Jack thought back to the repetitive lessons with Finbogie. They'd been fun for a while, but the need to practise so often had lost its appeal.

I wish she'd hurry up and find the start of this bridge, he thought, as the waves splashed his thighs.

Without warning, Morrigan gave a cry of triumph. Taking the sceptre from her cloak, she struck the rock face three times, each time calling, "Papa Legba!"

There was a moment of stillness after the third strike; even the waves seemed to stop. And in that period of tranquillity, Jack saw a frail old man appear, standing thigh-deep ahead of them. He limped up to Morrigan, and enquired in a thin reedy voice, "Are ye ready?"

"We are."

Dishevelled and grimy, he didn't look like he could achieve much; but there was something earthy about him – almost primal. He held up his hands, then brought them down together with a resounding clap. Numb as his freezing feet were, Jack felt the stones underneath him shift; and then he sank, quickly and wordlessly, beneath the waves.

Falling into the pit at the end of the giant's bridge had been weird: cold, slimy, and silent. This was different: it was cold, yes;

but this time there were screams and yells all around him, as the crew members tumbled down an icy chute. Furiously trying to keep a hold of his sword, Jack felt his satchel almost torn from him.

I'm not losing that! That's food for three weeks!

Jack came to rest in a heap, with bodies strewn around him.

"'Scuse me," said Enda apologetically, as he disentangled himself from Ossian and Daid.

There were groans and mutterings now, as those who had landed badly examined themselves for breakages.

"Come along!" the old man snapped.

Jack looked around. They were in some sort of cave. It wasn't dark, more ... gloomy. Jack could make out side walls, and a high roof. He was glad of the warm clothing Gilmore had provided.

The old man had set off, limping, on what looked like a rock path. Then, reaching two boulders a few paces on, he stopped, and turned.

"Line up!" The sharp order came in the same reedy voice.

"Right! By crews!" Enda shouted the order down the line at the thirty would-be travellers.

"Who's leading Dermot's crew?" Ossian challenged Enda.

"You take it. Kedge maybe isn't ready for that, and Arvin's not what you'd call a captain."

"I'll keep you dancing, though," laughed Arvin, shouldering his squeeze box.

"I thought Armina said only dark magycks could open the bridge," whispered Jack to his father. "That wasn't dark; the old man just clapped his hands."

"This is not the bridge," snapped Papa Legba, whose hearing

seemed remarkable. "You'll know when we break the seal what dark means."

Jack shuffled his feet awkwardly.

"The Bridge of Impossibilities can only be crossed by those true of spirit." Morrigan walked along the line of travellers, eyeing each carefully. "You," she snapped at one of the HebShian crewmen. "What is your name?"

"T . . . Tonald."

"Your spirit is weak. You shall lead the first group. Take two of your comrades."

Why? thought Jack. *Why put someone you think is weak in front? Unless . . .*

"We are about to break the seal and start on the bridge," drawled Morrigan in an imperious voice. "And not all of us will see Tula. Crossing the bridge entails certain . . . expenses."

She sounds just like her father. Jack's mind flitted back to his first sight of Briannan at the midsummer festival.

"Right! In threes!"

The old man stood on one of the two boulders, and indicated for the first group to come along. Taking a sceptre from his belt, he waved it over Tonald and his two HebShian friends. Jack was astonished to see a bubble encase the three of them: a flexible, clear bubble that moved as they did.

It's like . . . what's that stuff you see in the High Street all the time? The humans wrap things in it . . . Plastic.

Papa Legba now reached into the bubble with a fistful of weeds. His arm passed into and out of the bubble without breaking it.

"They'll replenish the air. You may be in there for a long time."

Jack heard Morrigan giggle, and turned to see her sneer at Armina. The enchantress, for her part, seemed powerless.

"Keep coming!" barked the old man. "Quickly now! You need to get into these pustulas."

Armina now stepped forward.

"This is foolishness! This girl cares for no one's interests but her own!"

"But we have no choice," urged Iain Dubh. "We must go this way."

"I will have no part of it," said Armina determinedly. "Let us return to the boats. Come, Jack!"

"Too late for that!" sneered Morrigan. "The gate above is closed; if you stay here, you will drown!"

There was an uncertain milling of bodies, as some pressed forward, and others joined Armina as she sought to find her way back. Morrigan's warning, however, proved to be accurate: a gush of sea water from the chute changed the minds of those who had decided to retreat.

Jack shuffled forward, but in the gloom and confusion he found he had been separated from his father. Worse, he was next to Fenrig. Papa Legba grabbed the two of them and shoved them next to one of the HebShians. In an instant they were encased in the bubble, and within a minute all the other travellers had been enclosed in threes in the pustulas.

The pustula was clear; and he could breathe all right; but the inner surface was greasy, and it smelt rank. It reminded Jack of when he'd had to clean Murkle's grimy stove. The HebShian clutched the weeds Papa Legba had thrust in.

"The pustulas will allow you to move and breathe on the bridge!" snapped Papa Legba. "You'll walk for six hours, and rest for one. Speak little; conserve the air within. Now one of you must open the bridge. Whose blood will pay the price?"

Morrigan stepped out of her bubble, drew her sword, and thrust it through Papa Legba's heart.

18

The Bridge of Impossibilities

As the old man's body crumpled to the ground, Morrigan stepped forward and snatched his sceptre.

"Papa Legba is dead! I control the entrance to the bridge! Does anyone dare challenge me?"

Though in his pustula, Jack could hear perfectly what Morrigan was saying. And it chilled him to his bones.

She killed him! He'd helped us, and she just killed him!

Armina manoeuvred her pustula over to Jack's, and said, "Keep a close watch. Remember the *Mapa*; and the ring. Be on your guard."

Jack looked furtively at Fenrig. Was he really going to have to share this bubble with Morrigan's brother?

"There's no time to lose!" shouted Morrigan, revelling in her power. "Everyone up to the boulders now!"

When the nine bubbles were packed in close together,

Morrigan pointed Papa Legba's sceptre at the rock floor and shouted, "*Brigadoom!*"

There was a soundless explosion, and the rock floor gave way. Suddenly, Jack felt his pustula drop; then float down for several seconds in increasingly cold water until they came to rest on what looked like a bridge – an old rickety wooden bridge, with rope sides. An old rickety *underwater* wooden bridge. Startled fish swam away as the pustulas floated down.

Shivering, Jack peered ahead. He could still breathe – the pustula sealed him off from the water; but the bridge led into darkness. Every now and then there was a glow ahead to one side of the rope handrails.

Seeing that all nine pustulas had landed safely, Morrigan indicated the way forward, shouting to Tonald and his comrades to take the lead. Clearly nervous, Tonald advanced cautiously forward. The sea made a strange glooping noise as the pustulas proceeded.

Jack's pustula was fourth in line. His father was just ahead of him, with Iain Dubh and Ishona; and Morrigan was in charge of the second pustula, with Fergus and Archie. Jack elbowed his way to the front of his pustula.

"Watch what you're doing!" snarled Fenrig. "It's foul enough in here without you shoving."

"Your sister says we've got to go this way. Are you going to argue with her?"

Caught in a dilemma, Fenrig opted not to reply, but fell into step behind Jack. Though adult, Cal the HebShian seemed reluctant to take the lead.

Jack could see past the pustulas in front: it was almost pitch dark, but the line was moving.

❀ 145 ❀

"What are those glowing things up ahead?" he asked.

"Ye'll see soon enough."

It was the first time Cal had spoken. His voice was soft, like a gently flowing stream. And he was right: within half a minute they were approaching the first glowing object. With a lurching feeling in his stomach, Jack saw that it was a skull. A human skull, lit from inside.

Jack's surprise was quickly followed by astonishment: he distinctly heard Morrigan cheer as she passed the skull, while Fenrig made retching noises behind him.

He's not joking: he's really feeling sick. And his sister's loving this!

"They're the drowned," said Cal quietly. "There's many that neffer reach their destination."

"What's your sister so happy about?" demanded Jack indignantly as they passed the skull.

Fenrig didn't reply. He looked unhappily at the glowing skull, then averted his gaze.

"Bit tough, your sister, isn't she?" Jack couldn't help twisting the knife in Fenrig's unhappiness.

Fenrig's silence was broken by Cal.

"We've some time in here; let's not argue."

"Have you done this before, then?" demanded Jack.

"Thiss? Neffer!"

"Then how'd you know about it?"

"Tales are told up and down the length of these islands. I know off your fisit to Ireland."

"But what d'you know about this bridge? Why's it take so long to cross it?"

"Time iss different down here, they say. It's ass long ass it needs to be. We must keep moving. And there are creatures who don't like anyone using this pridge."

"How can we get lost if the bridge is going to Tula?" Fenrig butted in.

"The pridge can go anywhere. Did you not think it strange that it happened to be chust where we were? The start and end can be anyplace – safe or dangerous: that's why you need spirit. Your sister wass right apout that."

"So why'd she send your mate in the first bubble then? She said he didn't have it."

In the gloom, Jack was almost sure he could *hear* Cal blush.

"Ass ye said; she's tough. And she's no fool."

By the time they had walked for . . . *how long? Let's see, we were to walk for six hours and rest for one; we've done that a few times . . . oh, a long time, I guess.*

Jack found his mind was surprisingly at ease, despite the intense cold. Cal was right: time felt different down here. He was well used to the swaying of the bridge, and the darkness around them.

It's sort of trance-like: just keep plodding on. He hummed to himself, one of Arvin's tunes. The glowing skulls didn't bother him now. Every now and then one would be attached to part or even all of a skeleton. *But after you've seen a few . . . well . . .*

Jack *was* almost in a trance. The three of them had adopted a steady coordinated pace that meant they were close enough behind his father's pustula, and far enough ahead of the three HebShian behind them that they weren't in danger of getting their heels clipped.

Just keep plodding on . . . step-two-three-four . . . Just keep plodding on . . . step-two-three-four . . .

Jack's mind began to wander. They'd been going for ages, but he wasn't hungry, or even particularly tired. He'd got used to his satchel and sword as they swayed with his movements; it was all going swimmingly.

Jack laughed to himself. *Swimmingly*. Fish had got used to the nine pustulas proceeding along the bridge, and swam up close for a look every now and then. Some had even swum alongside for a while. Even in the gloom, Jack had learnt to tell different fish apart. Emerging from his daydream, Jack looked round.

No fish.

None?! It's almost as if . . .

Without warning, a flash of navy light struck the bridge, and it swayed alarmingly. Jack was aware of dark shapes moving swiftly around the bridge, but their speed was so great that he had no idea what they were.

Then he saw the lead pustula pierced by three harpoons, and its inhabitants flailing madly as the seawater gushed in.

"Mer-attack!" Iain Dubh's voice carried along the line.

Jack could see them now. Hideous mutants, there were too many of them to count, and they surrounded the pustulas which halted as one on the bridge.

"Close up!" shouted Iain Dubh, but the pustula inhabitants needed no encouragement.

"Don't let them pierce the pustulas!" Morrigan's voice now carried a hint of concern. "Use your sceptres!"

What sceptres? thought Jack, then looked on with relief as Cal drew an emerald-tipped sceptre from his cloak, and brandished it against the pustula's inner wall. The emerald glowed, and the nearby merfolk seemed repulsed. The gruesome creatures waved harpoons mockingly, as if inviting the travellers out to fight.

Jack's relief was temporary, however: the merfolk seemed to be multiplying in number, and Cal could only face one way at a time. The attackers quickly realised that the pustula was vulnerable to its rear, and they swarmed around, keeping Cal guessing. As their boldness grew, so they started to stab their harpoons at the bubble wall . . . Closer . . . Cal frantically tried to fend them off . . . Harpoon ends prodded the pustula wall, but didn't break it.

That's a relief.

Then a gush of seawater: one stab had got through.

"Prush the wall!" shouted Cal. "The grease will seal it ofer!"

Jack did as he was instructed, and was thankful to see the hole repair itself. But it was a losing battle. The harpoon thrusts were coming in from several different sides now.

We can't fend this lot off for ever.

Jack was right. A determined harpoon plunge cut clean though the wall, stabbing Cal through his thigh. He fell, blood gushing from the wound.

"Fix the wall!" shouted Fenrig, handing Cal's sceptre up to Jack.

The young Brashat dropped to his knees, and scrabbled in his satchel for a moment. Then, removing a strip of cloth, he wound it round Cal's leg.

"Haemostat," he said simply, as Jack frantically smeared the inside wall, while moving the sceptre round so that the merfolk were kept at bay.

"There's too many of them!" shouted Jack. "We can't keep them away for much longer!"

"Well, what are you supposed to be good at?" demanded Fenrig. "Do that!"

Jack's mind raced. *No time to use the* Mapa Mundi *now; we know our true path anyway. Tamlina's ring's no use, I've used my three goes on that.*

True path. *That's to get the Kildashie out, before they bring a permanent winter; and to do that we must get the Raglan, and get to Novehowe. Marco said it was the right thing.*

Then his mind cleared.

Gosol!

He didn't even have to say the word, although it echoed in his head like a sharp cry. The stunned merfolk looked at one another, unsure what was happening.

But nothing was happening.

Then a blur, as a new shape appeared out of the gloom. Lots of shapes, in fact.

"It's the selkies!" Fenrig's voice almost broke with emotion. He looked down at Cal, who smiled weakly back.

The selkies now engaged in combat. Twice the size of the merfolk, they swam powerfully through the attacking force, snapping and biting, brushing aside the harpoons as if they were twigs. Though greater in number, the merfolk soon realised that they were no match for the selkies' speed and strength, and they beat a hasty retreat.

As the mutant forms disappeared into the gloom, the selkies surrounded the pustulas, examining the inhabitants with interest. In various states of disarray, they were sealing the holes where harpoon thrusts had found their way through, and examining themselves and each other for injuries.

Finding he could stand, Cal got to his feet. The bandage around his thigh looked clean.

"Ye did a grand chob there," he said to Fenrig. "I'd say ye were well taught."

"They're not hard to make," replied Fenrig.

If Jack hadn't known him better, he would have said Fenrig was blushing.

"Are you all right?" Phineas' frantic voice came from the next pustula.

"We're fine, Dad. The selkies came when I thought of Gosol. That's amazing! Even underwater!"

"How many are lost?" Iain Dubh's urgent call came from beside Phineas.

"Tonald iss gone," said Cal sadly. "They were hit sefferal times – they neffer got a chance to use their sceptres."

There was no sign of the lead pustula, which had slipped off the bridge and floated down to . . . wherever.

"And Murdo's killed: a harpoon got his heart. There was no time to treat him." Ossian spoke softly.

"I said there were dangers on the bridge!" snapped Morrigan. "Get rid of Murdo's body; it'll only slow you down."

"You mean we can't even bury him?"

"Don't be stupid. How can you move the pustula with a dead body in it?"

"Ask the selkies." Fenrig spoke calmly.

Indeed, the selkies were watching this debrief with fascination. One swam up to Fenrig, and stared at him. Fenrig and Jack stared back in astonishment as the selkie leant forward to show her left shoulder.

"She's been shot!" shouted Fenrig. "It's the one we treated back on Soabost!"

The creature inclined her head.

"Can you take our friend?" asked Fenrig. "We don't want to tip him over the side of the bridge for the fish to eat."

Two selkies swam to the last pustula, and waited while Ossian and Kedge pushed Murdo's body through the wall. Cradling the body between them, the two selkies swam away into the darkness.

"Now we must go!" barked Morrigan. "The bridge is not safe for those who linger!"

The eight pustulas started on their way, and Jack was relieved to see that the selkies appeared to form a guard on either side. As they recommenced their regular pace, Jack glanced back at Fenrig.

He got me to call on Gosol. And he treated Cal's leg; and he got the selkies to take Murdo away. He's almost . . . noble.

Fenrig intercepted Jack's glance. A half-smile passed over his face.

19

Fractals' Seer

The thrill of seeing off the merfolk lasted for a while; but after a few hours Jack realised that the end was not in sight. The marching was monotonous, almost hypnotic, and indeed Jack felt at times as if he was almost sleepwalking.

Step-two-three-four . . . just-keep-plodding-on . . . step-two-three-four . . .

Arvin had long since given up playing his squeeze box. The music had helped, even giving them a beat to march to; but he had evidently decided to use his energies for walking. Jack tried singing to himself, but he was too tired to concentrate. He had lost track of how many seventh-hour rests they had had, and his food and water stores were getting low.

We must've travelled miles. It can't be long now . . .

Jack felt his legs grow weak, and he stumbled. Without room to manoeuvre, Fenrig and Cal fell over him.

"Watch out!"

The pustula swayed on the bridge and threatened to fall over. Effortlessly, two selkies bore the pustula's weight until Jack found his feet again.

"Sorry," he mumbled, aware that Fenrig was glaring behind his back.

"Just watch your step, lad," cautioned Cal. "We've a way to go yet. D'ye want me to take the lead a whilie?"

"I need to rest."

"Yeah, me too," echoed Fenrig. "We've been going for days."

"Time's different here, I thought ye knew that." Cal didn't raise his voice.

"So how much longer?"

"A long way yet. I'll see if Iain Dubh will stop."

Cal whistled, and in the next pustula Iain Dubh looked back. He seemed to read Cal's mind.

"It's too dangerous. Even the hour rests are too long."

"They're just lads."

"No matter. If we stop, we're easy prey. It's not just the merfolk we have to worry about."

Cal shrugged. "You heard what Iain Dubh said. Just keep the rhythm going. After a while you can do it and sleep too."

If we're asleep we're not on our guard, thought Jack. *But I'm too tired to argue.*

Step-two-three-four, gotta-keep-go-ing, step-two-three-four . . .

The pace was relentless, and after a while Jack realised he could no longer actually feel his legs. For ages he didn't dare look down, in case they weren't there.

Why isn't there some kind of charm that can keep us going? Or make us get there? No, mustn't think; blank out thinking . . . just keep going.

In time it was apparent that Jack and Fenrig were not the only ones to feel exhausted. A growing rumble of discontent came from the other pustulas as time wore on, so that Iain Dubh eventually shouted to Morrigan to halt.

"We can't!" she snapped. "We must keep going."

"But people are falling over. Let them rest a while."

"No!" shouted Morrigan.

Her entreaties worked – but only for a while. The stumbling and tripping became more frequent, the oaths grew louder and more bad-tempered as shins were kicked and people were trampled on. Eventually Iain Dubh called a halt.

"You can go on if you want," he shouted at Morrigan. "The rest of us are having a proper rest."

Morrigan wailed, an eerie cry that made Jack shiver. It made him think of . . .

No. No, it couldn't be that.

But the thought was in his mind now, and as he sank down to rest, Jack's mind raced back to the Woods of Keldy. That day when they'd found Tamlina wounded, when he'd first seen Malevola . . . There was no doubt about it: Morrigan sounded just like her.

Jack looked at Fenrig, but if his old adversary had heard his sister, he wasn't bothered. In fact, he was snoring gently.

"Rest now," shouted Iain Dubh. "We'll take turns to watch. But when we move, we move on together."

The selkie guard appeared to understand, although some seemed eager to keep going.

Morrigan shouted and cursed, upbraiding Fergus and Archie within her pustula, but they too had had enough, and dropped down to rest. She was left, fuming impotently.

Why isn't she tired?
Jack felt his eyelids close.
Mmmm, that feels good . . .

"Arise; go quickly!"

Jack woke to the sound of a sweet voice whispering in his ear. He looked round, but there was nothing to see – at least, not in the pustula. A selkie was hovering outside, peering in intently. Then the voice came again, "Get up! Go now!"

Fenrig jumped, startled by the sound.

And a third time: "Rise quickly!"

It was Cal's turn to be startled. There was urgency, and yet at the same time a strange sense of peace in the words. The selkie continued to hover outside.

Jack looked each way along the line and saw that there was a selkie hovering by each pustula, creating enough turbulence in the water to waken their inhabitants.

Jack stood up. He had no idea of how long he'd been asleep; but he felt refreshed.

The words echoed in his head: *Go quickly!*

"Come on," he urged Fenrig. "It's time to go."

The message seemed to have permeated the consciousness of all the travellers, for the pustulas now started to move again.

Morrigan cursed under her breath.

She *couldn't get us moving; but the selkies did*, thought Jack. *If it was the selkies . . .*

It was a cheery thought, but one that had to sustain him for a long time. The rhythm of the march was soon resumed, and even with their seventh-hour stops, it seemed like they had been on the bridge for an eternity. Jack was down to his last fey biscuit,

✦ 156 ✦

and he had only a few drops of water left. Even worse, the weeds distributed by Papa Legba had shrivelled, and Jack was uncomfortably aware that there wasn't as much air inside the pustula. Breathing was getting difficult.

The selkies were a reassuring presence, but it didn't stop a few heart-thumping moments when a giant dark shape floated past, a mournful cry lingering in the water long after it had gone.

"What in Tua's name was that?" gasped Fenrig.

"Chust a whale," said Cal. "Though that kind wouldn't attack uss."

Jack wasn't sure if this was good to know or not. They'd beaten off merfolk – with the selkies' help – but whales were another matter. At Shian size, they would be little more than a snack to a whale.

And, thought Jack as he considered the diminishing water supply, *we'll be a dried snack before long*.

He wasn't the only one to notice. From further back came complaints from Enda's companions the Twa Tams.

"We're running out of air back here! How much further?"

Phineas looked back.

"There's only Ossian and Kedge behind you. One of you move into their pustula: there'll be more air in it."

"You mean go out into the water?"

"If you want more air, there's no choice," said Phineas emphatically.

The column paused to watch as one of the Tams took a deep breath, and stepped through his pustula wall and frantically jumped into the one behind him.

"Hey! It worked!"

The column moved on again, but it was soon clear that both air and drinking water were in short supply. Breathing became laboured, and as the last of the food and water were consumed, a sense of despair descended. Iain Dubh was faring badly, along with all his HebShian comrades. Stumbling, falling, cursing, they were a pathetic sight.

They were pretty scrawny to start with, thought Jack. *Now they look as if they're going to drop.*

Jack had just reached the point of thinking that he would rather sink down and die, when he heard a triumphant shriek from Morrigan. Even through the dark water there was clearly light ahead. A dim glow, no more, but light. Reinvigorated, the pustulas shuffled along, the pace quickening.

"Nice one, Mor," said Fenrig, as Morrigan turned round to gaze jubilantly at the exhausted travellers behind her. His lips were as dry as Jack's, and his face seemed hollow, but he looked delighted.

The pustula inhabitants hobbled the final stretch onto a rock platform, whereupon Morrigan brandished her sceptre and uttered, "*Claudopont!*"

The sea fell away from either side, taking the pustula walls with it.

Jack looked round. It was another cave, but there was light coming from somewhere. Iain Dubh and the other HebShian had collapsed; they looked like they might never get up.

"Is that daylight?" asked Daid, a note of relief in his voice.

"Of a kind," replied Phineas. "If this is Tula, there's little true light here in winter."

"Doesn't matter," gasped Armina. "I need fresh air. Let's get out of here."

Morrigan had run ahead, casting beams of light from her sceptre, searching for an exit. With a sharp cry, she blasted a hole in the rock, and the cave wall fell away.

But if the travellers had been expecting daylight and fresh air, they were disappointed. Within seconds they were engulfed in a grimy sulphurous fog that made breathing painful.

"What's this?" gasped Jack in fear and astonishment. His lungs felt like they were burning.

"It's air poison," explained Phineas between wheezes. "It's what happens when you upset the balance."

"Welcome to Tula!"

Morrigan alone seemed unconcerned at the environmental catastrophe that surrounded them. She appeared able to breathe without undue effort; even Fenrig was looking with astonishment as his sister leapt ahead.

"This way!" she exclaimed, leading them through the destroyed cave wall.

Phineas pulled Iain Dubh to his feet, while Kedge and Ossian helped the others. Jack brought up the rear, and was about to step through the wall, when he felt a tug on his sleeve. Turning round, he was astonished to see Papa Legba.

The old man put his finger to his lips, and showed Jack the ring he was wearing.

A triple-S spiral! Just like Tamlina's.

"It is not safe for you to take the *Mapa* onto this island. You must leave it here with me."

Jack pulled away from the old man, who continued to hold onto his sleeve.

"The creatures here will kill you for the *Mapa*," urged Papa Legba.

No, thought Jack. *It's one of the three treasures; and I've been entrusted to keep it. I can't give it to this . . . dark magycks master.*

"If you doubt me, look at the *Mapa*."

Jack quickly tugged the map free from Tamlina's ring, and held the flag out. As it curled up into a ball, Jack could see that it showed Papa Legba in one circle, and the *Mapa* in the other.

He must be telling the truth!

"Trust me. I'm with Gosol." The old man indicated his ring again.

A peaceful feeling came over Jack. Flicking the sphere back into a flag, he handed it over.

"Keep the ring in your pocket. Now, you must catch the others up." And with that, Papa Legba disappeared.

Jack hurried through the hole in the wall. The outside of the cave was even worse: the fog was thicker, darker, and even more sulphurous; and a biting wind cut through them. Jack took a step and nearly disappeared.

The foul smell seemed to come from the very swamp around them: a squelchy, putrid, nauseating wasteland that almost defied life. Ossian had doubled back to find Jack, and now hauled him out of the sticky foul-smelling gloop he'd stepped into. Jack got to his knees and checked that Trog's knife was still there.

Phew. Need to clean that when I can.

"It's bogland!" shouted Armina, as she sank in up to her knees. "We'll never get far in this!"

With low visibility, the bog seemed to stretch, featureless, in every direction. It was a place that reeked of death, decay, and despair. An icy wind bore down on the hapless travellers.

"Gilmore," begged Iain Dubh, shivering with the cold, "haven't you got anything we can wear to help us here?"

Jack thought back to Gilmore's early promises of charmed clothes that could do all sorts – even make you fly.

"I'm . . . sorry . . ." gasped Gilmore. "I . . . never . . . expected . . . this." Each breath was an effort.

"What can we get to eat here?" demanded Arvin.

"Eat? Can you see any animals living in this desert bog? Save your breath for walking, you dolt!" Kedge spat.

"Kedge is right. Breathe as slowly as you can. And keep moving," shouted Ossian. "In single file! Behind Morrigan!"

"Keep your swords clear of the bog-water!" urged Phineas. "We may need them before long! For Boabans, and the Cu-shee."

As Morrigan led them off into the murky expanse, Jack stumbled forward. He felt he hadn't eaten in a week. His head started to swim.

"Look!" shouted Cal, as a ghostly silhouette appeared in front of them.

It was a building: that much Jack could make out. But how far away it was, and how big, was impossible to tell. Three crows swooped down on the travellers, cawing raucously.

"Fractals' Seer!" shrieked Morrigan exuberantly.

"Is Murkle in there?" demanded Daid.

"Never mind him: have they got food?" demanded Ossian. "I'm starvin'."

"Everything that's needed is in there," replied Morrigan, heading for the gloomy silhouette.

The travellers, exhausted, and hungry beyond imagination, fell into line behind her. Except Enda, who held back, tugging at Phineas' sleeve.

"I don't like this. Where's all the horrible creatures they talked about, if not in there?"

"We can't stay out here," gasped Phineas. "If the air doesn't poison us, we'll die of hunger, or exposure. Nothing can live long out here; and it's nearly nightfall, anyway. They must have some way of keeping the air clean inside."

Enda looked askance at Phineas, but said nothing.

The silhouette grew larger with astonishing quickness, and even in the gloomy twilight Jack could see that it was a peculiar shape.

Like I saw in the Mapa Mundi, *when Grandpa got the Phosphan curse again . . . it's all pointy-shaped.*

As they neared the strange building, the crows left them, and a path became clearer, leading up to a large wooden door. In the occasional ray of the setting sun that permeated the fog, Jack thought he could make out carvings around the huge door. They were the oddest-looking beasts he had ever seen. And all the rocks that made up the towering wall were pointy-shaped. Jack's teeth chattered: he'd never been so cold. Gilmore's super-warm clothing was no protection here.

"Swords and sceptres ready!" cautioned Phineas. "If it's Boaban Shee or Cu-shee, aim for their ankles. If it's witches, use your sceptres!"

"This is for real," whispered Ossian to Jack, who couldn't help thinking that a nice battle was just what he needed to warm up. After he'd had something to eat and drink, of course. But then he looked around at his fellow travellers. Iain Dubh looked fit to drop; Daid wasn't much better . . . In fact, only Enda, Ossian, Kedge and his father looked in any state to fight.

And Morrigan, of course. Taking the lead as she had done for so long, she strode up to the door and struck it with her sceptre. A rumbling echo-ey sound came from within.

Nothing.

Morrigan struck the door again, with even greater force.

Still nothing.

"Shouldn't we just try the handle?" asked Fenrig.

He stepped up, and grasped the huge steel handle, but completely failed to shift it.

"Let me have a go," muttered Kedge.

Taking the handle in both hands, he wrenched it to the right, and the door creaked open.

A waft of fresh air hit them, and the travellers hurried inside.

"That's better!" beamed Armina, as they closed the door behind them. "That stuff outside is terrible."

The air inside *was* breathable. It smelt clean, if anything.

Jack looked around. They were inside a hall, with two burning staves on the wall. In the dim light, Jack could make out carved stone figures above the staves. Strange-looking women, contorted and gruesome.

"Mallisons!" shouted Morrigan. "Vitalise!"

The new arrivals had no time to react. In two seconds the carved figures had dropped from the walls. One of them walked up to Morrigan.

"I knew ye'd come."

20

Island Hospitality

Morrigan seemed to blush. She even curtsied.

"I am ready."

"And how many have ye brought?" It was a squeaky voice.

"A score, Endora; and my brother."

The travellers, except for Morrigan, shrank back into a huddle, facing the old women, whose staring eyes were disturbingly large.

Must be because it's so dark in here.

Jack gripped his sword so tightly he could feel his hand pulsing, but glancing to his side he could see that Ishona and Daid were on the point of fainting. From hunger or fear, it made no difference: the arrivals would offer little resistance.

"There's no need for weapons," said Endora, examining the group. "The laws of island hospitality demand that guests are not armed."

Phineas made to protest, but Iain Dubh held up a warning finger.

"Do as she says. They will not attack us."

"How can he be sure?" whispered Jack to his father.

"I don't know," hissed Phineas. "But throw down your sword noisily – create a disturbance."

Jack chucked his sword noisily onto the ground, at which the others did the same – except Phineas. In the clatter of steel hitting the cold stone floor he secreted his sword in his jacket, as he had done in Nebula.

"We will see that they are kept safe for you," croaked the other woman.

She threw her cloak onto the ground, and scooped up the swords into a bundle. "And don't think that your sceptres are of any use here: Tula does not work that way." Clutching the bundled swords, she hobbled away.

"Wait here," cackled Endora as she set off down the hall. "The Ashray will see you to the dining hall."

Morrigan kept pace with Endora, whispering urgently in her ear, as her fellow travellers shuffled their feet uneasily.

How come Morrigan knows her already? This place is supposed to be full of the worst kind of witch.

"She's right about the sceptres," said Cal. "There's no power here."

"It was always said to be desolate; but it beats me how anyone can live here at all. There wasn't a single tree outside," noted Arvin. "No life of any kind."

"The Kildashie burned the last of the trees."

Jack turned in astonishment to see a ghostly pale, stick-limbed creature standing by the wall. No higher than Jack's waist, the tiny Ashray had a haunted look.

"The Kildashie were here?!" demanded Phineas.

"They left last month. We never had much, but the Kildashie destroyed what little we had." Her voice was high-pitched, almost a squeak.

"And the fog?" asked Iain Dubh. "Is it worse now?"

"Worse than ever. The trees used to clear the swamp gas; or some of it. Now it's choking everything."

"They're up to their old tricks, then," noted Jack. "First the islands, then the area around Edinburgh; now here."

"And what of your mistresses here? Have they sided with the Kildashie?"

The Ashray looked at Phineas. "I'll say no more. I've to take you to the hall."

The wizened creature moved off down the gloomy hall, and the travellers fell into step behind her.

"Stick by me," muttered Phineas as he moved next to Jack. "I wouldn't trust these hags a minute."

Except the sceptres don't work here: your sword and Trog's knife is all we have.

Jack saw Ishona and Armina walking together, whispering feverishly. For all Iain Dubh's reassurance, Jack felt ill at ease. Everything he'd heard about this place was bad. And yet . . .

"Ye all will be hungry?" A young woman in a long flowing green dress greeted them as they neared the end of the hall. Like the old women, her big eyes bulged slightly. "I am Hema. We've food aplenty. Come in."

As the Ashray scuttled away, Hema opened a large wooden door to reveal a great dining room with a fireplace at the side. Flames from the fire and two wall-mounted staves threw some light, but it was still murky. And yet the fire was cheering, and the smell of nearby food made Jack feel faint. He wasn't alone: the travellers, famished and exhausted, fell into the room.

"It's not often we have guests. Make yourselves comfortable; the food won't be long. There's bowls of water there – you can wash." Hema waved a gloved hand. "Help yourselves to wine."

Kedge was first to the fireplace, which bore two large glowing logs. Sparks flew up the chimney and out onto the stone floor in equal measure.

"This is more like it. I'm famished: what d'ye think they'll feed us?" He poured some wine into a goblet.

Leading the rest of the travellers in, Phineas walked over and whispered to Kedge.

"Ach, never mind that," said the Rangie lad. "You might no' need food and a warm, but I do. They've been fine to us." He smiled ingratiatingly at the young woman who had shown them in.

Hema stood with her back to the closed door, and smiled back.

Within minutes a dozen young women had brought in trays of food, piled high with delicacies. Like Hema, they could have been called beautiful, but for their unnervingly large eyes.

Hurriedly washing their hands at a side table, the weary travellers fell on the food; whatever caution any had had about their surroundings, or the nature of their welcome, had been overcome. The atmosphere quickly relaxed.

"I hoped we could count on island hospitality," laughed Iain Dubh, draining another goblet of wine. "But to have so much food in the winter, it must be a feast day. It's not the solstice yet, is it?"

"Not yet," laughed Hema, as she fed him some fruit.

"Tonight we begin the midwinter celebrations. The solstice is in two days."

"Two days!" Ishona spluttered. "That means we were on the bridge for . . ."

"A long time," interrupted Morrigan, rejoining the group. "I told you time was different there. But I got you here, didn't I?"

"So, tell us, Morrigan: where is Murkle?" asked Phineas pointedly.

"He's been very helpful. You'll see him soon."

The mention of Murkle's name made Iain Dubh sit up. He frowned, as if trying to remember why he'd come here. Bleary-eyed, he looked around. His HebShian comrades, from being famished and exhausted, looked relaxed, and completely distracted by the attentions of the young women. Only Armina and Ishona seemed unaffected by the nature of the welcome. They sat together, watching the proceedings warily. Iain Dubh took another deep slurp of wine, and sat back.

The young women came and went so often that it was hard to say how many there were. Aged about twenty-five, each sported elbow-length gloves, and wore a flowing gown that trailed to the floor.

The one exception was a girl of about twelve, who stood outside the kitchen, half-hidden in the shadows. When instructed, she would place more food or drink on the tables and retrieve empty plates, but she never spoke, retreating instead to her shadowy recess.

Jack looked at the girl idly. Replete with food and drink, he felt fuzzily tired. There was something familiar about her, but he couldn't figure out what. Dark-haired, she seemed to be brooding, sullen; never quite looking up.

Jack wasn't sure whether to feel worried or grateful: after his limited diet of the last few weeks, and the icy smothering fog outside, he was glad to have been fed, and to feel warm; but something felt wrong.

"Dad, nobody's even asked who we are, or why we're here."

"I think they know already: they knew Morrigan, and she's been off somewhere. We must be careful; this is too good to be true."

"And what about the Cu-Shee – the Black Dogs? We haven't seen anything like that."

"Like I said, keep your guard up."

"Me and the Twa Tams are going to get changed out of these manky clothes," laughed Kedge, as he and two of the HebShian men were led away. "Then they're going to show us around."

"No! Stay here!" cautioned Phineas, but his warning had little effect. The three young men left, laughing with their female companions.

Jack saw that Ossian was talking animatedly with another young woman, and that Morrigan was looking on. Her eyes were narrowed, and she mouthed silently.

I don't fancy being in Ossian's shoes when she gets hold of him.

Despite Jack's unease, the party continued happily. What food was not eaten was now strewn carelessly around the tables. The place bore the hallmarks of having hosted a great party.

Jack felt his eyes closing, and he fought to keep himself awake.

"We'll show ye to yer quarters," announced Hema. Clapping her hands, she ushered her companions forward, and each led several of the guests away.

"Where are we going?" asked Jack.

"Ye can wash; then go to yer room," smiled Hema. "Sanguina will show ye and yer cousin. I'll take some o' the others."

How did she know Ossian's my cousin? thought Jack. Then he reflected, *It must've been Morrigan.*

"I'll come too," said Phineas emphatically. "Come on, Enda."

"The washroom's in here," indicated Sanguina, opening a door. "There's nightwear in the box."

The candle-lit washroom was gloomy, but even in the dim light Jack could see it was gigantic. He noted a large chest by the side wall, beside which was a small heap of dirty clothes. There was no sign of Kedge or the others.

The room had no windows, but it did have a row of four cubicles by the far wall, each with a large bath; towels hung on the partition walls. The four guests edged cautiously into the enormous room, and chose clean nightwear from the large chest.

"It'll take a while to wash us four at a time!" shouted Ossian happily, taking the first cubicle. He seemed at ease.

"Hema was taking Daid and some of the others to another room," replied Phineas.

Grateful to get his filthy clothes off (*how long have I had these on?*), Jack entered the next cubicle and slipped quietly into the bath. The water was warm, but it smelt kind of funny. Sort of . . . eggy.

"How'd they get hot water if the rest of the place is so cold?" he shouted through to Ossian.

"It must be geothermal – you know, from hot springs. That's why it smells funny."

Jack lay and luxuriated in the warm water for a while.

Phineas' voice came floating over the cubicle wall.

"Jack! Keep your things safe!"

Jack looked over at Trog's knife on the chair, beside his Sintura belt. *I'm not leaving them with my clothes.*

"And you've got a spare set of clothes in your satchel, haven't you?"

"Yes, Dad."

"Don't use the nightwear, then."

When they were all cleaned and dressed (*knife and Sintura belt strapped on*), they congregated outside the cubicles.

"Where's Kedge?" demanded Ossian.

"His clothes are there; and the Twa Tams'," replied Phineas. "They must have gone off to explore the place. We'll stay together, though. I don't want everyone getting separated."

Phineas put his cloak back on, and tucked his dirty clothes under his arm as Hema ushered the next batch of four in.

"Everything all right?" Iain Dubh swayed slightly as he spoke, and gave a small hiccup.

"Sure; but keep a watch. Remember why we're here," cautioned Phineas quietly, so that Hema couldn't hear. "And don't leave your clothes here."

As Sanguina led them along a cold, dark corridor to a large bedroom, Jack thought he could see the bulge of his father's sword under his cloak.

"So many visitors has us struggling for beds," admitted Sanguina, as she opened a door. "Some of ye'll share here; there's another room along the corridor. And the ladies are next door."

It was like a dormitory, with mattresses along each side wall. Logs crackled in the fireplace, throwing some warmth, but precious little light, around the room.

"I don't care. I just want to get some shut-eye," stated Ossian.

"I'll just check with Armina," said Phineas, leaving the room.

He came back a few minutes later, apparently happy.

"Armina and Ishona have beds, and they seem all right. I suggest we get some rest. But remember, the solstice is in two days. We must leave soon if we are to get to Novehowe."

"How far is it?" asked Jack.

"Impossible to say: no one knows where Tula is exactly."

"Will Morrigan know how to get away from here?" Jack's guts were telling him something was wrong.

"She got us here, didn't she?" said Ossian smugly.

"But she's not with Armina and Ishona," pointed out Phineas, placing his sword under his mattress, just out of sight. "She knows too much of this place. And she still hasn't told us where Murkle is."

"You said we needed someone who understood how they think here," pointed out Ossian.

"Yes, but to keep us right; not to help them. We have to find the Raglan, and the Gusog feather. We'll do some exploring tonight, when everyone's asleep."

"Everything's dark here," noted Jack. "There's not been a single room that was properly lit." He thought fondly of how the crystals sprayed the light around the Shian square in Edinburgh.

"They don't seem to like the light, right enough," mused Phineas. "I guess it's to do with being this far north – they're not used to it in the winter."

When Iain Dubh and the others came in twenty minutes later, Jack had just drifted off.

"There's several bathrooms," chortled Gilmore, throwing his clothes and belongings next to a mattress. "I've never felt so clean in my life."

"Cal, will you take first watch?" asked Phineas, as the others copied Gilmore's example.

"There's no need for watches," said Hema, entering silently. "Oh, excuse me gentlemen, I should have knocked."

She laughed, a raucous cackle that was at odds with her beauty.

"Ye may have noticed that some of yer companions are not here." A smile flickered over her lips. "They're rather busy just now. But never worry, we've someone else to keep ye company this night! Malicia!"

She clapped her hands, and in the gloom Jack glimpsed a wall-mounted stone figure dropping to the ground, just like when they had first arrived.

"Malicia, I'm sure ye will take care that these guests are comfortable?" Hema moved along the line of mattresses until she came to Phineas.

"Tut tut," she said mockingly, as she stooped down and retrieved Phineas' sword. "The laws of hospitality: don't you mainland savages know of these?"

She threw the sword over to the mallison, then looked down at Jack.

"I know what ye have, Shian boy. But I'll get it later – there's no fun in taking everything straight away. Now I trust that ye will all get some sleep. Don't let the bedbugs bite!"

Slowly, she took off her right glove, revealing long, sharp fingernails. Stained red. She cradled her right forefinger under Jack's chin, smiling cruelly down at him.

"Ye've brought us fresh blood," croaked Malicia.

With a sickening feeling, Jack understood.

They're all Boaban Shee!

21
The Cu-shee

In a flash Hema had drawn her wand from her cloak, and pointed it at the wall.

"*Incarceris!*"

The walls telescoped away. Hema and the mallison floated back towards the door, and the mattresses disappeared. Jack felt himself topple over as the room heaved. It was like being at sea again – only even colder.

When he sat up, Jack realised that the large bedroom, fireplace and all, had gone: this was a cell. The mallison sat on a chair just outside a barred gate. Wisps of fog came in through the single pane-less barred window on the side wall. Except for a candle at Malicia's foot, the room was in darkness.

The curses and oaths died down after a couple of minutes, as the prisoners righted themselves.

"Are you all right, Jack?"

"What happened?" Jack crawled towards the sound of his

father's voice. The floor was freezing, and his hands half-stuck to the icy surface.

"They've tricked us. So much for hospitality. And we haven't a sword between us."

"What're we going to do?"

"We'll have to get out of here, and get the swords," hissed Phineas. "Then we'll have a chance."

"How're we going to get past the mallison?"

"There's only one of her, so that's something. But that gate's the only way out."

Finbogie now edged towards them.

"I should've seen that coming. But so long on the bridge took more out of me than I realised."

"We were all off guard," reassured Phineas. "But we have to work out how to escape."

"This place is even worse than Nebula; none of the charms will work here," said Finbogie despondently. "Our sceptres are useless."

"I'm sorry," mumbled Iain Dubh. "The bridge near finished me; the temptation of the food and the wine was too much."

"We'll get there." Enda tried to sound reassuring. "But first we must get out of here."

"Hasn't anyone got a hex that will fix that mallison?"

"The only one is the ungula hex," replied Phineas. "And for that we need swords. Nothing else works here. Iain, you and your men are tired – get some rest. Enda and I will work out what to do."

"And me, Dad. I've still got Trog's knife."

"We might be able to use that to pick the lock, if the mallison ever goes to sleep."

"Couldn't we reach through the bars and cut her feet off?"

"She's out of reach; and any noise from her would bring the others."

A scream came from outside the room.

"What . . . what was that?" Daid's voice trembled.

"It sounded like Kedge," whispered Ossian. "I shouldn't have let him go."

The mallison cackled as another scream floated through the walls.

"That's one of the Tams, isn't it?" whispered Jack. "What're they doing to them?"

"Let's just concentrate on getting out of here, shall we?"

A gloomy silence descended. Jack was so sleepy, he found himself nodding off, despite the bitter cold. He had no idea how long he had been asleep when he came to with a start.

Jack looked round. Iain Dubh and the other Nebula men were asleep; so were the others from the Shian square. Even Enda was snoring gently.

"Dad," Jack tugged his father's arm. "The bars on the gate aren't that close together. I might be able to get through."

"You can't go on your own; we'll have to open the gate. And we've still to get past that mallison."

A figure stirred in the gloom.

"Jack," whispered Finbogie. "Have you got your jomo bag?"

A shaft of light in the darkness. Jack lifted his shirt to reveal the Sintura belt.

"Careful! Make sure she can't see," hissed Finbogie as Malicia stood up and peered through the bars of the gate.

The noise of voices seemed to raise the others. Enda and

Ossian, quickly sensing what was needed, formed a wall, blocking the mallison's line of sight.

"I've got it!" croaked Jack, wanting to shout.

"And has it got the three dirts?"

"Aye: from Dunvik, and Ilanbeg, and Antrim."

"You remember what to do?"

"Just fling them at her feet. She'll get confused. I've got everything else in here too!"

"The jomo should stun her," said Phineas doubtfully, "but it doesn't open the gate."

"I'm sure I can get through the bars; then maybe I can find a key," said Jack hopefully.

"Hema took the keys. I can't let you go on your own."

"Dad, we haven't any choice," urged Jack. "I'll go and find the swords, and bring them back."

"How are you going to find them?"

"I'll find a way. We can't just wait here and do nothing."

"Phin, he's right. If someone doesn't get out, we've no chance at all," said Enda. "Come away now; I'll get the mallison to the gate. Ready, Jack?"

Jack nodded, and Enda strode the few paces to the gate.

"I'm Irish; I demand to see the consul."

The mallison got up, and hobbled to the gate. Peering up at Enda, she scowled, and spat.

"Hah!"

Jack sprang forward, and threw the three mixed dirts at the mallison's feet.

There was a muffled *whump*, and a puff of smoke. When it cleared, the mallison stood by the gate.

"It hasn't worked," hissed Ossian.

Then the mallison fell. Dead to the world, she lay on her back, eyes closed, a bemused smile on her face.

"Quick!"

Jack knelt down, and squirmed into the gate. It was a tight fit. Gasping, he wriggled first one way, then the other.

Wish I hadn't eaten so much tonight . . .

Agonisingly slowly, Jack inched his way forward. The mallison sighed, and smacked her lips.

Holding his breath, Jack finally wriggled through the bars of the gate, collapsing on the other side. His shoulder hurt like anything, but he forgot this when he saw the mallison's eyes start to open. Grabbing his satchel with the haemostat bandages, he tiptoed past her, and found himself in a long dark corridor. He heard the mallison rise to her feet, and bellow at the prisoners.

"Get back to yer beds, scum. Enjoy yer last sleep!"

Jack felt the hairs on the back of his neck bristle. He hurried away down the corridor, but it was so dark, he wasn't sure where he was going.

Footsteps ahead! And voices!

Jack froze. In the gloom he could just make out the outline of a door. Hurriedly turning the handle, he entered.

A single candle flickered in the gloom. Jack heard a gasp of surprise, and reached down for Trog's knife.

"Shh!"

It was a high-pitched squeak of a voice . . .

I've heard that before.

A second candle was lit, and the room brightened. Jack could make out the Ashray, sitting on the side of a small wooden bed-frame. There was no mattress. The tiny creature looked famished.

"Will you take us away?" she asked, her voice trembling.

"I need to get our swords: d'you know where they are?"

"I'll show you if you promise to get us out."

"We've all got to get out of here; but I'll need your help to free the others. And we've to find our friends – the ones who left the meal early."

"Ahh . . ."

"What d'you mean?" demanded Jack, his voice rising. "What's happened to them?"

"Shh! Be quiet! Hema will hear you."

"Look," said Jack firmly, "I've got to find the swords and free the others. Can I trust you?" He paused. "Wait a minute. You said 'Take us away'. Who else is there?"

The Ashray put her finger to her lips, blew out one of the candles, and picked up the other.

"Come with me."

She led Jack through a connecting door. Putting the candle down on a bedside table, she shook a slumbering figure.

"Come on; we're going."

The figure stirred, then sat up. In the light of the flickering candle, Jack could see it was the girl who'd served them at supper.

"We've to show this boy to the storeroom; then we're going." The Ashray shook the girl's shoulder. "It's nearly dawn."

Rubbing her eyes and yawning, the girl got up, and threw a shawl over her shoulders.

"There's something else we need as well," said Jack. "Some grey sandstone, chipped off a bigger block. And a feather, with a golden tip."

"The Gusog?" squeaked the Ashray. "It's in Hema's room; but she'll be in the . . ." She paused, and looked at Jack. "She's busy. Let's go."

"What about the stone? We think Malevola brought it here."

"No. No stone."

The girl tugged the Ashray's arm, and indicated Jack with a nod of her head.

"What is your name?" asked the Ashray.

"Jack. Jack Shian. I'm from Edinburgh . . . well, Rangie."

A half-smile passed over the girl's face, and she beckoned them forward.

The three went back into the Ashray's room, then tiptoed out into the silent corridor.

"This way."

The Ashray turned right, then paused as she came to a corner.

"Have you got a sceptre?"

Jack shook his head. "Ours don't work here. And anyway, I'm not fourteen yet."

Tutting, the Ashray led them round the corner in the corridor, and up to a large wooden door.

"This is Hema's room. Let's hope the beastie isn't here."

She turned the handle cautiously. The door creaked as she peered in.

"It's all right; there's no one here." The Ashray led them in, leaving the door slightly ajar. Her candle fluttered as she walked up to a large glass-fronted cabinet.

"There's your feather."

Resting on a purple cushion was a single tattered white feather. There was no obvious colouring on it.

"Is that really the Gusog feather?" asked Jack incredulously. "I thought it had a golden tip."

There was a low growl from behind them. Jack spun round, and saw the silhouette of a huge dog . . . Only it was bigger than any dog he'd ever seen. Jet black, it slinked towards the three of them, its claws clicking on the stone floor.

The Ashray squeaked in alarm, and pulled the young girl aside. The dog advanced slowly on Jack, its yellow eyes fixing him with a cold stare.

Jack grabbed Trog's knife, and desperately tried to think . . .

Kynos hex? No chance, not on a beast this size . . . What was that Cu-shee hex Enda taught me on the boat?

He brandished the steel knife, and was about to swipe at the beast's paws when it sprang forward and struck Jack's right hand. Blood welled as the knife spun out of reach. The dog stood for a moment, staring at Jack. It growled again, a mesmerising, terrifying sound.

Jack backed up against the cabinet, his eyes darting frantically from side to side. He tried to ignore the saliva dripping from the great beast's jaws.

The dog advanced a pace, and then there was a loud yelp.

Jack looked to his left. The young girl stood, Trog's knife in her hand. Blood gushed from the dog's right haunch, and the beast turned round to face this new enemy.

The girl and the Ashray backed away, but the beast was on them instantly, growling and snapping. The Ashray squeaked in alarm, and the girl cowered as the beast stood over them. Its eyes glinted in the darkness.

It leapt, slashing at the girl's left arm with its razor-like claws.

A silent scream, as the claw sliced through flesh.

Jack reached quickly into his Sintura belt, grabbed the devil's shoestring, and slipped it onto his wrist.

"*Abcanidæ!*"

The beast sprawled, its front legs caving in.

"Quick! Throw me the knife!"

The girl slid the knife along the floor, and Jack grasped it quickly. In a flash he swept the blade horizontally, and cried out, "*Terra nasus!*"

Thank you Enda, thank you thank you thank you for teaching me that.

The dog's back paws flew to the side wall, and the beast slumped, yelping in pain. Turning round, it tried to jump at Jack, whose eyes grew as large as saucers. As the dog's head sailed towards him he half-closed his eyes and held the knife in front of his face.

There was a squelchy thudding bark as the blade entered through the lower jaw and emerged just between the beast's eyes. If such a creature can be said to look surprised, then the look on this beast's face was pure astonishment. A strangulated gurgling came from the back of its throat, as it jerked backwards and fell sideways, kicking madly with its back stumps. Blood spread quickly over the cold floor. The gurgling slowly subsided, the legs stopped thrashing, and the beast lay still.

Then, raising its head one last time, it howled.

A death-embracing, sickening howl that pierced Jack's brain.

"They'll know we're here now." The Ashray skipped over the corpse and opened the cabinet. Grabbing the feather (nearly as tall as she was), she made for the door, pausing only to grab a bunch of keys from a hook behind the door. "Come on."

"Just a minute." Jack wiped Trog's knife and reattached it to his calf, then reached into his satchel and withdrew two bandages. Beckoning the young girl, he wrapped one deftly around her bleeding arm, then the other around his right fist.

Finally, something useful from my lessons!

The girl looked at him and smiled.

"Hurry!" The Ashray's squeaky voice was urgent. Running further along the corridor, she opened the next door along, and indicated to Jack a stack of swords, loosely covered by a cloak.

"How many can ye carry?"

Jack grabbed two swords in each hand, but quickly realised that if he was to fight he could take no more. He looked helplessly at the Ashray for a moment. Intercepting his look, the girl stepped forward, and also grabbed four swords.

"We'll let the others out, then they can come back for the rest," smiled Jack. "Let's go."

The three hurried back along the corridor. It was hard running and carrying four swords, and Jack dropped one of them as they rounded the corner. As it clattered on the bare floor, Jack imagined the sound carrying everywhere.

He scooped the sword up again, and they made for the cell; but just as they neared it Malicia stepped into the corridor.

"So, ye got out, ye wee maggot. Sanguina!"

22

Cutting Off Witches' Feet

"Quick, Jack! The keys!"

Phineas' urgent shout came as Malicia, teeth bared, leapt up, her cloak floating as she soared forward.

Jack dropped three of the swords, and fell to the floor. As the mallison floated close, he swung the fourth sword at where he thought her feet should be.

"*Ungula!*"

There was a scream of rage and pain as the mallison's left foot flew off. Jack looked with horror at the foot on the floor . . .

It's not a foot! It's a hoof!

Malicia crumpled to the floor. Seeing this, the young girl grabbed the keys from the Ashray, and flung them towards Phineas' waiting hands. The barred door flew open as Sanguina turned into the corridor, her eyes ablaze. Blood dripped from her mouth.

"Ye let them escape!" she roared at the hapless Malicia, who spun around on the floor, cursing and weeping in equal measure.

"My foot! The little snake has taken my foot!"

"Get her other one!" shouted Finbogie, as the prisoners burst out of the cell and grabbed the swords.

Jack nimbly hopped over Malicia's trailing leg, and hacked at her right ankle.

"*Ungula!*"

As hoof parted company with ankle, Malicia gave a loud cry, and rolled over. Blood seeped from both stumps. Sanguina halted just yards away, and surveyed the scene. Phineas, Ossian, Enda and several others brandished swords, and began to advance on her. She withdrew her wand, but Phineas skipped forward and sliced it out of her hand before she could use it. With a cry of fury she flew back the way she had come, shouting for help.

"Where's she gone?" demanded Phineas.

"To the exanguine room," replied the Ashray. "They're busy with your friends."

"Let's get the others out, and then we can tackle them," shouted Ossian.

"Where are the other swords?" pleaded Enda. "We'll each need one."

"This way," said the Ashray. "I'll show you."

She handed the Gusog feather to Jack, and led Enda and Ossian back along the corridor.

While Phineas went to release the other prisoners, Jack approached Iain Dubh and presented him with the feather.

"Um, it's not gold; but the Ashray says this is it."

Iain Dubh cradled the feather, stroking it gently. His eyes sparkled.

"First the flag, then this. We're blessed." He tucked the feather in his waistband.

"We've yet to get out of here," noted Cal solemnly.

As Phineas returned with the other prisoners, Enda and Ossian arrived with the swords. Within a minute all the prisoners were assembled, swords in hand.

"Where's Morrigan?" demanded Fenrig.

"She wasn't in with us," replied Ishona softly, eyeing the Gusog feather. "She's with them."

"That's a lie!"

"There's one way to find out," replied Jack. "Where's this exanguine room?"

"We'll go through the big hall," said the Ashray. "That's the quickest way."

"Thank you for helping us," replied Phineas. "And you, too." He stopped, and looked at the young girl, who had remained silent throughout. A puzzled look came over his brow, as the young girl half-smiled up at him.

"The haemostat bandage worked really well," Jack informed Gilmore proudly.

"Well then, at least something works in this godforsaken place," said the tailor.

"Come on," urged Enda. "We haven't time to waste!" He set off along the corridor.

"We're taking them with us." Jack indicated the Ashray and the girl as he caught up with Enda. "They helped us escape, and I promised. The girl doesn't speak," he added.

"We have to get ourselves out too," said Enda grimly. "I don't like the sound of the exanguine room."

The narrow corridors, lit only by occasional wall-mounted

staves, seemed to double back on themselves. In the gloom the escaped prisoners found they were bumping into each other. They eventually emerged through a doorway into the dining hall. The fire had gone out, but the two wall staves still burned. Even in the dim light the remains of the banquet were still evident.

"One more scoop for good luck," grinned Ossian as he approached a goblet.

"I wouldn't," said the Ashray quietly.

Ossian took no notice, and tipped the contents down his throat. The liquid quickly found its way out again, in a great frothing fountain as Ossian struggled to get it clear.

"It's vinegar!" he exclaimed.

"Things don't last long here." The Ashray indicated the food.

Jack went over and prodded the remains of a pie. It crumbled like ash; in fact, it looked like ash.

"This place is cursed," he muttered.

"But you must admit, we throw one helluva party!"

Morrigan stood in the doorway, framed by a light behind her. She wore a long robe similar to Hema's, and sported the same type of elbow-length glove.

The prisoners readied their swords – except Fenrig. The young Brashat seemed torn.

"Mor, tell them it's all right," he pleaded. "Tell them you'll help us get out of here."

Morrigan eyed her brother.

"We're staying here, Fen. Until dad gets away from that hellhole these people put him in."

She withdrew a wand from her robe.

"Morrigan," implored Ossian, lowering his sword, and advancing. "It's me. You can't do this."

Morrigan's wand levelled in an instant, and the hex caught Ossian full in the chest, flinging him backwards. He lay still.

Sanguina appeared at Morrigan's shoulder.

"I hope you're being hospitable to our guests," she croaked in a loud stage whisper. "Or shall we just show them what we do to vermin?"

Holding her wand in her right hand, she entered the hall, dragging what looked like a grey sack behind her. In the gloom the prisoners backed away, swords at the ready.

"It's all right: the good news is they don't want to kill us," muttered Enda.

"What's the bad news?" hissed Jack.

"Ye'll find that out if ye let them win."

Contemptuously, Sanguina flung the sack at the retreating prisoners, and it slithered over the icy floor. Only it wasn't a sack. In the dim light, Jack made out a sunken face.

"It's Murkle!" shrieked Armina. "They've bled him!" She bent down and examined the body. When she looked up, her eyes had narrowed.

"Witch bitch!" She leapt at Sanguina, and swiped at her legs with her sword.

The Boaban Shee soared and swerved, avoiding the steel blade, and firing off hexes as fast as she could. In seconds, the hall was full of Boaban Shee, fighting in pairs as the prisoners slashed at flailing legs with swords.

"Take cover!" Jack shoved the Ashray and the girl to the side of the hall.

"You too, Jack!" shouted Phineas. "You and Fenrig can use the bandages!"

But Jack ignored his father's command, and he jumped into

the fray. Seeing Sanguina and another Boaban advance on Iain Dubh, Jack skipped behind them and sliced with his sword.

"*Ungula!*"

Sanguina's right hoof flew with such force that it hit the side wall. She spun round, cursing and shrieking, and levelled her wand at Jack.

As she opened her mouth to utter a hex, a blade appeared through her chest. Fergus stood behind her, a look of satisfaction on his face as he gripped his sword. Sanguina stopped, her eyes wide open with surprise. Then she grabbed the sticking-out blade, and pulled it further forward. Fergus, taken by surprise, was dragged into her back, his hand seemingly stuck to the sword handle.

"It has to be her feet!" shouted Iain Dubh.

The warning came too late. Sanguina turned her head and spat at Fergus.

"You're going to get a Tula facial!"

She reached over her shoulder with her wand, and cried out, "*Cædo-vis!*"

The hex hit Fergus full in the face, and he fell back, a hideous crater where his eyes and nose should have been. Sanguina, never once taking her eyes off Jack, pushed the blade back through her body, and it toppled onto the floor behind her, clattering as it fell.

"I'll pay you for that!" she spat, and thrust her wand forward again.

Jack dodged the first hex, but he could see that this strategy would not last long. And when the next hex hit him on the right hand, his sword flew.

He looked around frantically. The room was filled with

contests: Boabans firing hexes, and prisoners slicing and parrying with swords; but no one was free to help Jack. He backed away as Sanguina hopped forward, cackling evilly, clearly enjoying the prospect of impending execution.

There was a blur behind Sanguina as a small figure rolled over the icy floor. Jack just had time to see the young girl grasp his sword.

"*Ungula!*"

Sanguina's body shot into the air as leg and hoof parted company. Then, as her body crumpled to the floor, a spine-tingling moan filled the room.

Jack looked in astonishment at the girl.

She spoke!

"You spoke." Even as he said the words, they sounded strange.

The girl was wasting no time. She sprang into the fray, hacking, parrying hexes, slashing. Displaying skills that Jack had taken weeks to master back on Ilanbeg.

The Boabans were vicious, even courageous; but they were outnumbered. And while several hexes had found their mark, leaving prisoners apparently lifeless on the frozen floor, they could not defeat more than a dozen wielding swords. Boaban bodies too began to litter the floor, their oozing stumps protruding from long green cloaks. The floor was so cold that the sticky red fluid had little chance to spread: it chilled instantly, forming tacky patches.

Swordless, Jack tried to avoid the hexes that flew around. Then, stepping in one of the blood patches, he slid unceremoniously forward. As he landed, he saw Ossian's blue-cold face next to his own.

That's my big cousin!

Jack's blue eye burned fiercely. He grabbed Trog's knife from his calf, and hacked madly at a Boaban who was trying to hex Armina. Both hoofs came off, spraying Jack's face with blood. Wiping his face, he saw that there were just two Boabans left – and Morrigan.

"Give up!" roared Phineas. "And you may live. You can never hope to take all of us!"

"Ye haven't seen yer other friends," sneered Hema. Icily calm, she backed away, tugging at Morrigan's sleeve. "Show them, daughter."

Daughter?!

Morrigan clicked her fingers, and three bodies floated through the doorway into the hall; accompanied by Malicia.

"Ye think ye can really defeat us?" sneered Hema.

Jack stared with disbelief.

But I took Malicia's feet . . . hoofs . . . off. She's supposed to be dead.

"Yer puny Shian hexes don't last here," scoffed Malicia, hobbling into the room. "Oh, my feet may tak' a while to mend; but just look at what awaits ye!"

The three floating bodies fell to the floor.

Armina was first to them.

"It's Kedge! They've bled him too!"

Kedge gave a moan; and with good reason. Slash marks showed down his face, his neck . . . in fact, his entire deathly pale body.

"His friends didn't last long," commented Morrigan coldly, looking at the Twa Tams' bodies. "Too long on the bridge, I expect. Malnourished Nebula insects."

"You made sure we were starved!" shouted Jack. "And they were bad enough to start with!"

Slowly, the slain Boabans were starting to rise. Hobbling painfully, they joined Hema and Morrigan.

There was a stand-off for a moment while each side regrouped. Armina placed crystals on wounded prisoners' foreheads, and Gilmore busied himself using haemostat bandages on the prisoners' open wounds.

"As ye see, ye can niver kill us!" gloated Hema triumphantly. She put her arm around Morrigan's shoulder.

Fenrig broke ranks. Having cowered by the wall while there was fighting, he now strode furiously up to his sister, and slapped her.

Startled, Morrigan thrust her wand at Fenrig's face, and was about to utter her hex.

"She called you 'daughter'!"

The wand hovered. "Fen," she said softly, "did you never wonder?"

"Mum's dead!"

"Yours; not mine." Morrigan looked up at Hema, who smiled back lovingly. If a cold-hearted, callous, blood-sucking murderess can be called loving. "And you can see that *we* are all very alive!"

"Not all!" shouted Armina triumphantly. She pointed to one Boaban Shee who remained on the floor.

That's the one I got with Trog's knife . . .

Jack looked down at the blade he still had in his hand. What was it Marco had told him? Trog believed his knife knew what to do?

"Shian hexes may not work for long," he said slowly, "but I bet you don't like Norse steel."

For the very first time, a look of concern spread over Hema's face.

"There's been no Norse here for centuries," she said, trying to sound confident.

"Well, now you've seen their steel again."

In a flash, Jack had dived towards Malicia's legs, and he hacked at her stumps with the knife.

Taken by surprise, the mallison couldn't even scream as her stumps were reduced further. She rolled over, lifeless.

Jack scurried back to his father, and got up cautiously, holding Trog's bloodstained knife in front of him.

"We'll take you one by one if we have to. Or you can show us the way off this island."

"Ye think one knife can take all of us?" scoffed Hema, firing a rapid hex that floored Phineas. "Ye've nine to kill, brat."

"He's the one who killed Malevola," smirked Morrigan.

"Then I shall leave him 'til last."

Jack gulped. As the hoof-less Boabans began to advance, he sensed the Nebula men wilting at the thought that their swords could not finish them off. Even Enda seemed at a loss for words.

"Ye've been poor guests," mocked Hema, growing in confidence. "Eating and drinking yer fill. But we'll live off ye for a while."

"I'm keeping the big country boy." Morrigan eyed Ossian's recumbent body with satisfaction.

The prisoners began to back away.

"You're not keeping any of us," shouted Jack, as he tried to keep the panic inside him down. "We're leaving."

. . . *If we can. But how do we to get off Tula?*

"Enda?" he said hopefully, looking at the big Irishman; but Enda's shaking head told its own story.

"The Nautilus charm won't work here, Jack. This place is cursed."

Jack heard Ishona sobbing quietly.

"Without me to show you the way, you'd never last an hour out there," Morrigan mocked them, glancing at the window. "Even in the daylight."

Jack risked a look through the great window, and could make out the first glimpses of the dawn.

"Morrigan is right," crowed Hema. "The Kildashie and their Thanatos friends burned the last of our trees, before they scurried away with the Raglan stone; now no creature can survive on Tula outside these walls. Unless of course ye know the path to the Rainbow Bridge?"

The path . . . My path . . .

Jack felt instinctively for the *Mapa Mundi* around his neck – nothing. He saw Hema look at him sharply. *She must think I've got it – Morrigan will have told her.* He gulped hard.

There's no Mapa Mundi *. . . so who can show us our true path?*

Marco and Luka had talked of the power of the map; and the justice of Gosol. But they weren't here. Papa Legba? No sign of him . . .

Jack looked down. His father lay, motionless.

Oh no: not again.

It came to Jack in a flash.

Who had tried to steer them away from the Blue Men of the Minch? Who had followed them all the way from Ilanbeg to Lyosach?

"Our brother will help to guide you . . ." "Our brother John will be watching you, from a distance . . ."

The eagle! *He has the power of Gosol . . . He came when the Urisk was beating Caskill . . .*

Jack concentrated hard. Despite the cold, sweat broke out on his forehead.

We really – really *– need some help here.*

With a crash, the far wall imploded. Light flooded the room as the great bird flew in.

23

The Swamp

Jack shielded his eyes from the sudden brightness – but the shock to his system was nothing compared to the distress of the Boabans. Screaming and covering their eyes from the unaccustomed light, they made for the dark corridor behind them.

"It's *lumos!*" screeched Hema.

Jack risked a peek to see where his father was, but it was the young girl and Ashray who came into sight.

"This way!" squeaked the Ashray.

She and the girl stood by the shattered masonry, and indicated for the prisoners to join them.

The eagle, which had perched on the rubble, now flew into the dining room and dropped a tatty leather volume in front of Jack. Then it wheeled round with a raucous squawk, grabbed the inert bodies of Phineas, Ossian and Kedge, and made for the hole in the wall.

Jack picked the leather book up, and saw the faint lettering on the cover.

Gosol.

He felt a pulsing in his pocket . . .

Tamlina's ring!

Quickly he took it out. His jaw dropped as he saw the three spiral arms becoming bold once more.

"The ring's charging – I can feel it!" He slipped it on his finger.

"Iain! Gilmore!" called Enda. "Try your sceptres!"

"It works!" cried Iain Dubh exuberantly, pulling his sceptre out. Levelling it, he let fly with a volley of hexes that had the Boabans, still blinded by the light, cowering further back into doorways and recesses.

"Everyone! Make for the hole!" ordered Enda, as he joined Iain in firing holding hexes at the Boabans.

"Don't just stun them!" shouted Cal. "If they're spared, they'll come after us!"

"Fenrig!" shouted Morrigan. "Don't let them kill us!"

Fenrig looked over at his half-sister. Unlike the Boabans she had not been overcome by the sudden brightness, and now she knelt and implored her brother.

Fenrig was torn. His eyes fixed on his sister as he edged back to the hole in the wall.

"Mor," he began.

"Fenrig, get out," urged Jack, clasping the leather volume to his chest, and running for the hole.

The eagle, still clutching the three bodies, now flew off a short distance, and perched on a mound twenty yards away. The light in the dining hall had faded, and Jack found himself stumbling in the near-darkness. Enda, Finbogie and Cal had shouldered Murkle and the Twa Tams, and with the other prisoners they were now climbing over the rubble to get out. They emerged into a freezing sulphurous quagmire; once they were out, the swamp gas started to burn their eyes.

"We have to get off this island!" choked Armina. "Who can show us the way?" She gave a yelp as she stepped into an icy pool.

"Make for the eagle!" shouted Ishona.

As Jack neared the hole in the wall, he could see Fenrig sitting there, looking back at Morrigan. Alone, she looked around in vain: those of her comrades who hadn't been stunned had all fled into the darker recesses of Fractals' Seer. Morrigan withdrew her wand, and attempted to level it at the escaping prisoners; but Iain Dubh had seen her, and his hex caught her arm. Dropping the wand, she cursed loudly.

"Cal's right: we have to destroy this place!" shouted Iain Dubh.

"Fenrig!" urged Jack.

The young Brashat, sitting on broken masonry, seemed frozen to the spot.

"They were going to kill us all, Fenrig!"

"No. Mor wouldn't kill me."

"Fenrig, she's half Boaban. They were going to bleed all of us: it's how they live."

Fenrig was unable to move, even as his sister got to her feet and edged forward, her eyes narrowed. Jack grabbed Fenrig's shoulder, and pulled him roughly over the rubble.

"Get away!" shouted Enda. "We're taking this place down!"

The prisoners struggled in the murky wasteland to join the eagle, Jack half-dragging Fenrig along with him. When they reached the eagle, it hopped forward and grabbed the leather volume from Jack's grasp.

"John?" asked Jack.

The eagle squawked.

"The air's clear here!" exclaimed Ishona.

"Only around the eagle," said Jack. "He's protecting us."

He turned to look at the castle. In the misty gloom he could make out shapes moving in the broken wall.

"Enda! They're escaping!"

At a signal from the Irishman, all the able-bodied prisoners levelled their sceptres at Fractals' Seer, and shouted, "*Deleo Structor!*"

The light from a dozen hexes lit up the murky atmosphere for a few moments, and there was an almighty crash as the masonry imploded. Then it splintered, spiralling up into the sky, and was lost to sight.

"What's happened to it?" demanded Fenrig unhappily. "My sister's in there!"

"We had to," said Iain Dubh impatiently. "Did ye not realise they were going to bleed all of us?"

"We must go," squeaked the Ashray, as the eagle flew off again.

"Where'd it go?" coughed Arvin, as the suffocating sulphurous gas descended.

"Why'd he leave us?" mumbled Ossian, who, like Phineas and Kedge, had slowly come round.

"They don't usually intervene," said Jack. "Marco told me: they encourage people to do the right thing. Otherwise they keep out of the way."

"Bringing that wall down wasn't keeping out of the way."

Jack pondered this.

"I willed him in," he said eventually. "But now we've got to help ourselves."

The young girl tugged at Jack's arm, pulling him along a barely discernible path.

"D'you know the way?" he asked.

She nodded, and began to trot away.

"Jack's right!" shouted Enda happily. "The eagle wouldn't leave us without the means of getting away! Come on! Follow her!"

Ossian and Phineas, both recovered now, shouldered the Twa Tams' bodies, while Enda picked up Murkle's gaunt frame. In the early dawn light the escaping prisoners made their uncertain way through the boggy swampland. The sulphurous gas that rose from the ground stung their eyes, burned their lungs, and made them half-delirious. But, as Jack kept repeating to himself, the further they got away from Fractals' Seer the better.

As he stumbled after the young girl, he pondered.

What actually happened to the castle? It's like it was blown to . . . ach! What do the humans call it? . . . smithereens!

Jack was woken from his near reverie by a whistling sound, as a piece of jet-black stone whizzed past his ear. Flint-like, and razor sharp, it was followed by another, and another.

"Take cover!" shouted Iain Dubh.

"There is no cover!" yelled Ossian.

Indeed, the featureless swamp offered no protection against . . .

"What are those things?" demanded Phineas, as the dart-like stones rained in on them.

There was a circling cloud of stones now: almost silent, they whirled around, diving and swooping at the prisoners.

"Cal!" shouted Enda; but it was too late for the Nebula man. A stone had pierced his chest, and he rolled over, motionless.

Iain Dubh wriggled over to his fallen comrade and wrenched the dart from his chest.

"It's a piece of Fractals' Seer!" he exclaimed. "The castle's attacking us!"

The cloud above them seemed to intensify. Gilmore tried to use his sceptre to create a force-shield, but there was no power for Shian sceptres out in the swamp.

Jack looked up as the cloud divided into two. As the larger part flew a short distance off, the other circled above, still an angry, menacing weapon.

"What's it doing?"

The answer came as the larger cloud gathered in intensity, first swarmed up then rained down just fifty or so yards away.

"It's Fractals' Seer!" gasped Jack. "The castle's re-formed!"

And as the castle settled and shook itself slightly, Jack could see a figure crawling through the swamp towards them.

"Over here!" squeaked the Ashray. "We have to go down to go up!"

In the confusion, Jack had not noticed the girl edging away, but now he could see that the Ashray was frantically helping her to dig in a small hollow. Using their bare hands, they had already created a trench in the bogland.

Taking their cue, Ossian and Jack joined in, even as a new wave of darts rained down. The trench filled with bog-water that froze and stung the hands at the same time, but Jack worked frantically.

This girl knows something!

And she did. The other prisoners quickly joined in – even Fenrig. Leaving the bodies of their dead comrades aside, they dug furiously. Bog-water splashed up as a fresh wave of darts found the trench. Eventually, the base of the trench gave way, and they all tumbled through.

As with the fall into the cave at the start of the Bridge, there were screams and cries; but for Jack there was a great sense of relief that they were getting away from the darts, and whatever evil was coming out of Fractals' Seer. The air in the cave was – well, not exactly fresh; but it wasn't poisonous, like the swamp gas above.

As the bodies landed, Jack saw the girl pick the Ashray up and hug her. Then whisper in her ear.

She *can* talk!

The Ashray scuttled up to Jack.

"She says this is the Bridge of Impossibility."

"What?!" screeched Armina. "That's the evil bridge that brought us to this cursed island! And only dark magycks can open it!"

"No," said the Ashray firmly. "That's for coming here. Leaving is different."

"Listen," said Ossian, "we nearly starved to death on the bridge comin' here, and we're even worse off now than when we arrived."

"Ossian's right," said Gilmore, grimacing as water from above dripped down his neck. "The whole point of coming here was to get the Raglan stone; and now the Kildashie have taken it away. We have wasted valuable weeks."

"But we have the Gusog feather," said Iain Dubh.

"Your feather is not going to get us off this island!" shouted

Arvin. "Whatever time-tricks it plays for you on Nebula are no use to us now! The solstice starts tonight!"

Jack looked around. This wasn't the same cave they'd arrived in; so how could it be the Bridge of Impossibility?

"Iain Dubh," he said, "can the Gusog slow things down and give us more time to get away?"

"Gusog doesn't slow time," said Ishona impatiently. "It changes *us*."

"Then what are we to do?" demanded Gilmore. "We can't stay in this cave for ever. We've no food, and that blasted swamp-water keeps dripping in." He jumped sideways as another gush of water fell from above.

"Wait a minute," said Jack. "If this is the Bridge of Impossibilities, then it must be opened, right?"

"By dark magycks," said Armina ominously. "This is no place for children to be playing."

"I don't think this is some game!" shouted Jack angrily. "This bridge is our only way off here! We *must* open it."

"Why don't you use the *Mapa Mundi* to show us where to go?" demanded Finbogie.

"I . . . I haven't got it."

Armina let out a howl of dismay.

"But I can get it back," shouted Jack, trying to be heard above the wail.

He strode up to his father and put his hand out.

Smiling, Phineas handed him the sceptre.

"There's no power for them here without your eagle," said Gilmore gloomily; but Jack took it firmly, and then turned to the girl.

"Where do I summon him?"

The girl pointed at a pale rock in the cave wall. Jack marched sombrely forward, and hit the rock face three times.

"Papa Legba! Papa Legba! Papa Legba!"

The air seemed to hold its breath; and in that moment of stillness, the frail old man reappeared. He limped towards Jack.

"Are ye ready?"

It was the same thin reedy voice.

"We are."

"And how many are ye now?"

Jack did a quick headcount. "Seventeen. One was killed up in the swamp, and three more in the castle."

"But ye're nineteen," continued the old man.

Jack looked round, and started.

Morrigan and Hema stood by the opposite wall, brandishing their wands.

24

The Rainbow Bridge

Hema walked slowly up to Papa Legba and smiled.

"So good of you to let us have this." She indicated the *Mapa Mundi* around Papa Legba's neck. "My daughter fooled that Shian boy into bringing it here. Of course, you've met my daughter before – she opened the Bridge."

Papa Legba's lip curled.

"*I* open the Bridge."

"But Papa," continued Hema, "these pirates have attacked our castle. We gave them shelter and food, and they have done violence to our sisters. You must not allow them to escape."

"Oh, he won't."

In a flash Morrigan withdrew her sword, and thrust it through the old man's chest. As it had before, his body crumpled to the ground.

The prisoners stepped back, but Jack ran forward and crouched down. He cradled the old man's head, then turned to look at Morrigan. The fury inside him was so great that he couldn't even form words to spit at her.

Then the old man shivered, and Jack felt him shake his head.

He's alive!

As the old man levered himself up to a sitting position, there was a palpable change in mood. The escaping prisoners seemed to grow a little in stature, even as Morrigan shrank back.

"Ye have not learned yer lessons well enough," snarled Papa Legba, rising to his feet. "To leave Tula demands not only blood, but tears."

He turned to address the prisoners.

"Where are your dead friends?"

"Above in the swamp," replied Phineas. "We cannot leave their bodies there."

Papa Legba drew a sceptre from his coat, and directed it at the cave ceiling. With a whoosh! there was a collapse of stone and bog, and the four bodies floated down to the cave floor.

"Papa," said Hema ingratiatingly, "my daughter is young, and should have known better. But I will see she is punished for her rashness."

"*I* carry out the punishments."

Hema backed away as Papa Legba levelled his sceptre at Morrigan. As the bolt hit her, her sword flew out of her hand and into his own. With a nimble skip, he hopped over to her cowering body, and thrust the blade into her heart.

"*Cardilacrima!*"

Papa Legba withdrew the blood-stained sword, and Morrigan fell instantly.

"Mor!" Fenrig shouted, but even as he ran to kneel by her

body he knew it was too late. "She was my sister!" he yelled at Papa Legba.

"Good enough for me," said the old man simply, and he thrust the sword into the rock by Fenrig's knee, staining the ground.

A single tear rolled down the young Brashat's cheek, and splashed into the dark red ooze on the ground. There was a further tumble of stone and bog as a hole appeared in the ceiling, and a shaft of coloured light fell into the cave.

"The air's fresh!" shouted Jack.

"The Rainbow Bridge is open," said Papa Legba with satisfaction. "Ye and yer comrades will reach Novehowe by the solstice."

"What about the . . . the ones who died?"

"I'll bring them along," said the old man simply.

"Are you coming with us?"

"I am. And I'm takin' this old hag along wi' me."

Papa Legba now directed his sceptre towards Hema, who had started scrabbling at the cave wall, trying to climb up and out. The bolt hit her back, and she tumbled back onto the cave floor.

"What about my sister?" sobbed Fenrig.

"She'll stay here. This is where she belongs."

Phineas put his arm around Jack's shoulder.

"Ready for another journey?"

Jack nodded. "We should thank the girl – she knew about this cave."

The escapees were lining up now to step into the rainbow shaft. The Ashray disappeared into the light, but the girl held back, just on the edge of the rainbow's beams, and beckoned to Jack and his father. As they approached, she held out her hands, inviting Jack and Phineas to take them. As they held hands in their small circle, she looked slowly from one to the other, then gave a little cough before pulling them into the rainbow.

Jack felt himself pulled upwards, spinning at terrific speed. The low road was nothing to this – even when travelling solo. This was 100 times faster and colder. It was more disturbing, more . . . nauseating. Jack retched.

I haven't felt travel sick for ages . . .

Embarrassed by this feeling, Jack did not even dare to open his eyes for several minutes; and when he did, he could see little. Jack felt as if he was being spiralled and compressed at the same time. If his teeth were chattering, the wind whistling past drowned out the sound.

This wasn't like flying with the horses. This was . . . well, like nothing Jack had ever experienced before. What does light feel like as it passes through the air? Jack didn't know, but he was sure he felt something like that. He tried to focus, but it was impossible. A vague, pixillated shape must have been his father; and another, that must have been the girl. He clutched their hands firmly, closed his eyes again, and prayed for the journey to be over.

The spinning didn't slow down, but after a while Jack felt the coldness grow less intense, and he risked opening his eyes again. The pixillated figures were still there, and he was aware of light rushing past at great speed. His own velocity was so great that Jack had trouble distinguishing how much juddering was due to speed, and how much was just him shivering. He felt nauseated again, and closed his eyes.

With a jolt, they landed.

★　★　★

Jack gasped, trying to get his breath back. Although they were no longer airborne, it felt like the wind was trying to cut him in two. Shivering, Jack slowly opened his eyes. Without realising it, he had released his grip: the blurred figures of his father and the girl were further away. As his eyes found their focus, he could see that each was leaning against a large standing stone. A light dusting of snow was visible as the last rays of the rainbow faded. Storm clouds scudded by.

Jack looked round to find the others. Ossian was three stones to his right; and Enda was next to him, with Iain Dubh and Ishona further along. In fact, everyone was standing by a huge upright stone. Arranged in a circle, the twenty or so stones were irregularly spaced several yards apart.

The nausea slowly left Jack, and he saw his father stagger over to the girl, who still had her eyes tightly closed.

"I hate to break this up," announced Iain Dubh. "But we need to find some shelter fast. Those storm clouds are about to break. And Papa Legba's just arrived with his prisoner."

Papa Legba strode over, shoving Hema forward unceremoniously. Her hands were bound behind her back.

"I doubt we'll make Novehowe before that storm breaks; but there's a house not far away. We can shelter there."

The first raindrops started to fall as the group set off down the road. More standing stones loomed up on their left as they walked along – only three this time, but just as big.

"We're still Shian size, aren't we?" asked Jack. "Are they Shian stones?"

"They go back a long way. Back to when the Shian and the humans mixed freely," said his father.

"But what are they for?"

"Let's get to the shelter, shall we? We'll have time to talk there." He smiled encouragingly at the girl, who was limping slightly.

The rain had started to fall in earnest now. Great smudges of water that soaked and depressed spirits in equal measure. As the group hurried along, Ossian went and put his arm around Fenrig's shoulders. The young Brashat's eyes were moist, and he dabbed at his cheeks.

"I'm not crying," he said to Ossian.

His attempts to stem the flood were not enough, however, and the tears fell, mixing with the rain.

"Of course you're not."

The storm broke over them in earnest now. Ossian's own eyes were wet, but Jack couldn't be sure whether it was rain or tears. It was strange to see Ossian in this light. Walking down the road, comforting Fenrig. He was almost . . . tender.

It was a bedraggled group that finally made it to the house by the road. The sky was dark with clouds, and no lights showed from the windows.

"What is this place?" asked Armina.

"It's an old human mill. It won't be occupied at this time of year."

Papa Legba approached the building with confidence, still shoving Hema in front of him. Levelling his sceptre at the door, he fired a charm. The lock clicked, and the door swung open.

"We'll be safe in here."

"It's not the solstice, is it?" asked Finbogie.

"Not 'til tomorrow. We'll rest up here for the night. Novehowe's just across the road."

The group congregated in the front entrance.

"I've put a bell hex around the house – the humans won't know we're here. And you should all eat. Here – I've some fey biscuits."

"Where exactly are we?" asked Iain Dubh as he chewed thoughtfully.

"You mean you've never been to see the NorShian before?" demanded Papa Legba.

"Of course," said Ishona emphatically, "but never by the Rainbow Bridge. Did it really take the whole day to get here?"

"It's a short day," smiled Papa Legba. "It's midwinter."

"So where are the NorShian? And our comrades who were sailing here?"

"They're all preparing for tomorrow, as should we. First, I'm going to take care of this nuisance here."

He aimed his sceptre at Hema's head, and a hex felled her instantly.

"Have you killed her?" exclaimed Armina.

"Just saved her for tomorrow. She can put her case then."

"Speaking of tomorrow, we'll need to be up early," said Iain Dubh. "I'll take Ishona and the Nebula men, and we'll get some rest."

As the Nebula crew got up to leave, Arvin said, "We'll bring Kedge. Come on, Daid: give Finbogie and Gilmore a hand."

As the most tired of the travellers left to go and sleep, Enda took his sceptre out.

"Papa, we thank you for bringing us out of Tula. But we gathered that you . . ." His voice trailed off.

"You thought I only dealt with dark magycks?" replied the old man sadly. "Well, I must confess that until recently . . ."

He twirled the ring on his finger; then advanced towards Jack.

"I never got round to returning this to you," he said, handing the *Mapa Mundi* over. "It would never have been safe in Fractals' Seer. Those Boabans would have cut you to death and taken it."

Jack gratefully took the *Mapa Mundi* back and tied it around his neck.

"Your ring," he said. "It's the same as mine . . . as Tamlina's."

"It is." Papa Legba showed the ring on his finger to the assembled group. "She and I were old friends. We both came late to Gosol."

"I'm cold." The Ashray sneezed.

"We can get some heat from this." Finbogie wedged his sceptre in an umbrella stand, and muttered under his breath. It glowed, softly at first, then began to radiate a warmth that flowed through the cold house.

"Thank you for leading us away from the Boabans," said Jack to the Ashray. "And you," he added to the young girl. "You knew where the bridge was."

"We are indeed in your debt," added Phineas. "Thanks to you, we have reached Novehowe in time for the midwinter solstice."

The girl looked up at him shyly.

"Tell us about yourself," continued Phineas. "How come you ended up on Tula?"

"I am Cleo."

25

The Fourth Brother

There was a stunned silence. Phineas dropped to his knees in front of the young girl.

"Cleo?" His voice was no more than a whisper.

She squinted uncertainly at him, and nodded.

"Your mother is Sheena of Rangie?"

"She calls herself Adriana," said the girl in a strange accent. "But I know her name is Giovanna."

Giovanna?

Jack walked unsteadily over to the two of them. He felt like he was at sea again.

Phineas' brow was furrowed, then he smiled.

"It's the same name, in Italian. Were you brought up in Italy?"

The young girl nodded, and managed a half-smile.

"Near Roma. You are Phinny-us?"

"Phineas. Yes."

As Phineas reached out and took her hand, she held her other hand out towards Jack.

"And I know your name. You are Jeck."

"Jack," he corrected her.

"That's right: Jeck."

"But what happened to your mother? Why did you leave?"

Cleo sat down on the floor and hugged her knees.

"She wanted always to be with the humans. She lived with one."

Phineas nodded sadly.

"Lived?"

"He left. Perhaps once a year she would take me to the Shian places nearby. But when we got there she would argue, and we would not stay. I was never allowed to mix with the people there."

"So she brought you up as human?"

"She hated her old life. When I asked questions about the Shian, or my family, she got angry. One day, she said she would send me to see what Shian life was really like."

"You don't mean Tula?" gasped Jack. "Why didn't she just send you back to Rangie?"

"She never talked of it. But she said one place would cure me of wanting to live as a Shian."

"The girl is right," butted in Papa Legba. "It was just before Tamlina showed me the power of Gosol. I was summoned, and I took the girl to Tula."

Phineas' eyes narrowed.

"You mean you used dark magycks to spirit my daughter to that . . . hellhole?"

Papa Legba hung his head.

"It was the way I lived – in the past. I have tried to make amends: I found her again, and I showed her how to reach the cave. I hoped one day it would help her."

"How long were you on Tula?" Jack squeezed Cleo's hand.

"She came to me three years ago," squeaked the Ashray.

"You mean you've been there since you were nine?!"

Cleo nodded sadly. "I was bonded to the Boabans for seven years."

"My first friend for eighty-nine years," said the Ashray. "My bonding was forever. But when you all arrived, I knew we might escape."

"Did you know who we were?"

"Of course. Morrigan sent messages to her mother; she thought it was no danger to tell us. Hema believed none could escape."

"And did you know who I was? I mean, to you?" asked Phineas.

"Mama talked sometimes of family. I knew only your names. But she kept one thing – an old paper. It has your name."

Cleo handed Phineas a tattered parchment. Unfolding it carefully, he smiled; then frowned, dropping the document. Picking it up, Jack read aloud:

"If sphere and silver you would gain, the seat of pow'r you may attain,

But seek ye first the key to own: the Creator key, the Raglan stone."

"I found this document," continued Phineas, "when we opened up the square under the castle. The houses had been uninhabited for years – there was all sorts of stuff."

"And that's when you went to look for Tamlina, isn't it?" said Jack.

"Not straight away. Sheena must have taken the paper: she hated the thought of me going after 'Shian treasure'. I searched for ages; when I couldn't find it, I knew I had to find Tamlina."

"Mama hid it," added Cleo. "Then I think she forgot it."

"The curse of secrecy," said Phineas. "But I'm no better: I never showed it to my father, or my brothers. I wanted to be the one to find the Raglan stone. I knew that would make us powerful again."

"Only your family," Fenrig snorted. "It wasn't for all the Shian."

A loud knocking at the door startled everyone.

"I thought you said you'd put a bell hex around here?" shouted Finbogie at Papa Legba.

The old man's eyes showed fear.

"I . . . I did," he stammered.

"That's a human's knock," said Cleo.

Jack felt Tamlina's ring vibrate, and looked down.

"It's all right. We'll be safe."

He moved across to the door and opened it. An old man stood there, clutching a battered leather volume.

"John?"

"I see you worked it out." The old man smiled. "May I come in?"

"This is John," said Jack, ushering the old man in. "He's a shape . . . what I mean is, he's the eagle who flew above us when we were sailing. And who helped rescue us from Tula."

"Marco and Luka said you would watch over us," smiled Phineas. "If you're a teacher like them, maybe you can explain to Fenrig here what this old document means. He thinks I wanted it only for my family."

"So you worked out that the treasures cannot be held by any one group; that they must be shared by all."

"Our young Brashat here is not convinced."

John looked Fenrig square in the eye.

"I would have thought that the story of the King's Chalice would have persuaded you of that."

Fenrig tried to hold the old man's gaze, but found he could not.

"We wondered if you would work things out. Several documents were placed very carefully for you to find all those years ago. But it seems the ancient Shian habits of stealing and losing have not been lost." He eyed Fenrig sharply. "Where did this one end up?"

"With my mother, in Italy," admitted Cleo.

"She took it to stop me seeking the Raglan stone," said Phineas. "So I decided to go and ask Tamlina's advice. That's when the Grey captured me."

"Ah! Tamlina! She had had the Raglan for many years – it was the source of her power. Finally she accepted that it was one of the great treasures, and there for all."

"See?" smirked Fenrig.

"But not just Shian," added John, watching Fenrig's face fall. "We taught a number of you about the way three fits into one. Is that not right, Papa?"

Papa Legba had been silent since John's arrival. Now he knelt, a picture of subservience.

"There's no need for that," muttered John. "You do not serve me. Now Jack, do you remember what Tamlina told you about where creation meets?"

Jack looked at Tamlina's ring, and thought for a moment.

I didn't even notice her ring the first time . . . But when we went back to see her: me and Petros and Grandpa . . .

"She talked of 'her Raglan'," he said slowly. "She said something about it teaching her . . . That's right: 'In the heavens, and on the earth, and under the earth; all o' creation meets.'"

"And what does that mean, do you suppose?" asked John kindly.

"That we're all tied in; linked."

"But three in one. The Raglan – that's part of the Destiny Stone. And the King's Chalice – the cup that can move beyond death. And the *Mapa Mundi* – that shows believers their true path."

"Then why does the map only work for Jack?" demanded Fenrig.

"Oh, others can use it – if they believe. The treasures are not magyck charms."

"And they must be together to work at their best?" asked Jack.

"They're part of the same pattern. Like putting three spiral arms together."

Jack looked at Tamlina's ring. He smiled at Papa Legba.

"Used well, they can bring blessings to many. But they can add power to destructive forces too. Your quest is to defend creation. You have learnt that the Kildashie are destroying the places they inhabit?"

"We've heard stories," said Phineas. "Of land laid bare; and rivers poisoned."

"Exactly. They have forgotten their links to the earth. Now they harness the Creator Force to destroy. That is *infama*."

"Wait a moment," said Armina. "We've to get rid of the

Kildashie, and their allies. But what you said about all of creation: have we to take on the humans as well?"

"The Kildashie are no different to many humans, desecrating their surroundings. But let the good humans tackle the bad ones. Defeating the Kildashie is your task: stop them getting the Destiny Stone."

"And when are they going to try that?"

"Your friends will tell you that when you see them tomorrow."

"Is Grandpa here?" blurted Jack. "And Rana and Lizzie?"

"They're not far away. Your family have tales to tell, as well as you. But you'll see them at the solstice tomorrow. I'm sure you could all do with some rest now."

"And what of the men we left at Lyosach?" asked Enda. "With the boats?"

"They'll all join you tomorrow. The solstice will open up many routes, and many will be there, from countless places. So, rest well: you must be in Novehowe when the sun rises."

26

Midwinter Solstice

For the longest night of the year it was the shortest night's sleep Jack felt he'd ever had.

"Come on, Jack." Phineas was shaking his arm. "We need to get across the road."

"It's still dark – it must be the middle of the night."

"It's gone nine. Remember how far north we are." Cleo's soft voice broke through the darkness.

The weary Shian travellers emerged into the chilly pre-dawn light of Midwinter's Day. Mist hung over the house that had been their shelter for the night, and a cold frost lay on the ground.

"Where's John?" shivered Jack.

"He's gone," replied his father. "Before any of us were awake."

"So how do we know how to get to Novehowe?"

"It's not far."

Ossian was first to find the path.

"I can see Novehowe's entrance!" he shouted excitedly, after a while.

"That's where the humans get in," pointed out Finbogie, holding his glowing sceptre aloft. "And the midwinter light. The Shian entrance is from underneath."

The group made their way around the raised earthwork, and found a small depression in the ground.

"Ah," said Arvin with satisfaction. "Now we're in business."

He took his sceptre out, and directed it at the sunken ground.

"*Effodio!*"

The earth loosened, then fell away, allowing the group to pick their way down to a dark chamber below ground. When the last of them had entered, Finbogie's sceptre stopped glowing, and the hole above sealed itself over. Jack felt himself shrink down to Shian height.

"Has anyone got a light?"

"Careful!" said a strange voice. "You're not the only ones here!"

"Who's that?" asked Daid.

"I am Hogboy – and you're in my home. Who are you?"

"We're the Ilanbeg and Nebula Seelie," explained Jack, whose eyes had grown accustomed quickly to the dark. "We're supposed to meet with the rest of our family here – for midwinter."

"We are visitors here," added Phineas. "We have heard that the hogboons show great hospitality to strangers at this time of year."

"Ach, every year it is the same," grumbled Hogboy. "Shian visitors tumbling in. Very well, I'll take you through."

There was a scraping sound, and a small flame lit up the tiny chamber. Jack could see that Hogboy was much bigger than any of the new arrivals: a dark, grimy, hairy creature, with just a small cloth tied around his middle.

Hogboy lit the end of a wooden torch, and peered inquisitively at his new guests. Then he turned and pushed at the far wall. A stone gave way, and suddenly Jack could hear the sound of subdued voices.

"There they are!" Rana's excited voice cut through the hubbub. "We've been expecting you for ages!"

"Only two days," pointed out Lizzie.

In the flickering light offered by Hogboy's torch, Jack could see that the larger chamber was crammed with close to fifty Shian.

"Quiet, please!" commanded a voice. "The sun will lift soon. Hogboy, put your torch out now."

A mutter, and the flame died. Suddenly, everything was dark again.

"Welcome to our new visitors. Your arrival has been awaited with great anticipation. I am Magnus of the NorShian. We will have time later to talk; but now, let us greet the lifting sun. See! She rises!"

All the Shian in the chamber now stood up, and Jack had to crane his neck to see the tiny glow in the far wall.

"It's the entrance tunnel," whispered Armina. "The rising sun will find it and light up the chamber."

Almost imperceptibly, a beam of light inched down the tunnel. And then, with a soundless splash, the chamber blazed as direct sunlight hit the far wall. There was a great cheer, as people slapped backs, and hugged each other. Bottles and flagons were brought out, and a muddled exchange of drinks began.

Eventually, the light began to dim, but it was quickly replaced by several dozen glowing sceptres.

"Grandpa!" shouted Jack as he caught sight of his grandfather and cousins.

Grandpa Sandy was trying to find Jack in the crowd, but there was so little room that it was impossible to move.

"We'll repair to the big house!" shouted Magnus. "I'm sure Hogboy would like his home back. Until next year, my friend!"

The Shian walked along the entrance tunnel, emerging into the bright morning light.

"Why haven't we risen to human height?" asked Jack as he and Phineas emerged.

"It's a Shian festival day: with the sun risen, Shian rules apply. So we'll need to stay away from the humans today, but Magnus will have that organised."

Jack quickly found Rana, Lizzie and Petros, and made a half-embarrassed attempt to hug them. Lizzie was jumping up and down, clapping her hands.

Grandpa Sandy approached, knelt down and clasped Jack.

"I'm so glad to see you here."

Jack could feel the tears on the side of his grandfather's face.

"Father," said Phineas. "We're fine; although Tula was rough. And we've much news for you."

"Magnus has everything ready at the big house; it's not far. You can tell us your news there." Grandpa Sandy wiped his face and got to his feet again.

"No, father: there's something you must know right now."

Phineas reached out his hand and beckoned Cleo forward. Rana's puzzled expression said it all.

"This is Cleo. *Our* Cleo."

Grandpa Sandy was stunned.

"You mean Jack's sister?" asked Lizzie disbelievingly. "But where . . . ?"

"We rescued her from the Boaban Shee. Well, in fact, *she* helped *us* to escape."

Grandpa Sandy now found his voice. He dropped to his knees once more and gazed into his granddaughter's face.

"I wasn't sure I would ever see you again."

Cleo smiled self-consciously at the old man.

"Come on," said Jack. "It's getting cold. Let's get inside. Where's this 'big house'?"

"It's just past the stones," said Rana. She set off along the road Jack had travelled the night before, and followed the crowd up to the standing stone circle.

"But that's where we arrived," said Jack.

"Not there, silly! Behind it."

Jack saw the mound of earth behind the circle for the first time.

"It's a tumulus!" said Jack, as he caught sight of the large earthwork.

"Best of its kind inside, though," smiled Lizzie. "I'll show you around."

"No need to go deiseil here," laughed Rana as she ran down the spiral slope that led into the mound.

They were soon inside in the warmth. Cleo was exchanging news with Rana and Lizzie, while Phineas and Grandpa looked on contentedly. The happy chatter of stories – told, contradicted by others who were there too, and eventually agreed upon – filled the enormous hall. Tables groaned under the weight of food and drink, and Jack helped himself to a well-earned breakfast. He was ravenous, and as he wolfed down another pie, he caught sight of Iain Dubh and a large fair-haired man talking. Iain Dubh beckoned him over.

"You will be Jack Shian?" asked the fair-haired man. "I am Magnus. Welcome to our islands."

Jack tried to say 'thank you', but a spray of pastry came out instead. Magnus smiled.

"There will be time for all your news. We have a long day ahead of us. The midwinter solstice allows us to feast, after a time of hunger. Like our Nebula friends, our winters are lean: but today marks the start of our festival."

"Jack," said Iain Dubh, "Thank you for helping us on Tula. I don't think we'd have got here without you. And we wouldn't have this." He showed the Gusog feather.

Jack blushed, and he gulped down the last of the pie.

"We all did what we needed to do."

"But not all of us are here," said Iain Dubh sadly. "Cal and the others are in the chapel room. We should go and pay our respects."

Jack nodded, and went to get his father. It was sombre, having to see the corpses lined up on a table. He hadn't really got to know the Twa Tams; but Cal had been good to him in the pustula. And what was he to think of Murkle? Part of him thought of all the times he'd sat, bored to tears in Murkle's lessons, wishing the old tutor would just die. And there his body was: bloodless, as white as the sheet which had been covering it. Jack felt a surge of pity for his old tutor. Nobody deserved to die at the Boabans' hands.

"They knew the risks we were taking," said Phineas softly. "And that's all the more reason that we have to succeed now. We've come a long way."

Jack looked at Magnus.

"Then you will join us?"

"You must plead your case before the NorSeelie court: it is the way. But we can feast first – there's time for talking later."

"But you must help us," implored Jack. "The Kildashie . . ."

Phineas put his arm around Jack's shoulder.

"Later. We must respect their way of doing things. Let's go and see how the others are getting along."

When Jack entered the large chamber again, he could see that Ossian was getting ready for a wrestling contest. Over the next two hours, a series of bouts took place. Jack, his belly over-full, managed to avoid getting volunteered.

When the wrestlers had gone off to toast their victories or drown their sorrows, the musicians took centre stage again. Jack approached his cousins.

"It's great, isn't it? It reminds me of Cos-Howe. D'you remember? When Ossian took us the first time?"

Rana looked at him reproachfully.

"That's a bit mean, considering Cosmo's been holed up in Cos-Howe for months."

"I didn't mean that . . . I just meant . . ." but Jack got no further. Rana stalked off haughtily.

"Jack, have you still got the *Mapa Mundi*?" asked Petros. "Didn't the Boabans try and get it from you?"

"Papa Legba kept it safe while we were on Tula," he explained.

"You mean you let someone else take it?!"

"I knew he'd keep it safe. He's got a ring like Tamlina's." Jack showed the ring that once more kept the *Mapa Mundi* around his neck. "I figured, if he's got that, then he's on the right side."

"Malevola had that ring for a while, so that doesn't make sense."

"Well, something just made me trust him. And he *did* give it back to me when we got here."

"Where's he gone? I haven't seen him since yesterday."

"He took Hema away. Whatever she gets, it serves her right," said Lizzie. "From what Cleo's said, she was a right old witch."

"Not a witch," said Cleo. "The Boabans turn into witches when they don't get enough blood. She was still Boaban."

"The dancing and singing will go on for a while," said Phineas, joining the group. "People have come from all over, because the low roads are working again today."

Jack looked round the chamber. It *was* more crowded. And with people he'd never seen before.

"Where are *they* from?" he asked, indicating a group who were conversing with Iain Dubh and Ishona.

"They're from across the ocean," said Phineas. "These islands are a crossroads, you know. People have passed through this place for centuries. That's 'Grey Wolf'; and the one next to him is 'He Who Waits'."

"Are they Shian?" Jack couldn't be certain: Grey Wolf was quite a bit taller than the other.

"I think so. But remember what John told us: the Shian and human worlds are not so separate. This is a strange day: all sorts can end up here."

"You mean like him?" Jack pointed to a large figure who stood alone by one of the fireplaces. "He's enormous – almost like Caskill."

Clad in green, the half-giant held an axe in his right hand, and clutched a holly branch in his left. The flames from the fireplace crackled and spat as the figure leant against the mantelpiece.

"He looks like he could take anyone on," said Jack in awe.

"Looks like he might be about to," muttered Petros.

A cold blast blew through the large chamber, and Jack felt an icy chill grip his guts. Turning round he saw ... No, it couldn't be.

"Good of you to open the low road for us today," proclaimed a figure at the entrance. He moved quickly into the chamber, followed by a dozen others, all holding their sceptres at the ready.

"I am Stegos, of the Kildashie. And this," he brandished a triangular lump of granite, "is part of the Raglan stone. We know the *Mapa Mundi* is here; let us have it, and we'll be on our way."

27

The Green Man

Stegos quickly picked out Jack from the crowd.

"You have the *Mapa Mundi*, boy? Then hand it over."

The Kildashie held aloft the fragment of Raglan stone, and although Jack shrank back, Stegos was swiftly on him. He gripped Jack by the throat – but his arm was immediately beaten down.

Jack had not even been aware of the half-giant's movement from the fireplace; but he said a silent *thank you* as he dropped to the floor, rubbing his neck. Stegos was just as surprised, and he wheeled around in anger.

"I am Kildashie! We own the Shian treasures!"

The half-giant stared at him impassively.

"You deal with things that you do not understand," said Phineas, positioning himself between Stegos and Jack. "Splitting the Raglan makes its power unpredictable!"

Stegos eyed Phineas warily. "But it's part of the Destiny Stone; the rest has gone on to Edinburgh."

"The Destiny Stone cannot work properly if it's splintered. As the Raglan it was our best hope of uniting the treasures!"

"I don't believe you. This piece is proof the Kildashie are in charge. And my friend here –" he waved at one of his comrades "– has your season-wheel."

One of the Kildashie brandished a small wooden wheel which showed a winter setting.

"That's our season-wheel!" shouted Magnus. "Without its turning we cannot survive!"

"One word from me," said Stegos, "and he'll shatter it. Your winter will last ten years!"

"You splinter the Raglan stone; and you would break the season-wheel. You neither understand nor deserve such treasures."

"Enough with words! Give me the *Mapa* – or my friend here will bring a winter of death. Or maybe your children would rather have some heat?"

Several of the Kildashie now darted forward and grabbed prisoners – including Cleo, Rana and Fenrig. Igniting their sceptres, they held the burning end at each hostage's face.

"This is the midwinter solstice!" shouted Magnus. "This violates all our laws and customs!"

"We will be gone once we have the *Mapa*," said Stegos simply. "If you want to make sport, I will duel with the boy. This piece of the Raglan for his map!"

Phineas, Grandpa and the Nebula crew all moved forward to protect Jack.

"No!" said Phineas, withdrawing his sword. "You duel with me, not my son."

"Dad," said Jack hoarsely. "That's a piece of the Raglan. It can make hexes ten times stronger."

The splintered Raglan was erratic, yes – but not useless. Jack saw the wave of doubt spread over his father's face. Duelling was one thing; swords against strong hexes, that was death-waiting-to-happen.

But nobody found out what Phineas would have done next. The half-giant pushed himself forward again.

"One hex for one blow," said Magnus as the half-giant brandished his axe. "You go first, Kildashie."

Stegos stared at the man, his jaw dropping.

"What makes him think he'll get a blow in? I'll take his brains out – if he has any."

"One hex for one blow," repeated Magnus firmly. "Ten minutes' recovery time."

Stegos chuckled. "All right. And to show I'm a sport, there's the piece of Raglan stone." He placed the sandstone on the floor. "Now, if the *Mapa Mundi* goes there too, you're on!"

As the half-giant turned round to look at him, Jack could not read his face. It was impassive – almost dead. But looking at the hostages, cowering at the thought of their faces being scorched by the Kildashie's sceptres . . .

Fenrig looks like he's wet himself!

. . . Jack realised he had no alternative. Tugging Tamlina's ring from his neck, he untied the flag, and laid it next to the splintered Raglan stone.

The crowd had split into two: the Kildashie with their hostages by the entrance, and everyone else facing them. Stegos and the half-giant stood in the middle, eyeing each other up.

Stegos looked carefully at the axe in the great man's right

hand; then at the switch of holly branch in his left. Then, with a chuckle and a shake of his head, he swiftly raised his sceptre, and aimed it at the half-giant's face.

"*Decapitis!*"

There was a flash as the hex caught the huge man square in his face. An audible gasp ran round the chamber as the face burnt; and when the head toppled onto the ground, followed by the body, Jack felt an icy chill run through the room.

"Now, I take the *Mapa Mundi*!" shouted Stegos triumphantly.

"No!" commanded Magnus. "Ten minutes, remember."

"All right," laughed Stegos. "Ten minutes won't hurt." He looked round in triumph at his comrades.

Jack was desperately trying to think. There must be something he could do here ... Gosol had brought Grandpa back up at Dunvik; but he'd used the Chalice for that – and his grandfather hadn't been in bits.

If I could get the piece of Raglan stone ...

But Stegos was standing with his foot over the small fragment of sandstone, his sceptre still aimed at the giant's recumbent body. The other Kildashie were laughing, and two had even freed their hostages, confident that they would soon be on their way. Fenrig, released by his captor, scurried away.

The minutes ticked by, and there was nothing happening except a growing pool of blood by the slain half-giant's body. What had Magnus meant – ten minutes' recovery time? How do you recover from a severed head?

The minutes
   ticked
     by.
In silence.

Stegos glanced round, then stretched and yawned, and bent down to retrieve the *Mapa Mundi*. But he was halted by a flicker of movement from the half-giant's body.

Jack's eyes nearly popped out of his head. There was no doubt – the body had moved. The arms bent, and the body pushed itself up into a kneeling position. Blood continued to drip from the open neck.

The arms swept the floor in front until they encountered the severed head. Then cradling the head, feeling gently for the face, the half-giant stuck it firmly down onto his torso again. Then he picked up the switch of holly and axe, stood up, and faced Stegos.

The Kildashie had watched this display with a growing sense of disbelief. Disbelief gave way to incredulity – and then terror.

"One blow for one hex," stated Magnus firmly. "Stand ready. The ten minutes are not over."

Stegos' jaw moved up and down, but no sound came out. Whether he would have managed to say something eventually is a moot point, because the half-giant swung his axe, and cleaved head from trunk with a 'Tchock'.

Jack hadn't heard a 'Tchock' before; and he hadn't previously heard the sound which followed it: a kind of splushing noise as Stegos' head hit the floor, splattering out blood and brains. Next to those sounds, the 'whump' as Stegos' body hit the floor was a bit of an anticlimax.

The remaining Kildashie stood, stunned. Then two made a break for it, and escaped through the doorway, pulling the entrance down behind them. Their comrades, if they had entertained thoughts of escape, now saw that this was impossible. They were quickly disarmed, and the season-wheel recovered.

The prisoners were led away into the makeshift morgue next door.

"Shouldn't we go after the others?" shouted Jack, stooping down and retrieving the *Mapa Mundi*. As he picked up the sandstone lump it burnt his hand – but only briefly. It felt sort of . . . *zingy*. The flag around his neck tingled.

When the treasures come together, their power increases . . . even if the Raglan has been broken, and it's only a part of the Stone anyway . . .

"No," said Phineas, going over to comfort Cleo and Rana. "It's better if the story comes from them – that will put fear into the other Kildashie."

"And what'll happen to the others?" asked Jack, nodding towards the morgue.

"We can't kill them: it's the solstice, for one thing. And it's like at Dunvik: Gosol demands that we spare them."

"They were going to burn our faces off!" screamed Rana.

"But you're safe," explained Grandpa soothingly. He took the Raglan stone fragment from Jack, then knelt down and hugged Rana. "And we mustn't sink to their level."

Cleo's eyes showed indignant fury at her ordeal. She strode over to the half-giant, whose face, though still disfigured, showed a trace of a smile. Cleo gave a short curtsey, then walked off towards the morgue.

"Wait! Where are you going?" demanded Magnus.

Cleo stopped abruptly.

"I want to see them punished."

"Oh, they'll be punished – just not killed. Trust us: we wouldn't insult you by letting them off lightly. They abused all of us."

"He's right," said Phineas, putting his arm around Cleo. "Let's let them take care of the prisoners. Come on; the party's getting going again."

Stegos' body had been dragged away, and his head removed. As the music restarted, fresh earth was spread around to cover the blood. NorShian carried trays of food and drink around, and the atmosphere quickly returned to party mode.

"This place is amazin'," said Ossian. "You'd never think they'd just been attacked. It's like nothin' even happened."

Kedge, however, was not sharing the jollity. In fact, he was shaking.

"It's all right," said Lizzie soothingly. "They've gone. The ones who escaped aren't coming back."

Kedge's eyes showed that, however much he wanted to believe he was safe, the thought of Kildashies and beheadings chilled him to the very bone.

"Come on over to the warm," said Armina, taking Kedge over to the fire. "And we'll get you something to drink."

Jack watched as Kedge was led away. Painful memories had clearly been stirred.

That was just a taster, thought Jack. *When we take on Boreus and the rest of the Kildashie, we won't have a green man to save us*. He walked up to Magnus.

"You knew he would do that, didn't you?"

Magnus looked down kindly at Jack. His face was flushed; and it wasn't just from the roaring fire.

"As I recall, we haven't gone through the formalities yet. Did you have a request you wanted to make?"

Jack felt hot tears welling up inside.

"This isn't a game!" he shouted. "We've travelled hundreds of miles, some of us have died, and you want me to play?!"

"Jack." His father's voice was soothing. "They didn't know the Kildashie were going to attack. The green man is their totem. He's the sign that the year does turn."

"We're at the depths of midwinter," explained Magnus, cradling the season-wheel. "We have to believe that the dark days won't last forever."

"We know your green man is proof to you that winter will pass," said Phineas. Turning to Jack, he added, "He killed Stegos with an axe, but did you see what he held in his other hand?"

Jack thought. It *was* odd that the half-giant had held a switch from a bush.

"The holly bush is green isn't it? Even at midwinter?"

"Exactly. It's a sign that spring will return. If the green man hadn't got up, winter would have lasted forever."

"And if you knew our islands then you would know that that is what we fear most," said Magnus. "We would never survive that."

Iain Dubh had silently joined the group.

"Jack, you remember how bad things were at Nebula? After the Hallows' Eve party?"

Jack thought back to the grimness of Nebula. Thin-faced creatures, only just surviving the hardship of cold and near-starvation. He shivered.

"Well, Novehowe's much like that. It's a long hard winter. Only the prospect of spring returning makes it bearable."

"I'm sorry if making you wait a few hours to put your request was troublesome," said Magnus. "But we have waited months to share this time of festivity."

Jack looked down guiltily.

"So," continued Magnus generously, "I gather you have a request to make?"

"He does," said Iain Dubh. "And I promised Jack that the Nebula men would join him if he could persuade Magnus of Novehowe to do so. So, Jack, plead your case."

"We ... we wanted to ask if you would help us stop the Kildashie. If they get the Destiny Stone and the King's Chalice, they'll be able to control everything. It's freezing cold everywhere; and there's floods, and the woods are all getting burnt, and the waters are being poisoned ..." Jack heard his voice getting faster and faster.

"The Kildashie believe they can do whatever they like," added Phineas. "We've always known they could be *infama*; but from all we've heard, they really don't care."

Magnus looked across at the half-giant, who had resumed his place near the fire.

"For the Kildashie to challenge the green man and threaten to break our season-wheel *was infama*. But we are not so reckless as to join a battle without knowing what we fight. How big is the Kildashie force?"

Jack looked at his father and grandfather.

"The Kildashie and Thanatos occupy Edinburgh and most of the lands north of Keldy. The Boabans – well, they have Tula, but nowhere else. The Red Caps are in the Borders; and there's various Unseelie in the west."

"But how many Kildashie are there?" insisted Magnus.

"There were only thirty or so at the Oestre festival ..." began Jack.

"That was just their advance party," added Armina. "When they attacked the Congress, Boreus brought in many more."

"You see what we have here," said Magnus, "and this is us at our best, until spring at least."

"But we must defeat the Kildashie before the new year. That's when they'll try and get the Destiny Stone."

"By Hogmanay?!" laughed Magnus. "That's out of the question. We have no fighting force to lend you."

28
Stalled

Jack felt he was drowning. He struggled to take in a breath, and his head swam.

"Magnus," pleaded Phineas, "you know that we have come far to ask for your help. It is imperative that we stop the Kildashie from taking the Destiny Stone."

"It is not that we do not wish to help you, but see for yourself what we have here. A dozen fighting men, at most. Our community has not had the benefit of being near the Stone, like you have. And midwinter is hardly the time for such excursions."

"But we were told that many others would be here at midwinter," exclaimed Jack. "We have to join forces."

"The low road is open today," replied Magnus, "which is why you see some of our overseas friends here." He indicated small groups dotted around the chamber: Grey Wolf and the other Cree; a group of short painted men, who crouched low beside the fire; and the McCools.

"Then you can call others to join you," said Jack simply.

"But this is our solstice festival: a time for celebrating the passing of midwinter."

"Magnus, I do not doubt the integrity of these mainlanders," added Iain Dubh. "The boy has found the *Mapa Mundi*; they have retrieved the Shian flag from Ardmore, and even rescued the Gusog feather. I promised HebSeelie support if they could persuade you to join."

"Your honour is not in question, Black John. But our forces, even combined, are not enough to take on the Kildashie and all their allies. And especially not in winter."

"But if the Kildashie get the Destiny Stone, they could control the weather: and then it would be winter forever," pleaded Jack.

Magnus looked keenly at Jack.

"You mean they really control the seasons? And the weather?"

"We don't know how; but wherever they're in control, it's freezing. They've cut down most of the Shian woods, and they've caused flooding, even in the human places . . ."

Magnus looked down at the NorShian season-wheel.

"We'd heard that things were bad in some areas," he admitted. "But it's all so distant."

"It won't stay distant if they get the Stone," said Phineas firmly. "You saw the power this fragment of the Raglan gave to Stegos; the whole Raglan will be giving them much more. If they get the Destiny Stone itself – well, it's unimaginable."

"I suppose . . ." said Magnus; "I suppose I could call on our friends from the fjords. But there's time yet. The low road will be open for most of the next ten days."

"But we need to be in Edinburgh by Hogmanay. Otherwise the Kildashie will win."

"I can send a message to the fjords; but there's no guarantee they'll come. If they do, we can join you. If not, then attacking the Kildashie is suicide. I won't waste my men on a mission that's doomed to fail."

"D'you think they'll come?" Jack turned to a NorShian beside him.

The man shook his head slowly.

"Only if they think one of their own is in danger."

"What d'you mean, 'One of their own'?"

"The fjordsmen left traces wherever they sailed; including people. They look out for those who are still there. That knife on your leg is Norse, isn't it? It's an old one."

"An old soldier gave it to me; on Ilanbeg."

"Well, if an old Norse remnant like him was in danger, or harmed, then the old earls would come."

"Old earls?"

"Oh, Harald, and Rognvald. They used to bring warriors over here, back in the old days."

The man wandered off, leaving Jack feeling low; the NorShians' lack of enthusiasm was depressing. Spying Ossian talking with a group of Cree, he moved over.

"This guy's amazin'," said Ossian as Jack approached. "The stories he tells about huntin'. Three days goin' after a moose. I'm goin' over for a visit when all this is done."

Jack sipped a goblet of juice. That seemed like an optimistic assessment based on what he knew. If only there was some way of speeding things up.

Rana approached frowning.

"I thought Mum and the others were going to join us."

"That's right," said Lizzie. "The low road's open today – why haven't they come?"

"Back on Ilanbeg, Marco talked of the time being right," said Jack. "I guess they'll join us in Edinburgh."

Jack thought back to Ilanbeg: what had Marco and Luka taught him? They would defeat the Kildashie with the right force, and at the right time. But how were they to know?

"Silver shilling for your thoughts," said Rana mischievously.

"I was just wondering how we can persuade Magnus. That other guy said the Norse would come if they thought one of their kind was in danger."

"Well, the Novehowe lot *are* Norse. And so was Trog," stated Lizzie. "A lot of them mixed in with the local Shian, so you can't always tell."

"What d'you think, Cleo?"

"I should like to see Jeck's flag. The Kildashie that came – they knew it was important. But I have not seen it working."

"It's not like just lighting a candle," said Jack impatiently. "It has to be right for it to work."

"Then maybe *I* can make it work."

Jack pulled Tamlina's ring off, flicked the *Mapa Mundi* into a sphere, and handed it to Cleo. The two circles formed, and clearly visible in one was a Christmas tree.

"That's the High Street!" exclaimed Petros, looking over Jack's shoulder.

Jack didn't need to be told. The huge Christmas tree outside St Giles' Cathedral was up there for so long before Christmas that it was a familiar sight to Shian, even before they retreated inside for the 'great winter shutdown'.

Then the tree faded, and was replaced by the image of five lit candles: three purples, and one pink one forming a square; and a white one in the middle.

"They're all lit," shouted Lizzie excitedly. "That means it's Christmas Day!"

Jack frowned. *Is it telling us to go to Edinburgh on Christmas Day?*

A picture started to form in the other circle, and Jack gasped: a huge figure of a man ... no, more than a man ... a giant. Jack blinked, but there was no doubt about it. It was Caskill. And the charmstone was hanging loose in his chest.

"Who is that, Jeck?"

Jack's head was whirling. Half of him didn't want to believe what the other half was telling him. Then he made up his mind.

"We've to go to Edinburgh at Christmas. And help Caskill."

"Caskill?!" exclaimed Petros. "He went off to Nanog; or somewhere. But west: he was going to set off for the west."

"Well, he's going to be in Edinburgh on Christmas Day. And he needs our help."

"But we can't go until everyone else is ready," said Lizzie.

"Magnus is taking ages to decide," replied Jack. "He's said he'll ask the fjordsmen, but there's no guarantee they'll come."

"I would like to see a city at Christmas," said Cleo. "It will be nice to see all the lights again."

"I wouldn't mind going to Edinburgh," said Petros. "To the human spaces, I mean. The parties will be cool."

You've changed your tune, thought Jack, as he flicked the *Mapa* back to a flag. *You used to go on about the 'Dameves'.*

"I can take you to human places," added Cleo. "I know how to be part of a human crowd."

"So do I," said Petros. "I'm a quarter human, remember."

"It's too dangerous to go to Edinburgh," snapped Lizzie. "Besides, we'd never get away."

"There's people coming and going all the time," Jack pointed out. "We could easily slip out if the low road entrance is open. And be back before anyone notices."

"Edinburgh *is* dangerous," said Ossian. "You've just been tellin' everyone how bad the Kildashie are, and you know what the Thanatos did to Ploutter. Kedge won't go back. What makes you think you'd get away again?"

"Without Caskill we'd never have got this far. And if his charmstone's almost out, he needs our help."

"What are you youngsters up to?" enquired Phineas as he approached. He held a goblet, and his face was ruddy.

"Nothing," said Jack. "We were just wondering when Magnus was going to ask the fjordsmen to come."

"Not much joy there, I'm afraid. I'm sure we can persuade a few of the people here to join us, but it's not the army we need."

"What should we do, then? We can't sit here and do nothing." Jack's voice rose.

"Oh, I'm sure we'll think of something. But a word of advice: don't even think about travelling without the rest of us. We haven't come this far for you to risk it all on a whim." Phineas went off to join Armina and Daid by the fire.

"He must've heard you," hissed Petros. "We'll never get away if he's watching us."

"Uncle Phineas is right," stated Lizzie. "You can't go off into Kildashie territory without protection."

Oh, I'll take protection, don't you worry, thought Jack.

He was startled a moment later when Grey Wolf tugged his arm.

"I'll come with you."

29
Mustang Flight

Jack turned round in astonishment.

"You knew what I was thinking?"

"It is written on your face; and I heard you say 'Caskill'. But I see you have doubts."

"The Kildashie and the Thanatos are deadly; and I hate the cold. If the Kildashie have made Edinburgh as cold as we think . . ."

"They are breaking the circle: stopping the season-wheels turning is *macava*; you call this *infama*. We know it too: years ago men came and destroyed our homelands."

"Where *have* you come from?"

"Over the sea. But one of my ancestors came from these islands. From time to time some of us return to his birthplace."

"And you know Caskill?"

"We know of him. He bears a charmstone, I think: like this."

Grey Wolf pulled out a quartz piece held on a string around his neck.

"It's the same as the one we got for Caskill! The one that stops him sleeping!"

"We heard that you had rescued that; that's one of the reasons we came here. If Caskill is in the big city, then he will be in trouble. I will help you find him."

Jack steered Grey Wolf further away from the others and whispered, "I was going to take Rana and Lizzie's invisibility bonnets. I'm sure I can get to Edinburgh and back without being seen."

"I do not know this city, so I will need your help to keep safe there. But I have things that will help too. Let me tell He Who Waits."

"Cleo wants to come," butted in Petros as Grey Wolf left.

Jack was irritated that Petros had sneaked up on them.

"No way. I'm not taking her. This is about helping Caskill. She doesn't know anything about Edinburgh."

"But she knows about human spaces. If the Shian areas are dangerous, that could help."

Jack considered this for a moment.

"I still don't like it. It's going to be hard enough me slipping away. If she comes too, Dad's bound to notice."

"And me," said Petros. "I'm not missing out if there are some human parties."

"This isn't a family holiday!" snapped Jack. "I've got to get there and back quickly, and without Dad or the others noticing."

"Well, if your dad asks me, I might have to tell him where you've gone."

"You wouldn't!"

"Not up to me to lie for you," said Petros simply.

Jack ground his teeth. He felt like thumping Petros, but then he turned round and saw his father watching. He turned back.

"Well, how are we all going to get away without Dad and Grandpa knowing?"

"We could say you've gone to look at the human spaces here; he'll buy that. Don't worry, we'll think of something."

Over the next couple of days the Novehowe solstice celebrations seemed to have a mellowing effect on everyone. Despite Jack's concerns, and the continuing non-appearance of any support from the fjordsmen, the atmosphere was infectious enough for Jack to join in the parties. And the Novehowe lot *did* know how to party, Jack had to give them that. Like the McCools, most of them seemed to survive with just brief naps, returning to the festivities bleary-eyed but ready for more.

Phineas and Grandpa – in fact, all of those who had left Ilanbeg – had settled down into 'the Novehowe way', joining in the parties, the short walks outside, the music sessions. Where they betrayed their 'non-Novehowe-ness' was in the sleeping. The Nebula crew, more accustomed to island life, and thriving on the abundant food, had adapted well, and were in the full throes of the celebrations.

All kinds of Shian were making an appearance too. Not since the Hidden Commonwealth had been summoned at Dunvik had Jack seen such an array of creatures, not even on Ilanbeg: Darrigs, Elle-folk, Pisgies, even Phooka. Enda and the other McCools had quickly found the Phooka, and one corner of the great chamber became a little Irish enclave.

However it was the growth in the Cree numbers which most

fascinated Jack. He Who Waits and Grey Wolf had been quietly joined by several dozen friends. They had arrived unobtrusively, and made little obvious impact on the celebrations. But they were definitely *there*. Jack realised with a growing sense of optimism that this might make it a lot easier for Grey Wolf to disappear for a while without being noticed.

While this might get the Cree man away, Jack couldn't see how he and Cleo and Petros could escape without Phineas and Grandpa finding out. The answer came on Christmas Eve, when Enda pulled Jack away from the group of youngsters as they sat next to the fireplace.

"Jack, d'you fancy a jaunt out into the humans' world tomorrow? Ye'll niver believe this, but we've found an Irishwoman here, and she's said we can visit her home. We wouldn't touch the food – 'twould be disgustin', sure we know that. But have ye iver seen a human Christmas?"

Jack shook his head.

"Well, Connemara Mary will take us out after breakfast. Will ye come?"

Jack's smile was his reply.

Brilliant: a perfect excuse!

So it was that as Christmas Day dawned, Jack stashed the *Mapa Mundi* and Tamlina's ring in a kitchen cupboard, and then slipped unobtrusively into the girls' room.

Fast asleep! Good!

Relieving Rana and Lizzie's satchels of their green bonnets, he found Grey Wolf and handed one over. When Enda announced after breakfast that a crowd were leaving to go and celebrate the day with Connemara Mary, Jack, Petros, Cleo and Grey Wolf tagged along.

"Have a good time!" shouted Grandpa Sandy as they made for the tumulus entrance.

Once outside, however, they dropped to the back of the north-bound crowd, and as the advance group got further ahead Jack and the others turned round.

"It's freezing!" said Petros, as he shivered in his coat. "Should we go back and get some warmer clothes? Gilmore's got loads."

"We haven't time," said Jack, as he set off down the road. He was shivering too, but he resolved not to show this to Petros or Cleo. Grey Wolf, wrapped in a thin blanket, seemed unmoved by the bitter weather. He allowed Jack to lead, but kept a watchful eye on Cleo as she struggled in the strong wind.

They reached the three standing stones just as the rain started.

"Quick! Let's get away before we get soaked," pleaded Petros.

"The low road'll dry us anyway," said Jack impatiently, as he made for the dolmen in the centre. "Come on!"

He got the four standing in a circle, arms linked.

"We'll use the bonnets in turn to get out of the square. All right?"

The others nodded.

"*Wind flock castle!*"

A gust of icy rain swept over them.

"*Wind flock castle!*" shouted Jack.

No movement; nothing.

"Maybe the low road does not work today?" said Cleo.

"But Magnus said it would be open," protested Jack.

"Well, it's not open now," grumbled Petros. "And I'm getting wet."

"We're all wet!" shouted Jack.

"If the low road will not work, we must go another way. Come!" Grey Wolf set off at a jog back along the loch-side.

"Where are we going?" demanded Petros.

Grey Wolf indicated the large circle of standing stones ahead.

"It's the place for flying here, and leaving."

Jack turned to Petros as they jogged along, but Petros just shrugged.

"We have a saying where I come from," laughed Grey Wolf. "'You will run with horses'."

Reaching the first stone, he stopped and watched the others arriving out of breath.

"I think so many days of relaxation are not good for your health!" he laughed. "But these horses will take us where we need to go. What is the name of the place in the city for horses?"

"It's below Arthur's Seat," said Jack. "We used horses from there to get to France."

"Horses?" asked Cleo timidly.

"Haven't you ridden before?" A look of concern passed over Jack's face.

Cleo shook her head.

"Then you shall ride with me," said Grey Wolf.

He gave a low whistle, and two ghost-grey horses appeared.

"We ride without saddles."

"We're used to that," said Jack.

The four were quickly mounted. Cleo, sitting in front of Grey Wolf, covered by his blanket, hung on tightly to the horse's mane. Jack sat behind Petros, and gripped his waist.

The horses began to canter along the flat ground beside the loch, quickly getting up to a gallop. Jack waited for Grey Wolf to shout, "Horse and hattock!"

"*Mistatim!*"

The rise into the air was much more sudden than Jack had anticipated. The two horses sped upwards at terrific speed, and only the passing of the icy cold air kept Jack's grip on his cousin's waist firm.

"It's f . . . f . . . freezing!" he chattered.

Petros was concentrating on keeping a hold of the mane, and didn't turn round.

The air was so cold that Jack's eyes dried as soon as he opened them. He could feel ice starting to form on his nose, but didn't dare release his grip to wipe his face.

"How d'we know where we're going?" he eventually shouted at Grey Wolf.

"The horses know it's south; but you'll have to let me know when we get there."

But I've never flown to Edinburgh from the north before!

Jack's panic slowly settled, and he began to calculate.

Edinburgh to Claville last year took us about thirty minutes (and I thought that was cold!) . . . This is maybe a third of the distance . . . faster horses, but they don't know where they're going . . .

"It'll take ten minutes!" he shouted back. "We must keep the coast beneath us."

Jack forced himself to keep his eyes open, but he had to blink every second or two to stop his eyes drying out.

After seven or eight minutes Jack saw the firth.

"I recognise those bridges! We're nearly there! That's Arthur's Seat ahead."

Grey Wolf steered the horses towards the great volcanic outcrop overlooking Edinburgh, and brought the horses down to the field beneath it. They seemed none the worse for their flight.

Jack had expected the ground temperature to be warmer than the icy air above; but with a sinking feeling he realised: *This is what Kildashie cold is!*

It took Jack several moments before he could prise his frozen fingers from Petros' belt.

"That was fun!" exclaimed Cleo. She had emerged from the protection of Grey Wolf's blanket looking a lot warmer than Jack felt.

"Look, Jack," said Petros, as he rubbed his hands together, "me and Cleo will have a look around the human spaces. I promise we'll be OK. We'll meet you by the statue opposite St Giles' at eleven, yeah?"

With a sense of misgiving, Jack watched as Petros and Cleo set off towards the city centre.

They'd better not get found out . . .

"So," said Grey Wolf, "where do we find Caskill?"

A screech came from high above them.

"What in Tua's name is that?" screamed Jack as a great winged beast swooped down towards Arthur's Seat.

"It's a skoffin," replied Grey Wolf; "a dragon from the ice lands."

"What's it got in its claws?"

Whatever it was, it was soon plummeting to earth as the skoffin released its grip. There was a thud as a body fell onto an overhanging rock shelf near the summit of Arthur's Seat. The skoffin screeched, and soared away.

The body stirred, then sat up; but there were a dozen smaller creatures running towards it. The nearest one threw its cap at the body, and there was a roar of pain as the gory missile hit home.

I know that sound.

"It's Caskill!"

30

Temptation

"Those others are not there to greet him," said Grey Wolf. "What are they?"

"Dunters," replied Jack, with a sinking feeling in his stomach. "Red Caps. They're vile."

"There's no time to get the horses. Climb on my back."

Jack did as he was told, and was amazed at how quickly and smoothly Grey Wolf bounded along. It took only a few minutes to clamber up the slope, covered in ice as it was . . .

We've got to get to Caskill before they kill him!

. . . but even as they neared the top the situation looked hopeless. Caskill, covered in gore, had managed to force the Dunters back from the edge, and was scrambling for the frost-covered summit to give himself the advantage of height. But the Dunters' aim with their blood-soaked caps was too much for him, and he swung wearily at the small creatures which now pursued him up the hill. Several dead or stunned Dunters lay sprawled on the ground, but there were just too many of them. One leapt at Caskill, and began to claw at the charmstone in his chest.

Jack leapt from Grey Wolf's back, thrust out his right wrist and took aim.

"*Absango!*"

A bolt hit the Dunter square in the back. It disappeared without a sound.

If Jack was impressed with this, he was stunned at Grey Wolf's response. Retrieving the slimmest of bows from under his blanket, the Cree fixed a needle-fine arrow in place and let fly. *Ffffit!* In two seconds he had repeated the feat. Two Dunters fell dead.

Taken by surprise, their comrades turned round, and aimed their gory bonnets at the two arrivals.

"*Absango!*"

Jack was gratified to see another Dunter vanish. More fell as Grey Wolf's arrows found their mark.

We might just be in time to save Caskill after all!

Jack took aim again.

"*Absa . . .*"

The Dunter threw down a hex-stone . . .

"*Tarditas!*"

. . . and Jack's voice froze. In fact, everything froze.

Jack stepped beside his frozen body, and looked at it. His right arm was raised, and his mouth was open. But he looked like a statue . . . and so did Grey Wolf and the Dunter . . . and Caskill – frozen in the act of falling to the ground.

Jack racked his brains. What kind of a hex was this?

"It's quite simple." The voice was husky; the words spoken slowly. "The Dunter has stopped time."

Jack felt sick.

It can't be!

But when the grey-cloaked figure emerged from the mist, he knew it was.

"Ye're the one who brought back my sand timer after that Brashat wretch stole it."

The Grey advanced on Jack's disembodied figure.

Am I imagining this?

"I see ye do not have my sister's ring with ye; a shame. But yer determination shows ye have talent. I have watched yer progress these months, and would mak ye an offer."

In a second the Grey had advanced on Jack and scooped him up in her arms. Sweeping him up to a crest that looked over a colourless Edinburgh, she sat him down.

"I could use yer talents. Bring me the map and the ring, and I will give ye power and riches beyond yer wildest dreams!"

She waved her arm over the city, instantly transforming it into a bright colourful metropolis. Wealthy people paraded along fine avenues, displaying their opulence.

"Ye and the Kildashie can have the Shian world; and even the wealth of these humans will be yours if ye will join me."

To have as much as I could ever want . . .

A series of images flitted through Jack's mind. His family, living in grand style; the best food and clothes; Petros could even have all the human gadgets he wanted . . .

No; something's wrong. Jack shook his head, trying to clear his thoughts.

"And not just riches." The Grey swept her arm over the

cityscape again, and buildings shone in the warm sunlight. Jack felt the chill leave his bones, and a snug sense of wellbeing filled him.

"A life of comfort awaits."

The vision was so enticing. To be warm again, to shake the winter off . . . He *was* warm!

"All Shian creatures will be your servants; even the Kildashie will be at yer beck and call. Only give me the map and the ring, and pay me homage."

A candle ignited in Jack's brain. *No: if the Kildashie are still around the sunshine won't come back! And the Grey's . . . evil.*

Jack felt an eagle soaring overhead . . . He imagined it, claws outstretched, flying at the skoffin.

"No!"

The blow hit Jack right under the rib cage, knocking the breath out of him. Frozen again, he fell to his knees, gasping. He was aware of a succession of *Ffffts* as he merged back into his body, and looked up to see Grey Wolf despatch the last three Dunters.

The ground in front of them was littered with Dunters. Lying in a series of grotesque poses, each body displayed a fine arrow shaft. But near the very summit of Arthur's Seat, Caskill had fallen sideways, and was breathing slowly. Foul-smelling burns festered where the bloody caps had found their mark.

A low exhalation escaped, a throaty grunting sound.

"Caskill!" shouted Jack.

There was a flicker, and Caskill peered up. For a moment he didn't seem to see Jack. Then a smile spread across his face.

" 'Talis." He indicated the charmstone which now hung by a mere thread.

"That's right; I taught you that. But why did the skoffin bring you here?"

The giant's great fist patted the charmstone.

"'Talis. Dunte' wan'."

Grey Wolf now removed the amulet from around his own neck, and showed this to Caskill. As the giant saw the crescent moon shape, he smiled again. Then he winced in obvious pain. The stench from the burning flesh caught Jack's nostrils afresh, and he retched.

"No good." The giant rested his head down on the ground, and breathed heavily. "Die now."

Before Jack could stop him, Caskill reached for his charmstone, and tore it off. Pressing it into Jack's hands, he closed his eyes.

"Uuuuh."

A last throaty exhale; then nothing.

"He has been gathered up," said Grey Wolf. "We must encase him here."

He took out a small stone from a pouch, and laid this next to Caskill's body. Then he pulled Jack away.

"Sepelio!"

The ground beneath the giant subsided, and enveloped his great carcass. Almost as quickly, the earth sealed over him, finally ending the stench of putrid flesh. Just the outline of the giant's body remained visible.

"Your knife."

Grey Wolf indicated Trog's knife, still strapped to Jack's calf. Taking the steel blade, Grey Wolf strode to one of the dead Dunters, and sliced off his ear. He wrapped the gruesome relic in one of the caps before stuffing it into his pouch.

"These will show Magnus that the Unseelie have attacked Caskill."

"You mean Caskill's Norse?"

"His ancestors were." Grey Wolf looked round at the scattered Dunters. "We will need to remove these bodies."

He put his fingers to his lips and whistled. Moments later, three huge buzzards descended, and scooped the Dunter bodies up in their great talons. As the birds flew off silently, Grey Wolf eyed Jack curiously.

"I think you saw something here?"

Jack pondered this. What had he actually seen? It was like a dream . . .

"I had a memory of the Grey."

"That Red Cap threw a hex stone. It blinded me for a moment; then I killed him."

"A moment? We were talking for ages." Jack paused and thought. "She said something about stopping time."

"Then our quest is urgent. You have the charmstone?"

Jack showed the amulet to Grey Wolf. It was strange to think of the journey this charmstone had had since Gilravage had taken it from the 'laird' in Nebula.

"Let us go and find the others."

Grey Wolf set off down the slope, but while the bigger and much stronger Cree made light work of the descent, Jack found this hard. He stumbled and slipped several times as he tried to keep up. When they were both finally at the bottom, Jack stopped.

"I need to get my breath back," he gasped. A stitch in his side felt like it would split him open; but at least he was warm – despite the frost. Grey Wolf looked on in amusement.

When his heart rate had slowed down, Jack took in his surroundings.

"Cos-Howe's not far from here. I wonder how Cosmo and the others are getting on."

"We heard of Cos-Howe. Where is the gate?"

"That way." Jack indicated a path. "Past the human streets."

As the two left the comfort of the Shian space, Jack felt what was by now an unfamiliar sensation: rising up to human height.

Nearing the streets by Cos-Howe, they could see a few humans, well wrapped up against the snow.

"It's just up here."

Jack became increasingly confident as they got nearer the street which contained the secret entrance to Cos-Howe, but as they turned the corner into it he stopped and put his arm across Grey Wolf's chest. The muscles beside his eyes were twitching furiously.

"There's Shian nearby. They must be Kildashie." The two turned round and retraced their steps for a short distance.

"What d'you think?" Jack asked. "Should we try again?" He peered down the street.

A whistle from behind him made Jack spin round, and he just caught sight of a figure in a doorway.

"Jack! It's me!"

"Oobit?"

"You walked right past me!"

You're that skinny now you were easy to miss!

"I never saw you. How'd you get out?"

"There's another gate – the Kildashie are too stupid to find it. They can't work out why we haven't run out of food, but we've managed to find supplies – until now, anyway." Oobit shivered.

"We're all at Novehowe, with the NorShian."

"I know. The two Kildashie who got away really scared Boreus when they said what had happened. He's talking about pulling all his men in to defend Edinburgh."

"How many are there?"

"At least 100, split between the castle and guarding Cos-Howe. They're cocky, though, and stupid. They're drunk half the time; and they fight each other when they're bored. Without the Thanatos they wouldn't amount to much. Who's your pal?"

"I am Grey Wolf. We came because Caskill was in trouble."

Oobit and Grey Wolf exchanged greetings.

"Is Caskill OK?"

"The Dunters killed him. They were after his charmstone, but we got it." Jack showed Oobit the amulet.

"I heard about the charmstone. The Dunters would've given it to the Kildashie; crawlers. It's good you got it."

"How d'you hear about it?"

"Oh, we've got a spy in the square. But Cos-Howe can only last a few more days, Jack. It's getting hard for us to find food." He looked warily up the road, and rubbed his hands up and down his arms.

"Are the Kildashie going to try and get the Destiny Stone on Hogmanay?"

"Aye; they're planning a big celebration. We might've taken them on, only they've had Thanatos guarding Cos-Howe too. We can't tackle *them*."

"We heard what happened to Ploutter."

"He nearly made it, too. The Thanatos are vicious. They're only helping the Kildashie because they think they'll get the Chalice. The Kildashie told them it can stop death."

"And they believed that?!"

"They're desperate. You know they're nine-tenths dead? It means they don't fear those who are alive. But anything that might stop them going to Sheol is worth a try."

"Sheol? You mean Shian hell?"

"It's the worst punishment of all. Most of them know they'll not survive that – being nearly dead already."

"So who can defeat them?"

"The righteous dead, Cosmo says. Whatever that means."

"Like the ghosts at Dunvik? The Brashat didn't believe the ghosts would last after Hallows' Eve."

"We'd need an army of righteous ghosts – and I don't know where we'd get that in Edinburgh. Anyway, the main thing is to stop the Kildashie by Hogmanay. What're the chances of an attack by then?"

"Well, we've got McCools, and the Nebula crew up in Novehowe. There's Cree too, and we're trying to get the fjordsmen. Is it true the Kildashie have the Tassitus charm?"

Oobit looked at Jack in amazement.

"Tassitus? Of course not. They've worked out something worse, though: they've got the Tarditas hex. With that they can freeze time while they attack."

That's what the Dunter used on me!

"Is that how they attacked the Congress?"

"They were just practising then. They're boasting they'll have it perfected by Hogmanay, and then they'll take the Destiny Stone. It won't be lack of food that kills us if they get that."

"We'll be back by Hogmanay," said Jack firmly. "Say Happy Christmas to Cosmo for me, yeah? We've got to find my sister and Petros now – I don't want them getting scared because we're late."

"I'll tell Cosmo you're asking after him. You know the low roads are open today?"

"We came by horse; the low road wouldn't work."

"It's definitely working now. See you soon. I've got to find some food."

Oobit ran furtively up the street, and was lost to sight as he rounded a corner.

"Come on, the High Street's up here." Jack set off up towards the Royal Mile, along streets that were eerily quiet.

"This big city is not so busy," said Grey Wolf as they neared the Finisterre café bar.

"It's Christmas Day – most people are indoors."

They crossed the North Bridge intersection, encountering a few cheery human stragglers who wished them a happy Christmas.

"That's St Giles' up there," said Jack as a crowd of humans emerged from the cathedral.

"Jack!"

A shout from across the street.

"It's Petros," said Jack, starting to cross the road. "Hey, where's Cleo?"

Petros looked near to tears.

"I've lost her."

31
Thanatos Execution

Jack felt his stomach lurch.

Dad's going to kill me . . .

"Where did you last see her?" demanded Grey Wolf.

"In the New Town. I went to look at a shop window, and when I looked round she'd gone."

"I knew we shouldn't have brought you!" shouted Jack.

"It's not my fault," retorted Petros. "She wandered off."

"Shh! We must not draw attention to ourselves – there may be Unseelie spies," said Grey Wolf, looking around cautiously. "I will find her. Show me which direction you went. Her scent will be on the air."

"You mean you can smell her?"

"I'll feel her presence. But you must both get away: they will be missing you in Novehowe."

"I can't go back without my sister," said Jack.

"It's too dangerous to stay here. There's Unseelie about, I can sense them."

"They wouldn't have taken Cleo, would they?" asked Petros unhappily.

Grey Wolf shook his head. "She's human size; and she's used to blending in. The Unseelie won't realise who she is. Don't worry: I'll find her."

"We were about half a mile over there," said Petros, leading the others part way down the Mound, and indicating a section of Edinburgh's New Town. "You'll find her, yeah?"

"I will. And Jack: show this to Magnus." Grey Wolf untied the pouch from around his waist and handed it over.

Jack grimaced as he thought of what was inside.

"I'll bring the mustangs back. Your friend said the low road was working again – use that – and take this." Grey Wolf handed the invisibility bonnet to Petros.

"I don't fancy hanging around here any longer," said Petros.

You wait 'til my dad gets you, thought Jack. *Mind you, he'll kill me too . . .*

Grey Wolf set off quickly towards the New Town while Jack and Petros retraced their steps back up the Mound. Turning right, they headed for the castle esplanade.

"We'd better use the bonnets now," said Jack firmly.

"I know," replied Petros testily, "I'm not stupid."

Stupid enough to lose Cleo, thought Jack, but he knew better than to voice this.

Both youngsters placed the green bonnets on their heads, and disappeared from view. The esplanade was silent as the pair made their way to the Shian gate in the corner. Jack walked slightly faster than his cousin, and when Petros joined him on the gate Jack grabbed his shoulder.

"*Effatha!*"

The gate swung open. An icy blast hit them as they emerged gasping for breath at the top of the Shian square.

Kildashie cold again!

"There's no one about," whispered Jack. "Look: they've smashed half the square's crystals."

"I can see that." Petros peered into the gloom. "Let's get out of here." He started to march down towards the foot of the square.

"Wait a minute; I want to see what they've done to our house."

There were lights on in the house, but there was no sign of anyone as Jack approached. He crept up to the front window, and peered in.

Doxer!

Instinctively, Jack shrank down out of sight; then realised that this was ridiculous.

I'm invisible: he can't see me.

Jack raised his head again and looked in. Doxer was facing the window, right enough; and carrying a tray of drinks, which he offered to those seated.

That's Boreus!

The Kildashie leader was indeed sitting there, with several other figures in dark robes, their heads covered by cowls.

They must be Thanatos . . .

Facing them was a sorry-looking figure.

It looks like Freya's dad!

Involuntarily, Jack gripped the windowsill.

Just then Doxer looked up and stared out of the window. Again, Jack sank down.

But he can't see me!

Jack checked his green bonnet was still firmly on, then risked another look in, and saw that Boreus had risen from his chair.

"What is it?" demanded the Kildashie as he approached the window. "Is there someone there?"

Crouching down again with his back to the wall, Jack held his breath. He was sure he could feel Boreus standing there, just on the other side of the window.

Jack had counted to twenty before he allowed himself to exhale slowly.

I'm getting out of here!

As quietly as he could, Jack crept down to the house at the foot of the square.

"Where'd you get to?" hissed Petros angrily. "It's too dangerous to play silly sods."

"Well, you should know," Jack retorted.

There was a sound of a door slamming, and a man crying as blows rained down.

"What's happening up there?"

Jack risked a look.

"It's Festus – Freya and Purdy's dad. The Thanatos have got him."

Petros looked round from the shelter of the wall, and instantly wished he hadn't. The sight of someone you know being sliced by a Thanatos sword is not something you want to dwell on. He retched, and fell backwards.

They're doing the Kildashie's dirty work for them again, thought Jack as he dragged his cousin onto the low road mound.

"*Wind flock Novehowe!*"

The flight down had been cold; but at least it had been smooth. Jack and Petros were caught up in a whirlwind ride as they were whisked along the low road. The spinning, whirling, howling was worse than Jack could remember, even on the worst trip to Keldy. Jack clenched his teeth, and kept his eyes shut, praying that the moaning howl in his ears would go away. At the same time he felt as if he was about to be attacked . . .

Please, let us just get back to Novehowe safely . . . .

Jack's stomach heaved, and he thought he would vomit, but gradually the spinning slowed, and he dared to open his eyes.

We're over water . . .

With a lurch, they came to a standstill beside the stone circle. A fine rain was falling. Jack gasped for breath.

"That wasn't so bad," said Petros.

Jack's eyes narrowed as he looked across at his cousin.

He nearly fainted back there. He's just saying it to wind me up.

"Let's find Magnus." Jack set off for the tumulus.

By the time they reached it they were soaked and cold, and were happily anticipating the tumulus' warmth. But as they passed through the door, however, their reception was distinctly frosty.

"Where the hell have you been?"

Phineas' voice cut through Jack and Petros. Jack halted in his tracks.

"We . . . I mean I . . . We went to help Caskill."

"And where is Cleo?"

Jack looked across at Petros, but his cousin was finding the floor very interesting, and did not return eye contact.

"Grey Wolf's bringing her back. She wandered off in Edinburgh."

"You mean you lost her? In a city she has never been to before, a city crawling with Kildashie?"

Jack willed Petros to say something, but Petros was sticking to silence.

After an awkward pause, Jack continued, "But we've found out useful stuff. And Grey Wolf asked me to give this to Magnus. It's important."

Jack untied the pouch, and showed this to his father. Phineas beckoned one of the NorShian, and whispered urgently in his ear. The man left, and returned a few moments later with Magnus.

"Don't think I've finished with you yet," Phineas hissed as Magnus sat down.

"Please Magnus, Grey Wolf said to give you this." Jack tipped out the gory contents onto a table. "Caskill's dead; but he gave me this before he died." Jack showed the amulet.

Magnus inspected the charmstone first, then glanced at the Dunter's cap and the severed ear.

"I gather you have been to Edinburgh. What would take Caskill so far from his home to such a place?"

"Grey Wolf thinks the Kildashie heard about the amulet; and they got a dragon from the ice lands to kidnap Caskill and take him to Edinburgh."

"The Kildashie are using skoffins?!"

"There was only one; it flew away after it dropped Caskill. The Dunters were waiting for him. Grey Wolf and me got rid of them, but they'd already hurt Caskill badly . . . He died."

Magnus turned the charmstone over in his hand, and for a while said nothing. When he spoke, his voice sounded heavy.

"Do you know the meaning of this symbol?"

Jack shook his head. "I saw it on your season-wheel."

"The crescent moons are back-to-back: as the old moon dies the new moon is born; and so time moves on. If the Kildashie went to so much trouble to get this charmstone, then it appears that they do after all wish to halt the seasons."

"Why's that?"

"Because if all the charmstones and season-wheels are destroyed, then time will stop." Magnus looked across at the season-wheel which hung from the wall. "This is no longer a far-off problem."

"Grey Wolf told me that Caskill's ancestors were Norse."

"They were. And our Norse friends will be vexed at this news. Karl, go now urgently to the fjords. Tell our friends that the Unseelie have killed Caskill, and that they wish our winter to remain forever."

Karl nodded, and set off immediately.

"And have you other news for us?" asked Magnus.

"We saw Festus – one of our neighbours in the square. The Thanatos killed him."

"I trust you realise how dangerous it was to go to Edinburgh, then?"

"We saw one of the Cos-Howe men too," said Jack, keen to change the subject. "They can't hold out much longer. The Kildashie have the Tarditas hex – it means they can freeze people while they attack."

"The Tarditas?" Armina spoke up. "That does not freeze people – it freezes time."

"That's what I meant; it's how they attacked the Congress. You didn't hear them coming because they'd frozen time. And now they're going to use the Tarditas to get the Destiny Stone – at Hogmanay."

Magnus sat thoughtfully for a moment.

"Our hand is forced; we have no choice now," he said finally. "With this new evidence I am sure that the fjordsmen will come. You must be hungry; go through and eat. But tell me first: why did Grey Wolf not return with you?"

Jack shuffled his feet.

"He's . . . bringing Cleo back in a while."

"You mean you lost her."

Jack didn't reply.

"Grey Wolf would not have stayed unless he was sure he would find her. Now go and eat. The next few days will be busy."

As Jack went through to the kitchen, Phineas followed him.

"Jack, there's no sense in us arguing now. We must be united against the Unseelie. And if what you said about Cos-Howe is true, then things are truly urgent."

"Oobit said there were 100 Kildashie in the city; how many Norsemen d'you think will come?"

"I am sure Magnus knows what is needed. But we have others to worry about too: there's the Unseelie in the west; and the Thanatos."

"Oobit said the Thanatos don't fear the living."

"So?"

"Well, they might not like ghosts, then. We used them at Dunvik last year, when we beat Briannan."

"Even with the Norse ghosts to help them, Comgall and his monks would be no match for the Thanatos, Jack. Those ghosts could be called because of their link to the Chalice. We need something on a completely different scale here."

There was a crash as several McCools fell through the door.

"'Scuse us!" hiccupped Enda. "We found some more friends out there."

Dermot and the other Irishmen who had been left with the boats entered noisily.

"That Connemara Mary is a fine woman," sang Dara. "What a voice."

Phineas strode over and accosted Enda.

"The attack on Edinburgh is on. Sober your men up, and call for more help. The Norsemen have been sent for; we'll need every ally we can get."

Enda looked inquisitively at Phineas, then at Jack.

"Ye've been off enjoying yerself, haven't ye? Ye were meant to come with us this mornin'."

"Caskill's dead."

Enda stopped in his tracks.

"Ah now, I'm truly sorry to hear that. I liked the old rascal."

"He was killed for his charmstone. We gave it back to him, and somehow the Kildashie found out."

"I know Telos caused you problems on Nebula; but he was never out of our sight there. I'm certain he never contacted the Kildashie."

"Jack's not suggesting that one of your men betrayed him," said Phineas.

Jack looked away and shrugged. "Somebody must've."

"Ye may speak the truth. But it could have been Saorbeg from Nebula; or any one of a hundred spies the Kildashie have over the islands. Watch yer mouth, lad: a careless tongue will land ye in trouble."

"He's already in trouble," said Rana, who had heard the

argument and come in to see what was up. "He's stolen our invisibility bonnets; and he's left Cleo with the Kildashie."

"She's not with the Kildashie!" shouted Jack, his face reddening.

"No, she's not." Grey Wolf stood in the doorway. "And she's some news for you."

32
Preparations

Phineas was first over to the doorway. He clasped Cleo to his chest.

"Never run off like that again."

"I did not run off. I heard singing and I went to see; when I looked around, Petros was gone."

"It doesn't matter," said Phineas. "You're safe."

"Where d'you get to?" demanded Petros.

"I saw Italian flags, and I looked in; it was a restaurant. When I spoke in Italian, they invited me in."

"You mean you can eat that human food?" said Lizzie.

"I am used to that. They were nice people: a big family, together for Christmas. I said I was lost, and they gave me food. But afterwards, when they said they would call the police, I ran out."

"She wasn't hard to find, out in the open," said Grey Wolf. "But tell them, Cleo, what the humans told you."

"All the changes in the weather, the summer floods, and the winters that are warm then freezing – they're worried. They know it's not right."

"It's pollution," said Jack. "Daid told us, in one of his lessons."

"These changes happen in the human world too," said Grey Wolf, "when the balance with nature is lost. The Kildashie are like many humans – what you call *infama*."

"So the Kildashie hate the humans; but they're just like them?" said Jack.

"They have no respect. They believe they are masters of their world, not part of it. They will pay for their foolishness."

"Then we must make them pay." Grandpa Sandy had now joined the group. "The low road has allowed us to make contact with many friends, and they are on their way to help us."

"What about Ilanbeg?" squeaked Lizzie. "Can we go and see Mum?"

"Not until all the Shian areas are safe. Maybe once we secure Keldy, they can go there. You will be pleased to know that your Uncle Hart is restored to health; he will lead them. Others from Nebula and Lyosach will take on the Unseelie in the west."

"So the counter-attack's on, then?" Jack felt his heart racing.

"We have no choice. The Kildashie will try to get the Stone on Hogmanay. So: we must prepare. Today, we celebrate; tomorrow, we prepare for the fight. We will restore the Congress to its rightful place."

There was a cheer from the assembled crowd as Grandpa Sandy took his seat. The atmosphere in the chamber was hopeful, exuberant, joyful. Jack smiled.

If the Nebula crowd take on the western Unseelie, all we've got to worry about is Kildashie with the power to control time; and a fight to the death with Thanatos. Simple.

As the midwinter festivities gathered pace, so more arrivals appeared. The Lyosach took themselves off with Iain Dubh and the Nebulans to plan the western front. More McCools arrived and engaged in deep conversation with Enda and Dara about how they would recapture the border lands from the Dunters. Elle-folk and pisgies were marshalled into squads that would fetch supplies and carry messages as the various units dispersed. But best of all was the news that the 'friends from the fjords' would be arriving in a couple of days.

This news sealed the change in the atmosphere at Novehowe. Nearly 100 Norsemen – cousins of the Novehowe NorShian, but somehow more feared; more to be respected.

"Why do the Kildashie fear the Norsemen?" asked Jack of his father when they strolled outside the tumulus in the chilly dawn of Boxing Day.

"Because the Norsemen nearly wiped them out. They attacked the coastal areas, where the Kildashie were strong. But the Norsemen didn't go inland, so the Brashat escaped."

"So the Brashat just finished the Kildashie off after the Norsemen left?"

"Aye, the Brashat banished the Kildashie to their islands, but the Kildashie knew it was the Norsemen who'd nearly wiped them out. That memory lingered: what they feared most over the centuries was the Norsemen's return. You should ask Murkle . . ."

Jack looked at his father. Phineas gulped, and swallowed hard.

"That just came out. It's hard to remember sometimes that he's dead."

Jack started to feel sorry for his old Shian tales tutor. He couldn't claim to have ever liked him; but to have been bled by those Boabans . . . *Ugh!*

"Have you heard?" asked Ossian as Jack approached. "We're going to take the low road to Edinburgh, and get those Kildashie out."

"Not everyone," said Petros. "I heard Enda telling Dara the McCools and Lyosach will go and split up the western Unseelie."

"Dara says they fight each other given half a chance," added Jack.

"I can't wait to get tore into those Kildashie," said Ossian with relish. "Travel's all very well; but it's time to go home now."

Petros wrinkled his nose.

The optimistic atmosphere changed with the arrival of the 'fjordsmen' two days later. Harald quickly took charge, and impressed on everyone (but especially Magnus) that they all had the fight of their lives to come. Harald pointed out that the Kildashie would not simply melt away when faced with a Norse attack: they'd had over 1,000 years to get over that particular hang-up.

After the initial greetings and discussions, Harald summoned Jack.

"We have heard of your recovery of the *Mapa Mundi*. I should like to see it."

Jack looked nervously at his father, but Phineas just smiled back, nodding. Jack tugged Tamlina's ring loose, and unwound the flag from his neck. The Elfting leader inspected it carefully.

"But the circles are blank – they show nothing!"

"Only Jack has ever been able to make it work," explained Grandpa Sandy.

Harald looked pensive, then handed it back. "Perhaps you would show me?"

Jack flicked the *Mapa* into the Sphere. For a few moments there was nothing to see, then figures formed within the two circles.

"It's me, and the *Mapa*," said Jack. "With the rest of you in the great hall in Edinburgh castle."

Phineas looked over his shoulder.

"It's true: Jack's there with the rest of us. And there's bodies on the floor."

"Then he is clearly meant to be part of this army," concluded Harald, "although I doubt the wisdom of taking a boy on this quest."

Jack bridled. *A boy? I'll be fourteen in a few months!*

"The map never lies," said Phineas calmly. "It has often shown us our true path."

Harald consulted with some of his lieutenants, then shrugged his shoulders.

"It is not unheard of for a boy to come to war; at least, back in the old days."

"And he will bring the *Mapa* with him," stressed Phineas. "Who knows when it may be useful?"

"Have you any idea of how dangerous that is?" roared Harald. "To take the treasure that the Kildashie seek right into their stronghold?"

"The *Mapa* shows us our true path: we cannot succeed without it. And only Jack can make it work."

Harald paused briefly. "Very well; but the boy and the *Mapa* must stay in the rear, and you are responsible for them."

While the atmosphere over the next couple of days could not be said to be light-hearted, the new arrivals certainly galvanised everyone. About 100 strong, they swamped Novehowe. Jack and the others found themselves training in a dim recess with Finbogie as the much bigger (and better armed) Norsemen went through their paces.

"Have you seen their sceptres?" gasped Lizzie as she watched a squad of Norsemen training. "They're the most powerful ones ever."

"They're the Elfting army – that's like our Congress," said Jack. "Only there's more of them over there."

"They don't mind the cold, do they?" Rana shivered as she joined her sister outside to watch the display.

"That's just as well. Edinburgh's freezing." Jack shuddered at the thought of his recent trip.

"Good news," announced Harald, emerging from the tumulus. "The Kildashie have pulled back from Keldy – it's undefended."

"Are you sure?" asked Rana.

"Certain. We sent some men down there, and they say the Kildashie have pulled in all their men to Edinburgh. They're planning a big celebration on Hogmanay."

"So Mum can get as far as Keldy?" asked Lizzie hopefully.

"If Keldy is undefended, then there's nothing to stop her."

"Does that mean the other Unseelie will still fight?" asked Rana.

"Once they see the Kildashie have abandoned them, most of the Unseelie won't be hard to tackle. You've seen how bold the Nebulans are now with their flag and the Gusog feather."

"So Edinburgh's all we've got to worry about?" asked Jack.

"My fjordsmen can take the Kildashie on, but we'll not underestimate them: they're well-trained, and used to the cold."

This could not be denied; but doubts gnawed away at Jack's mind.

"What about the Thanatos?"

"Nobody really knows what they'll do. But if the Kildashie use the Tarditas hex to take the Stone at Hogmanay, we can't afford to wait. Has Finbogie trained you well?"

Jack eagerly explained the manoeuvres that Finbogie had passed on to the youngsters, the girls included.

"We cannot let these girls come to Edinburgh," said Harald emphatically. "A war is no place for girls."

"That's not fair!" shouted Rana. "We've been training the same as Jack and Petros; and we were at the battle at Dunvik."

"I heard your father kept you away from the fighting," stressed Harald. "You shall go to Keldy. When Edinburgh is secure, you can join us." He turned on his heel and swept away before Rana or Lizzie could mount a challenge.

"He's right, you know," said Jack. "It's going to be tough in Edinburgh."

"Then why are you going?" retorted Rana. "You're still not old enough to use a sceptre."

"I can make the Sphere work," said Jack simply. "And Finbogie's taught me enough counter-hexes – they'll keep me right."

"It's still not fair. They're taking Armina and Arvin, and they don't fight."

"I want to see my dad," added Lizzie.

"Gettin' excited?" asked Ossian as he approached. "I can't wait to get at those Kildashie."

"Harald says we can't go to Edinburgh," moaned Rana.

"He's right, though. His men are goin' to get the worst of it. There's no point bein' there if you can't fight."

"We'll see," replied Lizzie.

"What about Magnus?" asked Jack.

"He's comin' with me to Cos-Howe. Him and Harald don't get on, you can tell. They're better apart."

"So it's fjordsmen and Cree against the Kildashie?"

"Don't forget the Thanatos," added Jack. "But we've got Dad and Grandpa and the others."

Things at least seemed straightforward when Harald read out the attack plan: his men and the Cree would attack the castle, while Ossian and Magnus went to relieve Cos-Howe. The Lyosach and Nebulan forces were to free the west, while the McCools would liberate the border lands with the Warfrins. Together, it was felt that they could defeat the Red Caps.

"Will the west really be so easy?" asked Jack of Iain Dubh.

"It was only the Kildashie uniting the Unseelie that kept them so powerful, but they're not all one group. In fact, some of the factions there hate each other."

"So you reckon it won't be a problem?"

Iain Dubh smiled. "There's enough Seelie that *will* help us – we'll be all right. Our Gusog feather gives us life in the winter. And the flag from Ardmore is our battle totem."

Jack blushed. "It was Caskill who got your flag back."

"You had to free him from the cave first. No Jack, those of you going to Edinburgh will have a much harder battle – I'm glad you're going to be kept in the rear."

"And who're the Warfrins? Harald said they were going to help the McCools free the border lands."

"They're from the low lands, and they've got some special power against the Red Caps. Thins their blood – something like that."

Jack found it hard to get to sleep that night. The Kildashie were mean, and the Thanatos vicious. Who knew if the newly-arrived Warfrins would help defeat the Red Caps? Or the islands-men defeat the Unseelie? He felt a tight fist in the pit of his stomach: in just over a day it would all be over. They would have recovered the Stone – or be dead.

33

The Edinburgh Coach

Jack was first out of the tumulus, closely followed by Ossian.

"The mustangs were brilliant! We made it to Edinburgh in ten minutes."

Ossian overtook Jack as they raced up to the standing stones, and was there waiting when Jack arrived, panting, his breath visible in the cold still air. Horses whinnied, and some pawed the ground. Others shivered, but Jack guessed it wasn't the cold. They were finally on their way!

As the Seelie army grew, Jack waited irritably. Why was Petros so slow? Surely he wanted to get going?

When Petros finally arrived, Jack could almost feel his lack of enthusiasm.

What's the matter with him? We're about to get our homes back; and he'll see his dad again.

Jack stopped.

He's scared about his dad . . . He thinks what happened to Festus will . . .

A wave of guilt washed over Jack. He had been so excited finally to get going; and at least *he'd* found *his* father . . .

"Come along!" shouted Phineas at the stragglers. "Edinburgh crew over here; Keldy lot – you're over there."

The groups were soon marshalled and mounted, and at a signal from Grey Wolf the Keldy crew cantered, then galloped, and disappeared into the air. Once they were out of sight Grey Wolf signalled to the Edinburgh-bound crew.

It was just as Jack had remembered it from a few days earlier. Gripping Petros' waistband tightly, he felt the sudden rise in height (and fall in temperature) as the freezing winter air whipped his face. He was grateful that this time he had Gilmore's warm cloak. Charmed clothes had a lot going for them.

They were soon in the clouds, and the other horses and riders were lost to view. Jack could only trust that the mustangs knew their way – there were no landmarks in this grey desert. As the intense cold gripped Jack, the memory of the first trip came back to him: it had been no picnic. He tried to concentrate on not falling off.

After several minutes a loud shout from He Who Waits alerted Jack to a change in direction. The flyers were soon in a break in the clouds, and Jack could make out the dim outline of a shoreline below.

"Which coast is it?" he shouted, shaking Petros' waist.

His cousin did not answer, and Jack could only hope that the coastline meant they were nearly there. However, the visibility soon disappeared in another swirl of clouds, and Jack suddenly felt his horse pull to the right.

"What's the matter? What's happening?" Petros had found his voice again.

"I don't know. It was like the horse didn't want to go any further. I think we're heading inland."

They were definitely losing height. The horses, used to travelling together, had wheeled west then north-west as one, and were taking the riders steadily down. This wasn't supposed to be happening. With a sinking feeling, Jack saw the ground get nearer, but his mood changed as familiar sights came in view.

"Hey! That's the River Keldy! I recognise the bridge."

Within minutes the horses had deposited the riders in the field near Ossian's house. While cold, it felt a lot warmer than being in the air – and was nothing like as cold as Edinburgh had been a few days earlier. Jack patted his warm jacket.

Those riders who were supposed to be in Keldy had already dismounted, and were looking in astonishment at the new arrivals.

"What's happened?" demanded Rana. "You were supposed to go straight to Edinburgh."

"Something stopped us," replied Phineas. "When we got to the Forth the horses turned and made for here."

Grandpa Sandy consulted with He Who Waits before turning to the crowd.

"It's a campanilus hex."

"What's that?" demanded Ossian.

"Like a bell hex, only much stronger. The Kildashie must've raised it when they retreated. The horses can't get through; it'll block the low roads too."

"So how are we supposed to get to Edinburgh?" asked Grey Wolf.

"We'll send out scouts and see if it really goes all the way round. If it does, that's good in one sense, because it means the

Kildashie have given up on the rest of the country. But it also means we're stuck."

"You mean we don't have a way in?" asked Iain Dubh incredulously. "I thought Harald was supposed to help us defeat the Kildashie; he can't even get us to Edinburgh!"

Jack felt a buzzing at his neck. His right hand rose and grabbed Tamlina's ring. Hurriedly, he tugged the *Mapa Mundi* from around his neck, and flicked it into the Sphere. The two circles formed, blank – or was it snow? Jack stared hard at them.

They must show us our true path! They must*!*

The snowy picture faded, clearing to show the distinctive outline of Edinburgh Castle in one, and a humans' coach in the other.

Ossian and his parents came down to see us by bus! The Kildashie won't be expecting that.

"We can do it! We'll take the coach the humans use!"

"This is a Shian struggle," asserted Iain Dubh. "Moving into the human sphere will not work."

"This problem will become the humans' if we do not stop the Kildashie," said Jack. "And everyone knows that when *they* have a problem, *we* suffer. In any case, the *Mapa Mundi* always shows our true path."

"Jack's right: the campanilus won't stop a human coach," said Phineas. "It'll take a while, but we should just make it."

"Does that mean we can come?" asked Lizzie hopefully.

"Certainly not. Keldy is safe: you must stay here."

"You were allowed here because the Kildashie had left," added Grandpa; "but here is where you'll stay – for now. The rest of us will go by coach."

"Will that be big enough for us all?" asked Petros.

"We'll have to manage; and there's little chance the Kildashie will be looking at buses," replied Phineas. "They may even be safer than flying in to Arthur's Seat."

"But much slower," pressed Grey Wolf. "We must get to the castle before this evening." He shivered as an icy gust swept down from the hills.

"I've got the invisibility cloaks too," added Gilmore.

Jack hadn't noticed the huge bag his tutor had lugged down from the horse.

"I'll take one," said Ossian. "There's a coach depot not far from here, but they'll all be in use tonight. If I'm invisible, I may be able to borrow one before they all go. Grey Wolf, you come with me."

The two set off at pace, and were soon lost to view.

Time

passed

slowly.

Jack's spirits had risen and fallen with every sound from the path taken by Ossian and Grey Wolf. Had they really come this far, only to fail?

Nine o'clock. Nothing.

Half past. A light rain began to fall.

This is worse than waiting for Caskill at Ardmore!

With an overwhelming sense of relief Jack heard his cousin's voice breaking through the darkness.

"Come on! The coach is over in the human space!"

The Shian crowd quickly made their way along the path until it came to a short tunnel running beneath a railway line.

"Watch out!" shouted Gilmore, as he was sent spinning near the tunnel entrance.

His sack dropped to the ground, and there was a flurry of activity as those around him helped him to his feet. Gilmore grabbed his sack, and dusted himself down.

"I thought it was the Kildashie we were supposed to be fighting," he muttered, starting for the tunnel again.

As he passed through the tunnel, Jack felt himself rise to human height.

"That's me," said Petros as they emerged at the other side. "I'm going back to Keldy."

He turned and started back down the tunnel.

"Hey! What's wrong?" Jack doubled back after his cousin, dodging the crowd coming the other way, and dropping back down to Shian height.

"I can't." Petros had sat down on a rock, breathing heavily. "The Thanatos will kill me."

"It's your dad, isn't it?" spat Jack. "You're scared about what's happened to him. Well, if I can get my dad back from the Grey, you can help rescue yours from Edinburgh."

It was no use: Petros was white as a sheet. Jack could see him replaying his dad's capture – and Festus' death – in his mind. Jack watched him for a moment, then turned on his heel.

When he emerged from the tunnel he could see the crowd boarding a large coach in the car park. Daid stood by the door, a huge smile on his face.

"They could only get one bus. Come on, all aboard."

He's been waiting years to deliver that line, groaned Jack, as he clambered up the steps.

"All right, Jack?" His grandfather sat beside him.

"Won't the campanilus stop the coach?"

"We're human size, Jack – it's the wrong kind of hex.

I'll bet the Kildashie aren't bright enough to work out a back-up."

True enough, the coach passed through the campanilus hex as they crossed the Forth Road Bridge. The air turned noticeably colder too – frost formed on the windows, and Jack could see ice on the road. Winds howled around the coach, which slowed to a near halt as it encountered heavy traffic. The whole world seemed to be descending on the city for Hogmanay.

The coach came to a halt in a side street, double parked over a row of cars. As the door opened a bone-chilling gust swept in, causing gasps of horror. Even Jack winced in surprise: he'd almost forgotten how bitterly cold Edinburgh had been just a few days earlier.

Jack made his way to the door, pulling Gilmore's warm cloak around him. It was tempting to stay inside and just drive off somewhere nice and hot . . .

But we're not going back now . . .

"We won't be using the coach again, will we?" he said as they disembarked.

Grey Wolf looked at him curiously.

"From here on we are Shian. We do not look back."

34

Storming the Castle

The crowds were horrendous – even at midsummer Jack couldn't remember the streets being this crowded. Coupled with the icy roads and the howling wind, walking was a real problem. Almost every other step brought a slip or a stumble. Getting to Edinburgh Castle before midnight looked an impossible task.

On the other hand, Grandpa had been right. In a crowd of thousands, another 100 or so made no difference. Even if the Kildashie spies were out, their chances of being spotted were almost nil. Given the humans' ability to ignore everyone else in a crowd, the Seelie army made its way unobtrusively up to the back of the castle.

"It's not quite so bustly here," explained Phineas as they turned to head up the slope. "And it's a bit more sheltered from the wind."

The shelter, such as it was, came from the castle rock, which loomed high above them.

The sound of distant – but loud – music bounced off nearby

buildings. Sizable human crowds still provided cover, but without the intense pressure of the Princes Street throng. As the group neared the Royal Mile, they divided into two: Magnus and Ossian turned right for Cos-Howe while Harald's sections continued to head uphill. As agreed, Jack followed at the rear with his father, shivering as a fresh gust of snow hit him.

There was no sign of Unseelie, and it was only as they were moving past the crowds up towards the castle gate that Jack got the first inkling that something was up. The crowd was still jostling from every side; but there was an extra jostle that made him shake. This shove felt different. *Meant*, somehow.

"Jack!" a voice hissed. "Will you get us in?"

Jack spun round, trying to identify the source of the voice. He recognised it, sure; but it didn't make any sense.

And then he stopped: *Of course it makes sense. They'll do exactly what they're not supposed to do.*

"Where are you?" he whispered.

"Just behind. Don't let on to Uncle Phineas – he'll go spare."

He's not the only one, thought Jack. *None of the section commanders wanted kids along. I'm only here because they know I can make the* Mapa Mundi *work.*

As the Seelie shuffled up through the human crowd, Jack tried to think how he would explain this one to his father.

. . . I can't, he concluded. *Not if he sees them. The only chance is to keep them hidden.*

But arc lights shone over the esplanade, and Jack suddenly realised that he wasn't hidden himself.

"Dad! That's one of the Kildashie! I think he's seen us."

Phineas saw that Jack was serious, and he pulled Grey Wolf's arm.

"We must take the Shian gate!"

Up ahead, Harald continued on unaware to the main castle gate. The rear section edged through the crowd towards the Shian gate in the esplanade corner.

"*Effatha!*"

The gate groaned as it accommodated this larger-than-usual group, but they landed safely in the darkness of the Shian square. Jack put his arms behind him and checked his cousins were there.

"Did the Kildashie see us come this way?" enquired Grey Wolf.

"I don't think so. The human crowd hid us at the right time."

Indeed, the gloomy Shian square was deserted.

"They've smashed most of the crystals," exclaimed Armina. "Savages."

Through the gloom, one solitary light shone.

"That's my room!" Jack said indignantly as he saw the glow.

"Did ye think your room would not be taken?" snapped Finbogie. "Every space here will have been trashed by the Kildashie. Scum!" He spat.

Jack moved involuntarily towards his house, but was restrained by his father's arm.

"Careful, Jack. It could be a trap."

But Jack wriggled free, and made a dart for his house. He was there in seconds, and had peered in the front window before Phineas could catch him.

"Jack! You could give the whole game away." Phineas dragged Jack around the side of the house.

The peace was disturbed by a commotion from within the

house: indignant shouts, and taunts, followed by a thump–
whump as something (or somebody) fell down stairs. When the
front door opened moments later, it was to reveal a sorry-looking
Doxer, his nose bleeding and his face scratched.

"Pax!" he shouted, as he stumbled forward.

He spoke!

Doxer collapsed in a heap, accompanied by an unmistakeable
peal of laughter.

"Rana!" roared Phineas. "Show yourself now, or I'll blast you
out!"

The threat was enough, and Rana and Lizzie sheepishly
removed their invisibility bonnets.

"How in Tua's name did you get here?!" demanded Phineas, as
Grandpa Sandy approached.

"We missed out on going to Tula!" protested Rana. "And we
want to find our dad."

"Your bravery does you credit," said Grey Wolf. "But these are
not games." He turned to Doxer. "What do you do here?"

Doxer looked nonplussed . . . No: terrified.

"What . . . do . . . you . . . do . . . here?" he echoed.

"Are you trying to be funny?" demanded Grey Wolf.

Doxer looked lost.

"You're helping the Kildashie, aren't you?" Jack accosted him.
"I saw you here the other day – serving drinks to them."

Doxer raised his hands in explanation, but said nothing.

"Is he mute?" enquired He Who Waits.

"No, he shouted when Rana pushed him out," said Jack.

He Who Waits stood in front of Doxer, and made a sign: two
fingers to the lips, and the back of the right hand to left palm.

Doxer nodded.

"He only speaks under duress," explained He Who Waits.

"Ask him what he's doing with the Kildashie," demanded Jack. "I've seen him with them."

He Who Waits signed again to Doxer, who seemed bashful, but signed a reply.

"He says he was captured by them. And he has information about a prisoner. Toonya?"

"Doonya," corrected Sandy. "What does he know?"

"Let us conduct this interrogation indoors," said Phineas. "Others may be in the square."

"Phineas is right," said Grandpa. "Take the young man in and interrogate him. We'll make our way to the Stone."

He Who Waits led Doxer indoors, followed by Jack and his cousins. Phineas followed, shutting the door behind him.

Doxer was led to a chair and made to sit down. Jack glared at his apprentice colleague, trying to work out what he knew. Was he just putting on an act?

He Who Waits pulled up another chair and sat opposite the youngster. Signing to him again, He Who Waits began to relate the story to the others.

"He says the Kildashie and Thanatos are up in the castle. They are waiting for midnight to get the Stone – they believe that is the time that it will become free of the iron rings."

"Then why is he here?" demanded Jack. "Why doesn't he escape?"

He Who Waits signed again.

"He is looking after the prisoner."

"Dad?!" squeaked Lizzie. "Where is he? Is he all right?"

Doxer made to put his hand in his pocket, but Phineas' sceptre was quickly at his throat.

"Easy does it," he said. "What's in your pocket?"

Doxer's eyes grew larger, and his hands began to shake.

"Raglan," he croaked.

"See? If you scare him, he can talk," said Rana with evident satisfaction. "Let me have a go."

"This isn't a game, Rana," scolded Phineas. "Do you have any idea of how worried your mother will be? She's probably in Keldy by now."

"What d'you mean, the Raglan?" demanded Jack.

Doxer indicated his pocket, and as Phineas trained his sceptre on the youngster, Jack reached inside his pocket and retrieved a lump of sandstone.

"It's like the one Stegos brought to Novehowe!" Jack's hand tingled.

"How did you get this?" enquired Phineas. "The Kildashie must know it's missing."

Doxer signed again to He Who Waits.

"He says the Raglan was broken into three pieces – he stole this one."

Jack recalled the missing corner of the Destiny Stone. *So that corner's been broken into three: this one, the one Stegos had; and Boreus must have the other!*

"He says it has kept him alive. The Kildashie do not feed him much, and he has to work long hours. And he has shared it with Doonya."

"What's he know about Dad?" squeaked Lizzie.

"He's kept in the cellar in the house next door," said He Who Waits, as Doxer signed again. "But the guards have all gone up to the hall tonight."

"Well, let's get him," said Rana.

"I'll go," said Phineas. "Doxer will show us the way. The others will need to get up above. It's nearly midnight."

They were just about to leave when Doxer bolted upstairs.

"Get him!" shouted Jack.

He Who Waits bounded upstairs after Doxer, and hauled him down quickly.

"He says he has something for you, Jack."

Doxer proffered a linen bag to Jack, and nodded encouragingly.

"What is it?" demanded Rana.

Jack reached inside and withdrew the vococorn.

"It's the one Tamlina gave you!" exclaimed Lizzie.

Jack cradled the large ram's horn. It had been too bulky to take when they'd had to evacuate the square. But it had summoned the monks and the Norse ghosts at Dunvik: without it they couldn't have defeated the Brashat.

"Tamlina said it would help us to summon allies in our quest," said Jack softly. "But we've got the fjordsmen already. Who else is there?"

Doxer nodded again eagerly.

"We haven't time for this now," noted Phineas. "Grey Wolf, take Jack up above with the others. I'll take the girls to see their father. They can't go up where there's fighting in any case."

The group left the house and parted. Phineas, Rana and Lizzie followed Doxer and He Who Waits next door while Grey Wolf and Jack rejoined the others at the side of the square.

"You took your time," hissed a fjordsman as Jack approached. "And who's the boy?"

"Doxer. I used to work with him, in Gilmore's workshop. He says he's been kept as a prisoner . . ."

"So where's he taking the others?"

"He says Uncle Doonya's locked up next door. Dad's gone to get him."

"We must get up above. Harald will need our help. Jack, you wait here for Phineas and the others."

A sudden feeling of stillness; and silence; then, "Arrp!"

A shout from the foot of the square, and Doxer came running up, his face showing real concern.

"Tarditas! Kildashie . . ."

"What!?"

Doxer tried to explain, but the words came out as a jumble. He Who Waits ran up, and watched as Doxer signed frantically.

"He says the Kildashie have stopped time. It will slow down Harald's men, but not the Unseelie."

"Then there's no time to waste," said Grey Wolf.

The Seelie crew leant up against the rock wall, and at the signal, passed up through the Shian gate to the castle chapel. A freezing wind hit them first, followed by the realisation that something was badly wrong. By the light of several burning torches they could see fjordsmen and Cree sprawled everywhere, while dark-cloaked figures sped among the remaining soldiers, their flashing swords making mayhem.

Jack's heart jumped up his throat. This wasn't supposed to be happening!

The new arrivals had no time to adjust. Caught in the Tarditas hex, they all but froze – even Shian sceptres were easy targets for Thanatos swords, and Jack couldn't even think of counter-hexes. Jack grasped the sandstone lump in his fist, and scrambled to the war memorial porch, then collapsed. The door was bolted shut.

No chance of sheltering inside, then.

The sound of fighting from the great hall reached Jack, and he guessed that Harald and Grandpa had made it that far.

They must've got in before the Tarditas hex could be used . . .

But the castle courtyard before him wasn't a pretty sight. Thanatos were felling the fjordsmen and Cree with indecent ease. The skoffin – no longer tiny – was swooping down and snatching away Seelie soldiers before they could organise and fight back. Even some humans – *unlucky souls: caught up in this –* lay sprawled on the ground, their bodies frozen.

The fight was as good as lost, even if some Seelie had made it into the great hall. Outside in the courtyard the fjordsmen just couldn't get past the Thanatos. A fleeing fjordsman, nearing the shelter of the porch, was felled by a sword blow. He fell before Jack: blood gushed from a head wound, splashing the war memorial steps.

As the blood splattered onto the flagstones, the dark ooze seemed to seep into the stone . . . and the stone groaned, as if it had been injured itself.

Jack's eyes opened wide with disbelief as the Thanatos reeled back.

The stones are speaking!

"Jack!" shouted Grey Wolf frantically as he joined him. "Summon the allies!"

Jack peered blankly for a second. Allies?

Then, without consciously thinking it, Jack reached into his cloak and withdrew the vococorn. Putting it to his lips, he blew steadily.

Nothing: for a few seconds anyway. Then a soft shimmering sound that sped across to the castle's great hall and echoed back again. The wooden door behind Jack creaked open, and two misty figures emerged.

Jack gasped: the door behind him had definitely been bolted. "Who are you?"

"226296, Parker," said one. "You summoned us."

And with that hundreds of wispy figures sped out into the freezing night.

35

Deliverance

The misty figures poured from the war memorial hall. Where each fallen Seelie lay, a figure would swoop down, embracing it. And around each body there was a soft murmuring from the flagstones. The sound got louder and louder, driving the skoffin into the icy air, where it continued to circle around, calling raucously.

The Thanatos, repelled by the swelling sound, fell back into a protective circle in the centre of the courtyard, their swords a blur in front of them. But the misty figures paid little heed: they swept in among the Thanatos like wind through autumn trees. The Thanatos began to fall – soundlessly.

"What are they?" gasped Jack.

"Your allies. Remember you told your father the Thanatos would not stand against ghosts?"

"But he said we couldn't call Comgall."

"That's right: because we'd need an army to defeat the

Thanatos," prompted Grey Wolf. "The ghosts of men who died fighting oppression. This is their memorial."

A righteous army; right.

As shapeless as smoke, as fast as the wind, the ghostly torrent swept through the diminishing Thanatos force, until just three remained. 226296, Parker flew back towards Jack and reformed as a recognisable human shape.

"They are *infama*. They have desecrated our memorial with their executions. We fought against tyranny; now you must do so too. Finish them off."

"He's right," prompted Grey Wolf, handing Jack his sceptre. "Otherwise they will come back to haunt you."

Jack stumbled over towards the trio, who seemed pinned back by the swirling ghostly forms.

"What kind of hex do I use?"

Jack aimed the sceptre, but his mind went blank.

If only Dad was here. Why doesn't he hurry up and bring Uncle Doonya up?

Jack gripped the sandstone lump in his pocket.

It's one of the treasures – or part of one. I've got the Mapa Mundi; *and we retrieved the Chalice. What puts them all together?*

A squawk from above as an eagle swooped down and attacked the skoffin. As it did so, a leather-bound volume dropped to Jack's feet.

It can't be!

But as Tamlina's ring at his throat began to vibrate, Jack knew it was. He saw the letters firmly stamped on the book's front cover, and his mind cleared. All the things Marco and Luka had said . . .

"Your cause is just . . ."

This was the fight against the Unseelie, the instigators of *infama*. Jack flicked the sceptre back to Grey Wolf, and thrust out his right wrist.

"*Gosol!*"

The bolt flew from his hand, a silver glow that quickly encased the remaining Thanatos. With a strangled cry they slumped to the ground, and folded.

The triumph was broken by a resounding clash from within the hall.

"Come on!"

Jack picked up the leather volume, and made for the great hall's doorway. The remaining fjordsmen and Cree were quickly behind him, and they burst into the hall.

A scene of chaos met their eyes. The sign 'Private Function' on the way in hadn't really registered with Jack, but now he understood. Dinner-jacketed men and ballroom-gowned women were frozen at their tables, only most of the tables were tipped over, their contents strewn over the surrounding floor. But if the humans were frozen, the Shian were not. Met by a volley of hexes, Jack dropped the leather volume and dived for cover behind a barricade of upturned tables near the door, where Harald, Grandpa and the others cowered.

Not all had made the shelter of the barricade: many Seelie lay, motionless, on the ground, while the Kildashie fired hex after hex from the far end of the hall. Grandpa put his arm protectively around Jack's back, wincing as a hex flew and splintered the edge of a protecting table.

"Don't your sceptres work?" bellowed Jack above the din.

"A little; but the Tarditas slows us down. The Kildashie are drunk; but even so, they've worked out how to make time work for them. The only thing that's saved us is this." Grandpa showed Jack the Raglan fragment that Stegos had taken to Novehowe.

"I've got Doxer's one, Grandpa."

Jack took the sandstone lump from his pocket. As Grandpa held out his own fragment, the two glowed briefly, then clamped together in his hand, like magnets.

"They've fused!" exclaimed Jack.

"The Stone must want to reform. This gives us more strength."

Jack peered out from beside the barricade.

"Are the humans dead?"

"No – their time is frozen; but not like we do it. The Kildashie want to separate their time and ours."

Another loud crash as a fire hex set alight the splintered debris beside them. Phineas burst in the door, and crouched down instantly beside Jack.

"The girls have got Doonya. He's weak, but he'll live."

Jack looked frantically around.

I'm not sure we will . . .

Harald and his soldiers crouched behind an upturned table, along with the remaining Cree, and even though quite a number of Kildashie had been felled (a result of drunkenly-inspired over-confidence), it still looked like an even contest.

"Stone watchers!" called out Boreus. "Midnight draws on. Rise and see your precious treasure delivered to us!"

An eerie silence descended as the Seelie considered this.

"Is it a trap?" whispered Jack.

"I don't know," said his grandfather, peering out from the side of the barricade.

"Come out and see!" called Boreus. "As midnight approaches, the Stone will appear!"

"They've done it. They've worked out how to get the Stone out of the Stone Room. The power they'll get from that will make them unstoppable," said Harald dejectedly.

Great, thought Jack. *He was supposed to be our trump card.*

"But we've still got the double Raglan fragment," said Grandpa, winking at Jack. He seemed very relaxed, given the situation.

The hexes had stopped, and Jack risked a peek out from the side of the barricade.

"They're not hiding," he hissed.

The Kildashie had emerged from behind their shelters at the far end of the great hall, sceptres still at the ready, but clearly not lacking confidence. Many of them clutched goblets of wine, and staggered slightly.

"I don't trust them," said Phineas. "Stay where you are."

Jack didn't need to be told. His gut was telling him that the Kildashie were what they'd always been: treacherous. And drunk or not, they outnumbered the Seelie force. But for some reason Grandpa Sandy felt bolder than that: he emerged from the side of the barricade, strode to the centre of the hall, then paused.

"What do you want of us?"

"Only your attention while we demonstrate who's in charge," said Boreus, grinning widely.

"Grandpa! Come back!" whispered Jack.

But Grandpa showed no sign of hearing. He advanced another few steps.

"Behold your famous Stone!" cackled Boreus, as twelve chimes sounded.

He pointed his sceptre at the end of the great hall, and fired a bolt. A glow emanated from the fireplace, and slowly the Stone appeared.

There were gasps from the Seelie army, peering out from behind their barricades. The Stone! And without the iron rings at either end! Even Grandpa Sandy seemed perturbed at this. He stepped back briefly, but found himself caught as a dozen or more hexes flew all over the place.

They are *drunk!*

As Grandpa fell sideways, Boreus strode forward and stood over his apparently lifeless body. Then, reaching down into Grandpa's cloak, he withdrew the Raglan fragment. Holding it aloft in triumph Boreus called out, "The fragment stolen from my brother Stegos!"

He withdrew another Stone fragment from within the folds of his own cloak, and held the two pieces. Just as before, the two clamped together.

"See! The Stone re-forms!"

Jack gulped. *If the Raglan and Destiny Stones merge together, then they'll have huge power . . .* He tugged nervously at the *Mapa Mundi* around his neck.

And if they get this, they'll have the full set.

"Now where is the third treasure?" roared Boreus. "Come out, pup, and face your destiny!"

With his back to the barricade, Jack flicked the *Mapa Mundi* into the Sphere. The circles remained blank . . . for ages.

Has the Tarditas hex got to the Mapa *as well?!*

Furtively, Jack peeked around and surveyed the hall.

I've seen this before somewhere . . .

With a sickening feeling Jack realised where. The time the third spiral arm had moved he had witnessed this – and Boreus was about to kill him. Jack stared at the circles again. Slowly the *Mapa Mundi* began to appear in one ... and the King's Chalice ... and the Stone of Destiny, iron rings and all. And in the second circle was Jack, clutching a leather-bound book –

I didn't notice that before ...

– but he wasn't alone. With a stomach-churning sensation Jack saw that the second figure was Boreus, holding a sword. There was no mistaking the message: he tied the flag around his neck once more, and stooped down to pick up the leather volume.

This is what must happen.

"Jack! What are you doing?" hissed Phineas.

"No, Jack," shouted Grey Wolf. "You can't trust them."

But Jack stepped around the side of the barricade, and stood for a moment surveying the scene.

Yup, this is it.

Without the power of the Raglan to counteract the Tarditas, Jack moved slowly forward.

"Grandpa."

The old man's eyes flickered, and he looked up at Jack.

"It's all right Grandpa. You can go back to the others now."

Looking dazed, Sandy stood up. Then, shuffling back towards the remnants of the Seelie army, he collapsed behind the barricade.

"I've failed him," he mumbled.

"Come here, child," ordered Boreus, and Jack took another few hesitant paces towards the Kildashie leader, stepping over a prostrate human. "Give me the Sphere. I know you have it. Isn't that right, boy? Boy?! Where's my wine steward?"

A dishevelled Doxer appeared at the head of the hall and scurried forward holding a goblet, his head bowed. Boreus placed the Raglan on a table, snatched the goblet and drained the contents in a single go. He staggered slightly as he dropped the vessel.

He's drunk too!

Boreus turned round and leered at the hapless Doxer.

Doxer! That snake in the grass! I should never have trusted him!

With his head bowed, it was hard to tell what Doxer was thinking. Jack racked his brains to think of a hex or a curse that would fit, but nothing came to mind. And the Tarditas made every movement painfully slow. He'd never get away with anything. Aware that several Kildashie had their sceptres trained on him, Jack continued to edge forward, but less sure of himself now. The *Mapa's* message had been clear: but why?

"Give me the Sphere, child." Boreus held out his left hand.

Jack hesitated, and saw Boreus turn and strike Doxer hard across the face with the flat of his sword. Doxer fell, howling.

At least he's got his voice back . . .

Kildashie soldiers jostled each other drunkenly.

"The rest of you, throw down your weapons, or the boy gets it!"

There was an uneasy pause behind him while the Seelie army debated this; but then the clatter of swords and sceptres confirmed to Jack that his comrades had indeed surrendered their arms.

"The Sphere, child, or we will kill you all. Did you think you could defeat us once we had the Stone and the Chalice?"

Boreus turned and looked again at the Stone in the fireplace. And now Jack saw the King's Chalice appear beside it. One of the Kildashie lieutenants strode over and grasped the ancient cup, holding it aloft.

"Soon all the Shian treasures will belong to us!" Boreus crowed triumphantly, and picked up his sceptre again in his left hand.

Jack could think of no way out. Miserably, he edged forward.

The Raglan pieces belonged together . . . Just like the treasures belong together . . .

"Kneel, child. I think a fitting deliverance would be to separate your neck from your body."

Jack dropped the leather volume as a hand shoved him roughly down onto his knees. Boreus stood before him, a broadsword in his hand . . .

The Raglan re-formed itself . . . Some things are meant to be together . . . Something binds them together . . .

The sword was raised.

What binds them together?

"No!"

The voice came from behind him . . . His father's voice. Jack glanced behind, and saw Phineas staggering up.

"He saved my life – spare him. I will take his place."

Before Jack could respond, his father had shoved him aside, and was kneeling down.

Boreus looked down on this scene with evident pleasure.

"No matter; and the Sphere shall be ours anyway . . ." He raised the sword again.

He's going to die in my place!

Jack's mind raced back to his vision from Tamlina's ring. He was still kneeling, waiting for the sword to fall, but a voice in his head kept repeating: "And the father shall die for the son . . . the father shall die for the son . . ." He'd opened his eyes then, to stop himself seeing any more.

"Prepare to die, Seelie!"

"No!" Another shout from behind him – only this time it was his grandfather's voice. "I do not deserve to live if my son dies. The father shall die for the son."

Grandpa Sandy now tottered forward, and pulled Phineas back. Awkwardly, he knelt down in front of Boreus.

Jack's mind raced: *which father was going to die for which son? Three generations . . . three treasures . . . Bound together by . . .*

And then another thought flashed, unbidden, through his mind.

The Raglan re-formed itself . . . If it's meant to be part of the Stone, the whole Raglan would fly to the Destiny Stone . . . Unless . . .!

Jack looked at the Stone in the fireplace as the broadsword was raised again.

No rings!

"It isn't the real Stone!"

Jack scrambled to his feet, and stepped forward so that he faced Boreus. With an angry shout Boreus swiped at him with his sceptre, which flew to the ground. Jack stood up, and as Boreus raised the sword again Jack planted himself purposefully in front of his grandfather.

"It isn't the real Stone!" Jack's voice was almost a sneer.

A memory of feverish dreams now swept through Jack . . . What was it he'd heard back in the *cailleach*'s cottage? The creator force? Jack looked down at the leather volume at his feet. John's book; like the ones Marco and Luka had had; and Matthew.

"*Gosol!*"

The word leapt from Jack's mouth before he had even thought of it.

The Kildashie leader gasped and staggered back, dropping his sword. His reaction flashed through the Kildashie force: seeing their leader suddenly vulnerable, drunken confusion replaced drunken confidence in seconds.

Now Jack reached down and grasped Trog's knife, and waved it tauntingly at the confused Kildashie.

"Norse steel!"

Confusion morphed into panic.

In an instant, Doxer had scampered forward and grabbed the Raglan stone from the table. Flicking it forwards he called out, "Jack!"

Jack caught the Raglan – *wow, it's hot, and heavy!* – and raised it above his head.

"Seelie!"

With a crash, the doors were flung open and the Cos-Howe contingent poured in. As the Tarditas hex hit them and they slowed right down, Jack's mind went back to the occasions when time had been slowed down – and speeded up. Midsummer . . . Oestre . . . Konan's timepiece in the pit of torment . . .

Time.

His mind cleared. He grabbed Boreus' sceptre, aimed it at the Kildashie leader and shouted, "*Fugitemp!*"

36

The Defeat of the Ancient Order of Plutocrats

The great hall of Edinburgh Castle has seen some wild sights in its time. Over the centuries, its walls have witnessed intrigues, plots, conspiracies and celebrations. The private function organised by the Ancient Order of Plutocrats (Surrey branch, established 1928) would be remembered by those attending for a long time, but for all the wrong reasons. The disturbance experienced by its well-heeled associates was an inconvenience, certainly; and they hadn't paid exorbitant sums to have their New Year shindig spoiled by a bunch of hooligans. But in their minds, that's what happened. As the Cos-Howe crew burst in, however, they were still frozen in time, aware only that unexpected visitors had disturbed their 'bash'.

What really happened was far more significant.

Jack's reversal of the Tarditas hex, and the sudden arrival of

Cosmo and his Cos-Howe crew swept away any chance of the Kildashie regaining the upper hand. Jack's challenge to Boreus had already sown doubt in the minds of the inebriated Kildashie foot soldiers, and their leader's dumbfounded reaction confirmed to them – slow of brain as some of them were – that all was not well. Distracted by the appearance of the new arrivals, they missed the fjordsmen and Cree grabbing their discarded weapons.

As some of Boreus' henchmen flailed at Jack for his imper-tinence, Phineas waded in to protect his son; and Grandpa Sandy recovered to wrench the Chalice from the stunned Kildashie lieutenant.

"It's not even the real Chalice," he said grimly, holding the cup disconsolately.

Confused and quickly surrounded, the Kildashie threw down their arms with little resistance.

"Did we miss all the fun?" asked Cosmo, advancing on Jack.

"Ossian and Magnus got you out OK, then?"

"Sure. As we were forcing our way out, these ghosts appeared and swirled around the Thanatos. They just vanished."

Parker's mates.

"You arranged that, didn't you?" Cosmo smiled down at Jack.

"I used the vococorn Tamlina gave me. It summoned the ghosts. Doxer gave it to me."

Jack looked round to see Doxer.

"He's over here," called Phineas softly.

He was crouched down, holding Doxer's body in close. Jack started quickly towards them, then halted, seeing the look on his father's face.

"What is it?" His voice trembled.

"The Kildashie's parting shot." Phineas indicated Doxer's bloodstained chest. "One of Boreus' henchmen decided to repay him."

Jack knelt down and looked into his colleague's eyes. They flickered, but there was no sign of recognition.

"Can't we use the Chalice?"

"It's not the real one, Jack; like the Stone. The Kildashie formed the images, even created a fake Chalice to wave in front of us."

"You mean they never got them at all?"

"I reckon they got in and touched the Stone, just like Daid did last Oestre. But they couldn't move it."

Doxer gave a gasp, and his eyes closed.

"I'm sorry, Jack; he's gone. He was brave to help us. We'll honour him."

Jack's eyes welled up with tears, and he looked away.

"How?"

"We can discuss it in the Stone Room."

Phineas stood up, and spoke briefly with Grandpa Sandy. They beckoned Grey Wolf over.

"Jack, you and Cosmo come with us."

The five made their way out to the courtyard, still littered with bodies. The icy night air clawed at Jack – he hadn't realised how warm he had just been, without even knowing it.

"We must re-set the humans' time as well. It's dangerous for our times to be separate for too long." Phineas spoke authoritatively as he escorted Jack and the others over to the stairwell that led to the Stone Room. Reaching the wooden door facing the courtyard Phineas called out, *"Perlignum!"*

The group were pulled forward. Jack gasped, but instantly recognised the stairs leading up to the alarmed door. He was astonished to see John standing there.

"Hello, Jack, Cosmo. I hope it's all right if I join you."

Cosmo shook John warmly by the hand, while Jack looked on, open-mouthed. Phineas took out his sceptre and aimed it at the solid steel door. The sceptre's ruby glowed, and there was a soft shimmering sound. The centre of the door melted away, leaving just enough room for them to jump through. Once inside, the door reappeared with a whooshing sound.

The buzz in the room was unmistakable – and much stronger than Jack remembered it. The *Mapa Mundi* around his neck grew warm, and the cabinet glowed.

"It's working, isn't it?" said Phineas. "The three treasures together."

Jack looked at the Stone and the Chalice. He'd been right: the image conjured up by Boreus down in the hall hadn't been the real Stone of Destiny.

"How close were the Kildashie to getting the real Stone?" he asked.

"They managed to halt human time with the Tarditas," explained Grandpa. "That's why the humans in the hall froze. Poor devils: all they wanted was to ring in midnight."

"But the Tarditas slowed us down too."

"We're Seelie, Jack. Our ties with the human world mean we get affected by what happens to them."

"So it's midnight for Shian, but not for humans?"

"You'll know the human's midnight because they let off loads of fireworks outside," explained Cosmo.

He looks so thin; he can't have eaten in ages.

"But it's *infama* for the two times to be different," went on Cosmo. "The Fugitemp speeded Shian time up, not the humans': we must correct it – and soon."

"Quite so," added John. "But we have a few moments. We should honour all those who did not survive, including Jack's comrade."

Jack started guiltily. He'd barely known Doxer, though he'd worked with him for ages; and he'd believed more than once that Doxer was a traitor, when that clearly wasn't true.

"This is one of those 'thin' times, when Shian can reach in and touch the Stone," said Grandpa. "It will be until the human's midnight arrives."

"If the Raglan is part of the real Stone, do we have to return it?" asked Jack.

"Why don't you try?" John smiled back.

Jack held out the Raglan – warm and heavy – but nothing happened.

"I thought it would fly to the Stone. I thought it didn't join the Stone downstairs because that was a fake."

"It *is* a fake," replied John. "But it didn't join because it's not meant to: the Raglan belongs in the Shian world. For you, it *is* the Destiny Stone."

"Then it will give strength to our new Congress," said Grandpa.

Jack looked at the iron rings on the Stone in the cabinet. The image the Kildashie had conjured up didn't have them.

They could only imagine having the Stone without the rings. Maybe they even fooled themselves they had it . . .

"Let's see all three treasures together," said Cosmo.

Obligingly, Jack flicked the *Mapa Mundi* into the Sphere, and held it up beside the glass cabinet along with the Raglan. The room glowed again.

"All together," whispered Grandpa Sandy reverently. "I never thought I would live to see this."

"Good things come in threes," added John. "And good things are connected. The Raglan's creator force gives you life; the Sphere shows your true path; and the Chalice shows that death is not the end. Together they give you life and truth."

"This will make your Congress strong," said Grey Wolf; "but we have only a few moments here."

Jack handed the Sphere to his grandfather, then reached in and touched the Stone. Whatever buzz he'd felt just being in the room was nothing compared to the kick he got on contact.

"Wow! It feels . . . zingy. Like the Raglan."

John laughed. "Well, they're both powerful – for Shian the Raglan is the Creator key. But think now, Jack. Young Doxer died helping you – along with many others tonight. How should we honour them all?"

Jack thought for a moment, then drew out Trog's knife from his leg. Leaning into the glass cabinet, he scored a small cross in the Stone, near one end.

"I saw that in the books Marco and Luka had."

Jack's mind suddenly raced . . .

John's book! I dropped it in the great hall!

He put his hand to his mouth.

"Don't worry, I've got the book," said Cosmo. "Are you done here?"

Jack nodded. He took a good look at the Stone, and at the King's Chalice, and turned to go.

"We can come back, yeah? When we've sorted everything out?"

"It's not so important now that we have the Raglan." His grandfather handed him back the *Mapa Mundi*. "But I promise we'll be back. And it will be our turn to host the Chalice soon."

"The Thanatos could've just waited for that. I mean, that's what they were after."

"If the Kildashie *had* got the Chalice, there's no guarantee they would have shared it. They're treacherous, remember. But come on: we must even up the human and Shian times."

As the six shivered their way back over to the great hall, a team of Elle-folk was busy clearing away the last debris of the fight. It was cold – but not Baltic like before. They entered to find the human scene just as they had left it – tables overturned, food scattered and drinks spilled.

The Shian scene was one of calm: while Armina tended to injured Seelie, the Kildashie had been made to kneel before the great fireplace. Though numerically superior, their drunken confidence had burst with their leader's downfall. Cowed and confused, they presented a pitiful spectacle. Boreus alone held his head up – but his rediscovered confidence had come too late.

Oobit was right: the Kildashie aren't that special.

"This will not take long," called out Harald as Jack and the others arrived. "You must establish the authority of your new Congress. Summon the Seelie!"

And, crowded as the great hall already was, it was suddenly filled with a great multitude of Shian creatures – Pisgies, Dwarves, Darrigs, the lot.

Just like at Dunvik. Cool.

As the people and creatures of the hidden Commonwealth sat or perched where they could, Grandpa Sandy strode in front of the assembly.

"My friends, after a long time we have returned to our homes here, and we have finally joined the three great Shian treasures."

"The Stone and the Chalice still belong to the humans, dolt!" spat Boreus.

"The Stone in the glass cabinet upstairs may belong to the humans, but it still gives us energy and power. And more than that, we have the Raglan – the Shian Destiny Stone!"

"And to celebrate, you'll execute us," sneered Boreus. "I have no fear of death."

"Men of Kildashie, you have desecrated this place with your murder and theft. Your alliances with the Thanatos and the Dunters have brought ruin to the entire Shian people."

Grandpa Sandy was in full flow, no trace now of the doubt and shame that had so recently reduced him to a mumbling wreck.

"For the murder of Atholmor and Samara from the Congress, and young Ploutter and Doxer; and many more besides, you will be banished into Sheol."

There was a gasp around the room. War among the Shian was one thing; and execution or suspension was the usual penalty.

Jack looked at his father.

"Suspended is bad enough – I should know. But Sheol is 100 times worse."

There is *a fate worse than death, then,* thought Jack.

"... sent immediately and without appeal for a period of thirty years." Grandpa looked round carefully at the assembled throng. "Is the Commonwealth in agreement?"

Whereas at Dunvik there had been some debate – even some defence – before the Brashat were suspended, it was evident that no one felt inclined to prolong these proceedings. There was a murmur of approval, and together Grandpa Sandy, Phineas and Harald levelled their sceptres at the cowering Kildashie.

"*Ifrinn!*"

The Kildashie were encased in a fiery glow. There was no sound, however; and after the prisoners had faded into nothingness, the only sign of their presence (bar the mess) was a faint singeing on the floor.

As John stepped forward there was excited chatter from the Hidden Commonwealth.

"Friends," he said, "you have witnessed the defeat of a terrible evil. And make no mistake, there are others around the country who will still cling to the Kildashie's ways. But my brothers have arrived to report that your friends and colleagues have subdued the Unseelie and the Red Caps."

Turning round, Jack saw Marco, Luka and Matthew by the door. A cheer rose from the crowd.

"Your friends will join you tomorrow," continued John. "I gather there will be a New Year celebration in the square down below. Celebrate your victory; but be vigilant: evil does not sleep for long."

As Cosmo stepped forward and tried to hand the leather-bound volume back to John, the old man beckoned Jack forward.

"You have accomplished a great deal, young man. My brothers and I have watched you for some time now. Please accept this." He handed Jack the book. "Take good care of it, for it's very old. But I'm sure you'll find it instructive."

Jack's eyes welled up with tears for the second time that night.

He swallowed hard, but found the lump in his throat wouldn't go away.

"You have triumphed over a formidable enemy. Clearly you learnt well the lessons we taught you," added Marco.

"And some of your Shian lessons too," laughed Matthew. "Good Fugitemp charm."

"We'll leave now," added Luka. "Take care, young man. Remember the power of Gosol. You trusted the Sphere, even when it showed danger. That's real belief."

"Farewell, friends," echoed Marco; and Matthew and Luka waved as they left the hall.

"It's not exactly tidy, but we can live with that," said Ossian, viewing the disrupted party with evident satisfaction. "Anyway, this lot don't deserve much better." He carefully tipped over a wine glass that had somehow escaped the recent disturbance.

"How did you get past the Thanatos, Grandpa?"

"The invisibility cloaks worked – but only outside. Some of us got into the great hall, but then the Kildashie used the Tarditas. We could barely fight. I take it those left outside did not survive?"

Jack nodded. "When we got to the courtyard there were bodies everywhere."

"But your arrival saved us, there's no doubt about that."

"Come along," said Phineas, "we'll need to leave this scene for the humans to deal with. It's time we evened up time."

He led Jack and the others out of the hall, across the now clear courtyard (barring a few toppled humans), and up to the castle chapel.

"In turns, quick."

In twos and threes the assembled Shian filed through the gate to the square below.

"Jack, you come last with me," said Grandpa. "You should see this."

After the rest had all passed through the gate, Grandpa pointed his sceptre to the sky and called out in a clear voice, "*Synchronos!*"

There was a peal of thunder, and a shaking that made Jack think of an earthquake. Then a chime from a church clock.

"Wasn't there supposed to be fireworks?" asked Jack.

"We skipped past midnight – it's one o'clock now. Let's get below, quick."

Grandpa Sandy pulled Jack up to the chapel wall.

"*Effatha!*"

Epilogue

"Jack! Come and see Dad!"

With a surge of relief Jack saw Rana and Lizzie clinging onto Uncle Doonya, and raced across to greet them. Momentarily perturbed by his uncle's gaunt features, his relief was restored when he saw Grandpa and Phineas arrive to hug Doonya.

"The house is a mess, but we'll soon get that sorted," announced Lizzie. "Mum and Auntie Dorcas will be through tomorrow – a grig told us. Uncle Hart and Petros are bringing them all."

Petros, thought Jack. *He didn't exactly cover himself with glory here, did he?*

Then he brushed away that thought. They were home; the Kildashie were defeated and banished; the Stone and Chalice were safe; and now they had the Raglan – the Shian Destiny Stone – to go with the Sphere.

Jack tugged at his neck. He'd got so used to the flag being there that he often forgot about it completely.

But it really saved us tonight – even when I couldn't understand why it was sending me towards Boreus.

"Jack, can I see the *Mapa*?" asked Phineas.

Jack handed the flag over to his father, who flicked it into a Sphere. Jack watched in amazement as the circles formed to show the *Mapa* flying on a flag pole, with the Raglan embedded at the base.

"You made the Sphere work!"

"The magycks are working again, Jack. Sure you don't mind sharing it?"

A wave of relief surged through Jack. Finally, he could stop worrying about somebody trying to take the *Mapa* from him.

"It'll be our totem," continued his father. "Grandpa's got the Raglan, and a new Congress will be elected tomorrow evening. Things are looking up, lad, thanks to you."

Even as Phineas spoke, the Shian square's crystals and warren pipes started working again. People and creatures were arriving all the time, news was being exchanged, stories swapped, and tales told of hardship endured and deliverance won. Iain Dubh and a band of Nebulans arrived to tell of the freedom of the west . . .

". . . Turns out the Unseelie groups couldn't wait to get stuck into each other. Once they knew the Kildashie were gone it was easy to split them up. Piece of cake . . ."

Enda and the McCools turned up with tales of triumph over the Red Caps . . .

"Those Warfrins made short work of the Dunters, I can tell ye. I wish we'd some of them back in Ireland . . ."

The night passed so quickly; Jack didn't even get time to feel tired.

When Cleo arrived at first light with Petros and the rest of the Keldy crew, Jack still hadn't been to bed, and although he was now dog tired, he was still too excited to think about going to sleep.

"D'you fancy coming out for a walk?" he asked Cleo.

"I would love that. I remember this is a fine city."

The two emerged onto a deserted castle esplanade that was littered with bottles, cans, and the occasional scarf. A chilly winter sun materialised from behind thin clouds, shedding little real warmth, but warming the heart nonetheless.

It's cold; but like it should be on New Year's Day. Not Baltic like when the Kildashie were in charge.

Jack and Cleo waded through the evidence of the previous night's party and made their way down the High Street to the top of the Mound. A street cleaner was busy sweeping hundreds of bottles and cans into a huge sack.

"What happened to the fireworks last night?" asked Jack mischievously.

"Cancelled. Too cold, and too windy. Still, some party, eh?"

Jack looked around, and saw the buildings glisten in the sunlight.

If only you knew.